BREAKING FREE

THE HEART OF BATH, BOOK 2

Jenny Worstall

ARE YOU SIGNED UP FOR DRAGONBLADE'S BLOG?

You'll get the latest news and information on exclusive giveaways, exclusive excerpts, coming releases, sales, free books, cover reveals and more.

Check out our complete list of authors, too!

No spam, no junk. That's a promise!

Sign Up Here

www.dragonbladepublishing.com

Dearest Reader;

Thank you for your support of a small press. At Dragonblade Publishing, we strive to bring you the highest quality Historical Romance from some of the best authors in the business. Without your support, there is no 'us', so we sincerely hope you adore these stories and find some new favorite authors along the way.

Happy Reading!

CEO, Dragonblade Publishing

CHAPTER ONE

Selina

WHAT A NINCOMPOOP! Miss Selina Templeton scrutinized the guest sitting next to her at the dinner table. The candlelight highlighted Mr. George Fitzgerald's already dazzlingly fair hair, and his green eyes glittered with amusement as he spun his tale—featuring himself as the hero.

"And I placed a bet then, for I had a good hand of cards, you see, and felt confident I would be successful. False modesty has no place here—I am an expert at the gaming tables. Have I mentioned this before?"

Cards! Bets! And gambling. Was this all he was interested in? And how boastful the man was.

Selina had harbored such high hopes for this dinner. She had been thrilled when her brother Henry, recently married to her best friend Kitty, had invited Selina to dine with them. Imagine— she was to be a guest at Henry and Kitty's first dinner as a married couple. Only twelve people had been invited. That in itself was exciting enough—and a great honor—but when Henry had revealed that George Fitzgerald had also accepted an invitation to dinner, Selina thought her happiness was complete.

Henry's friend George had occupied Selina's thoughts right through the recent Christmas period, and she'd been quite wild for more chances to see him, hoping to converse at length and discover more about his character. . . and admire his handsome countenance.

Selina flipped off her tight embroidered slippers under the table and rubbed her toes together in their silk stockings before stretching them out as wide as she could. Ah! That felt better. Lord! She wished she never had to wear shoes again.

"Are you all right, Selina?" her brother Henry said from the end of the table.

"Fine!" Selina said cheerfully. "Thank you for asking. I assure you I am in the best of health."

Apart from the ache in my heart—for I had stupidly thought George would be the one for me. However, now I find he is a pompous fool who can talk of nothing but cards—and himself.

How quickly love could turn to hate. Or perhaps that was putting it a little too strongly. How quickly attraction—a strong, intensely powerful physical attraction—could turn to boredom when one spent long enough with the object of one's heart's desire. And in this case, sitting next to George for an hour or so at dinner was quite long enough.

No longer would George be her Greek god, her Adonis, the man to fulfil her dreams. Why, Selina had even foolishly imagined that she might one day walk up the aisle with him. Not that she entirely believed in marriage.

For why would I allow a man to rule over me?

And yet before Christmas, George had made her feel as if he might be that man. The one who could break through her hard shell and find a softer, more gentle character underneath, a person who wanted what everyone else in the whole world wanted—someone to love, someone to care for. And to be loved and cared for in return.

No, George had revealed himself to be a dullard with precious little conversation beyond blabbing about his prowess at cards. To say he was disappointing was understating it. His character was nothing like his appearance.

Selina stifled a yawn.

"Is it time?" Henry smiled at his wife Kitty, and she nodded.

"Yes, my dear," she said. "If the ladies would like to follow me upstairs, we will go to the withdrawing room. You men will doubtless have much to discuss."

Heavens! That look between Henry and Kitty—the warmth, the mutual affection. If only . . .

Selina jumped to her feet, then dove under the table upon realizing she needed to retrieve her slippers.

"Selina," Henry said with a laugh, "you have not changed since you were a small girl. I remember Mama reprimanding you many a time for your habit of removing your shoes during meals."

Selina grinned at her brother. "I have never found ladies' shoes comfortable. However, I am sure all you lucky gentlemen at the table are wearing more agreeable footwear."

Henry put his head in his hands and groaned unconvincingly. "No! Please do not start on one of your speeches."

"Whatever do you mean?" Selina asked in mock astonishment.

"He means," Kitty said, "when you start going on about everything being unfair and how much better it would be if ladies could wear breeches instead of skirts. And more substantial clothes for evening dress too, not low-cut necklines that leave us at the mercy of draughts."

"Ah, yes," Selina said. "I have oft thought we should wear jackets at dinner, like the gentlemen, rather than gowns festooned with frills and furbelows. And cravats—for would they not keep our necks warm?"

There was much merriment round the table at this exchange, and a general conversation broke out. Most of the ladies exclaimed that they thoroughly agreed with Selina and found it annoying that their formal wear was ill-equipped to cope with the cold and damp January weather in England.

"Well, we men are delighted you ladies are all wearing low-cut dresses this evening," said one of the bolder gentlemen at the table, "otherwise where else would our eyes—"

"I think 'tis time for the ladies to withdraw," Henry said, cutting into the conversation not a moment too soon.

"Quite right, my dear," Kitty said with a fleeting frown as she got to her feet. "Come, ladies. Let us go upstairs."

Selina followed at the end of the procession, her shoes now firmly on her feet. Turning round at the door, she inadvertently caught George's eye. Why was he looking at her? And in such an odd manner. Perchance he disapproved of her speaking her mind? He seemed depressingly conventional and predictable.

Selina could smell the heavy, sickly port that was already being poured for the gentlemen. How absurd it was that at a certain point in every dinner the ladies were banished upstairs so that the men could begin drinking in earnest and exchanging all sorts of stories not suitable for women's ears. When Selina was married—if she ever decided to marry—she would make new rules. The gentlemen would be forced to drink tepid tea upstairs while the ladies were left in the dining room in possession of the drinks cabinet. The fairer sex would sample all types of strong alcohol and generally let their hair down. Figuratively speaking. Although it would actually be quite amusing if they literally let their hair down—pulled out all the hairpins and ribbons, tossed their locks around their shoulders and generally made themselves totally comfortable and dishevelled. Perhaps corsets could be loosened—and shoes would, of course, be optional.

Once upstairs, two of the ladies started playing a pianoforte duet, and tea was bought in on a silver tray by a servant. Selina sat down on one of the sofas, and Kitty joined her.

"We are so pleased you could come this evening," Kitty said, clasping Selina's hand. "Has the evening been everything you had hoped for?"

What could Selina say? Henry and Kitty had been kind enough to ask her to dinner, knowing how much she wanted to see George. How could she say to Kitty, her best friend in all the world, that the evening had been a disappointment? And that her dreams of romance with Mr. George Fitzgerald—of a future even—now lay in ruins.

"You did not seem . . ." Kitty hesitated. "You did not seem entirely *enthralled* with George this evening. Are you well? Is anything wrong?"

"Nothing is wrong," Selina said. "You and Henry have been so kind and thoughtful to invite me. I am thrilled to be a guest at your first dinner as a married couple—and overjoyed that you have married my brother."

The two friends embraced warmly.

"Of course, Kitty dearest," Selina said with a smile, "you are far too good for Henry. All the same, I believe the two of you are a perfect match and will have much happiness in your life together."

Kitty's cheeks went pink. "Henry makes me very happy. I cannot describe what it is like to be married except to say that it is like being in heaven every single day. And every . . ." Kitty stopped abruptly.

Interesting! Had Kitty been about to say every *night*? Every night was heaven with Selina's brother?

At some point, might Selina and Kitty have a conversation about this? They had spent much time together through their childhood years, indeed had more or less grown up together. *What happens when you get married* had been an endless topic of conversation between them, causing much speculation and mirth. When they had both been thirteen, they had made a solemn pledge to each other that whichever of them married first would give the other a full account of all that went on in the privacy of the marriage bed.

Of course, this conversation could not possibly take place now they were grown up. And even if it could, the withdrawing room, with so many other ladies and servants present, was hardly the right venue. In reality, the two friends would probably never speak of the subject again, for now Kitty was married, it was as if she had crossed over to a secret place that Selina had no entry to.

"We will still be the best of friends, you know," Kitty said.

Selina smiled. She might have predicted Kitty would know what she was thinking.

"I know," Selina said. "You will always be my best friend. And you are my sister now too, and that brings me more happiness than I can ever express."

"What about you and George?" Kitty said. "Henry and I had high hopes that a romance might blossom between you. Before Christmas, there seemed to be a mutual attraction."

"I would be lying if I did not say I'd cherished those hopes myself," Selina said. "And yes, it seemed there was attraction on both sides—but until this evening I didn't know the real George."

"What do you mean?" Kitty said. "Have you not known him for some time as Henry's friend? They were at university together, were they not?"

"Yes, they were," Selina said, "and I have seen him at social events over the years too, but I had not really *noticed* him until, until . . ."

"Until he saved the day in the Octagon," Kitty said. "I will never forget that. How George managed to unmask the vile Lord Steyne as a card shark."

"Yes, George was magnificent on that occasion," Selina said. "He talked eloquently and played the cards so skilfully, managing to reel in his victim and expose him for the villainous creature he is."

"George will always have my most sincere gratitude," Kitty said, "for from that day on, the *ton* turned their back on Lord Steyne."

"And good riddance, I say, for when I think of what Lord Steyne did, leaving Henry for dead at Waterloo and trying to ruin your family's happiness, why, it fair makes my blood boil in my veins."

"It's over," Kitty said. "Lord Steyne has left Bath and we are all safe. There is no need for any more boiling blood."

Selina sighed. "I have seen George on other admittedly rather short occasions since that time in the Octagon. Our paths crossed at various social events in the city, and he was always most charming. We even danced at a ball in the Upper Rooms, which was heaven—and chatted a little at your wedding, too. But where is that friendly, lively George this evening? Where is the witty, articulate man we saw in action in the Octagon in December? He barely talked at all this evening for the first two courses of the meal—not even to comment on the delicious food your cook had prepared. And when he did finally speak, it was to show off and boast about how good he is at cards."

"I did not notice he was quiet," Kitty said, "or then boastful."

"Doubtless you were too busy being the perfect hostess. You did brilliantly with all your guests, making them feel welcome and keeping the conversation going. No one would have guessed this was the very first dinner party you had hosted."

"Thank you," Kitty said. "I must admit to feeling a little apprehensive before the occasion. However, with Henry at the end of the table and the full support of all my friends, I think I managed tolerably well. And hopefully the evening has been a success, so far at least. Except for you, dear Selina. I am sorry to hear George was not very forthcoming—and then hogged the conversation with a speech about himself. Perhaps he is not well? We deliberately sat him next to you for the meal, hoping you would both enjoy the opportunity to get to know one another better."

"I think I have been a little foolish," Selina said. "George is a very handsome young man, and perhaps I allowed my feelings to run away with me. I know now that what I felt for him in the past was a mere physical attraction, whereas I am looking for a true soulmate. Someone I can love and cherish, someone I have much in common with, someone I will be able to talk to freely, right into my dotage, a best friend and partner in life . . ."

Selina could scarcely believe it, but tears were forming in her eyes.

"You have been more affected by this than I thought," Kitty

said. "This was not a mere infatuation. I believe you are in love with George."

"I am not!" Selina whispered. "I could never love a man who sits silent as the grave, glowering at the dinner table and looking as if he disapproves of everything, and then drones on about his card games."

Could I?

"Selina, dearest," Kitty said. "Please, take my handkerchief."

"Thank you." Selina gave a small sob.

"And you're not to worry about George," Kitty said. "If he is not the right man for you, it matters not how silent or boastful he is. There are plenty of others for you to meet and fall in love with. Henry knows many fine young men who are looking for romance and a marriage partner."

"I will be fine," Selina said, as her natural good humor and sunny disposition took over again. "'Twas a fleeting disappointment, that is all. I was infatuated with a person who did not really exist—a dream I had allowed to build up in my mind—and all because I was impressed with how George spoke in the Octagon before Christmas and how he stood up to Lord Steyne and defeated him."

George truly was magnificent that day. He looked so very handsome, too, silhouetted against the yellow walls of the Octagon, the candlelight illuminating his fine figure . . .

Kitty smiled. "I will make it my business this season to make sure you find a suitable husband. I want you to enjoy the happiness that I enjoy with my dear Henry."

Just then, the door to the withdrawing room opened and the men trooped in, some with rather flushed cheeks. The port had obviously been flowing freely.

And there George was, standing tall in the crowd, his manly bearing and noble profile outshining all the others, his blond locks crying out to be stroked, chiselled lips begging to be kissed . . .

Not that Selina was looking out for him. Why would she? He meant nothing to her.

If only that were true.

George

GEORGE'S EYES RAKED the room until he found her. Selina! How exquisite she looked sitting next to Kitty, her complexion radiant, eyes shining. She was perfection! Everything he had always wanted in a woman—beautiful, lively, individual, and not afraid to speak her mind.

When Selina had tossed off her shoes under the table without a care, George had noticed immediately and had admired her for her spirited behavior. How refreshing that she did not let the conventions of society constrain her. At that point, if George could have done exactly what he wanted, he would have dived under the mahogany table and kissed her shoes, before moving on to her stockinged feet . . .

George had been in love with Selina for more years than he could remember. He had seen her at many events in Bath but had always been too shy to talk to her. Due to her wonderfully extroverted nature, she attracted people like bees to a honeypot and was always surrounded by an admiring, vibrant crowd. Many were the times George had stood on the margins of a group at a ball in the refreshment room, longing to be able to claim Selina as a friend—maybe more. But she had never noticed him.

Why is it that I find women so difficult to talk to?

And this situation did not change until that fateful day in the Octagon before Christmas. At first, George had not been aware that Selina had been in the room when he was busy exposing Lord Steyne as a card cheat. This was definitely a good thing, for if George *had* been aware of Selina's presence, it might have put him off his stride—he surely would not have been able to succeed in his aim, namely, to draw Lord Steyne into the card game, then reveal that the man had three cards hidden in a pocket. Lord

Steyne had cheated from the very beginning, and now here was the incontrovertible proof. The man was nothing but a dishonorable wretch, a stain upon society, and a disgrace to the *ton*.

George smiled ruefully at the memory. He had put his shyness aside on that occasion, so concerned was he to achieve justice for his friend Henry, and for Kitty and her family. Surprising even himself by holding forth so eloquently, he had outlined exactly how Lord Steyne had cheated not only in this card game but doubtless in many others before. George felt it was his duty to speak out—an important service to the community in Bath and beyond, a service he could perform for all the people Lord Steyne had cheated and ruined. 'Twas a fitting punishment for all the evil he had done.

Then, once his speech was over, George had noticed Selina staring at him with admiration etched into her face—or so it had seemed at the time. This had seemed to be the beginning of something wonderful, a beautiful true romance and a welcome answer to George's prayers—which up 'til then God had neglected to answer.

As luck would have it, George had bumped into Selina a few times at social occasions after this and had also managed to exchange quite a few sentences with her at Henry and Kitty's wedding on Christmas Day. Since then, he had been racking his brains to work out how he could take things further but felt too unsure to ask his friends for advice.

George was all at sea in the world of romance, for having given his heart to Selina when he was but a very young man, he had never felt the need to pursue other women. He had not wanted to practice his seduction techniques on the young ladies of Bath, nor avail himself of the opportunities for purely physical encounters, as so many of his friends thought was the correct path.

I have always wanted to woo Selina—but do not know how to court a young woman. How easy and natural it seems for others.

Just then, George was conscious of Selina's eyes upon him as he stood near the door of the withdrawing room. Kitty seemed to be whispering something in Selina's ear, and now she was vacating the seat next to Selina on the sofa. Perhaps George could take her place?

I need to find some courage.

George had done his best at dinner to engage with Selina but at first knew not what to talk about. Thus it was that after a few pleasantries he had reverted to his usual taciturn self, the shy persona he generally adopted in the presence of the fairer sex. After a while, George remembered how Selina had seemed to admire him during the incident in the Octagon before Christmas—this made him decide to risk talking about cards and gambling. He probably went on about it at too great a length— had he even remembered to allow a pause in the conversation in case there was anything Selina herself wished to say?

Sadly, George now recollected he had left out the part of his narrative that explained his utter fascination with the patterns and logic of the cards—how for him it wasn't the gambling that mattered, it was the mathematics of it all. George seldom played for blunt, and when he did, it was for mere pennies. Curses! He might unintentionally have given Selina the impression he lived for gambling—that he was, in fact, an addict. He might also have come across as rather swollen headed.

George decided to be bold and made for the sofa.

"Would you mind if I sat next to you?" he asked Selina.

"Of course not," she said. "Pray sit down, Mr. Fitzgerald."

Zounds! This was rather formal—and did not bode well.

"I see you have your shoes on again," George attempted.

Selina's brow darkened. 'Twas probably a mistake to make such a personal comment, yet what was a man supposed to say? How could George find the words to achieve that light chitter chatter and froth so beloved by society?

"I, I did not mean to offend you," George said. "I only meant . . ."

"What *did* you mean?" Selina said.

"I only meant how much I admired your spirit, the freedom to take your shoes off—to put aside the normal inhibitions people feel. You are your own person. I admire that. More people should have your courage."

This was better. Selina's luscious lips were curving and her eyes sparkling again. Perhaps she liked being admired? What might George comment on next? His eyes fell to her delicious curves . . .

No! There are certain things a gentleman may think—but not articulate.

"Your hair . . ." George mumbled.

"What is wrong with my hair?"

"Why, nothing," George said. "I like the way it is swept up . . . er, pinned? And with the ribbon threaded through. I am wondering how that is achieved. How does it stay like that? Ahem! What I mean to say is—your hair is very neat. A nice color. And pretty."

"Thank you," Selina said.

Was it strictly necessary for her to curl her lip in that odd manner? George already knew he had expressed his admiration in a shockingly ill-judged and bizarre fashion.

Should George attempt to talk about cards again and gambling? Perhaps not, for 'twas fair to say Selina had not seemed enthralled when he'd attempted this topic of conversation at dinner earlier. No, the subject was best avoided.

"What do you like to do?" Selina asked. "I mean, apart from playing cards."

"What do I like doing?"

"Yes!"

George paused. Would discussing his medical work be considered unsuitable in the drawing room? He shook his head. 'Twould be better to discuss a different interest.

"I like helping out with the horses at my father's stables and riding my horse, Trigger. I'm very fond of him; he's like a friend to me."

Silence. Then,

"Have you traveled much, Mr. Fitzgerald? I have always longed to spread my wings. How I would love to go to the Continent—for I have an intense desire to see the ruins of Pompeii. Mr. Fitzgerald? You have heard of these Roman ruins?"

By Jove, she was beautiful! The fire in her eyes when she was animated . . .

I can see her now standing amongst the columns of a ruined temple in Southern Italy, the soft, golden evening sun creating a halo round her head and rendering her muslin dress opaque . . .

George swallowed hard. Pull yourself together, man!

"I have not yet had the good fortune to visit the Continent," he said, "though I do like to travel, especially by horseback. I love the feeling of the wind on my back, the freedom of being out with Trigger."

Why was George babbling like an imbecile about his horse? Selina would think he was a complete dunderhead.

George had always been happy to be the only child of his parents; however, at this point he would have given anything to have had sisters, the more the merrier. In fact, he felt he would be quite content to have been brought up with five or possibly six sisters—for then he might have felt more at ease in the company of the fairer sex. And know what they expected from a man in the way of conversation.

Damnation! This evening was not going according to plan. Selina did not look impressed. And during dinner, she had stifled a yawn. But who could criticize her for that, trapped as she had been, sitting next to the most tedious man in Bath?

"George!" Henry slapped him on the back. "I was wondering where you'd gotten to. Glad to see you're getting on so well with my sister. What have you two been talking about?"

"Mr. Fitzgerald has been telling me about Trigger," Selina said.

"Has he indeed!" Henry raised an eyebrow. "Well, Trigger is a fine horse. If you remember, Selina, Trigger was the horse I borrowed from George when I went to rescue Kitty from Lord

Steyne's clutches."

Selina's eyes blazed. "I remember! How could anyone forget that time?" She turned to George. "We will always be grateful that you allowed Henry to take Trigger at a time of great crisis. Kitty is my dearest friend in all the world, and her life was in peril. Trigger is a noble horse, and I am not surprised you love the creature so dearly."

She understands my affection for my horse—promising.

"I saw many brave and noble horses at Waterloo last summer," Henry said. "And much suffering."

"There is no need to speak of that now, brother dearest," Selina interrupted. "All is over; all is well. Come, 'tis time for some music. Look! I do believe people are expecting you to play a duet with Kitty."

Henry walked over to the pianoforte and sat down beside his wife. The Mozart duet unfolded like a busily decorated fan, full of charm and detail. And like the fan, the music was able to convey subtle meaning and significance when interpreted correctly. Such honeyed sounds . . . ah, Henry had what George most wanted in the world—an easy intimacy, friendship, and love with a woman he adored. Two souls journeying through life together in perfect harmony.

Next, Kitty played some Bach, and George was transported by the rise and fall of the melodies, the precise cadences, and the busy textures.

Music to him was like cards—an intricate mathematical puzzle—everything in its place, both complex and highly organized. George closed his eyes to more clearly see the intricate web weaving in and out, building, transforming, and adding up to the harmonious sound of musical bliss.

When he opened his eyes again at the end of the piece, George found that Selina had disappeared. He could not blame her, for there was no evidence that she enjoyed his company. Why would she? His conversation was dull and his personality so hidden beneath shyness that most women would take the chance to escape as soon as they could. She must have been delighted when he had lowered his lids for a few minutes.

Selina was on the other side of the room now, giggling, surrounded by a group of her friends. What were they talking about? Not George, for sure—he could have made no impression upon her this evening. The interest Selina had shown in him on other occasions had vaporized. Or had it perchance always been a figment of his imagination?

George wanted to reach out to the other side of the room, to pull Selina into his arms and whisper his private thoughts to her. Distressingly, there was an invisible barrier preventing him, a sheet of unbreakable glass. Would he always be on the outside looking in?

How utterly devastating! George had been looking forward to this dinner from the moment Henry had issued the invitation. When he had heard that Selina would also be present, he was overjoyed.

George had spent a considerable time getting ready before he came this evening—not something he usually did. His manservant had been somewhat surprised that George had first wanted to have his cravat tied in a particular way and was then anxious that a speck of dust was brushed off the shoulder of his jacket.

As he left his home in Devonshire Buildings, George had looked much smarter than usual. He traveled across the city on horseback—which, in hindsight, might have been a mistake. George looked down at his breeches. 'Twas a shame the weather had been inclement, for there appeared to be a few mud stains. Did ladies mind this sort of thing? George knew very few ladies. And he didn't really know Selina at all.

That was the trouble when one fell in love. Love is blind. One could worship them and want to be with them forever, all before one knew what their tastes were. However, everything George had observed about Selina had led him to believe that she was not some shallow young woman, concerned about a bit of mud. She was easy going, a free spirit.

Wasn't she?

Selina was the sort of person George would like to be—if only he had the courage.

Ye gods! Selina was singing now, accompanied by Kitty. She was utterly entrancing as she enunciated the words of a Handel air, her bosom rising and falling with her breath.

"Let the bright seraphim . . ."

She was wearing a diaphanous white dress and, if George was not very much mistaken, had removed her shoes again. He looked carefully at the hem of her dress. Yes, her adorable stockinged feet could be glimpsed. Ah! Her exquisite ankles . . .

George was not even fit to touch her feet or the hem of her dress. She was perfection, she was unobtainable—she was a goddess.

She is everything I want in a woman—and regrettably I seem to be the exact opposite of what she admires.

Selina

ENTHUSIASTIC APPLAUSE GREETED the end of Selina's performance. She was a talented singer, and her musicianship was much respected at private musical gatherings.

"Encore, encore!" Henry said.

"Doesn't she have a lovely voice?" one of the guests remarked.

"Indeed. Such talent," another said. "I'm particularly fond of that Handel air—and I've never heard it performed better."

"I must find out who her music teacher is," one lady said. "Perhaps he would be interested in teaching my daughter?"

"I can tell you who he is," Kitty said. "Signor Allegretto. I have had some lessons with him as well. Perchance you have heard of him?"

"Signor Allegretto!" another lady said. "His name is known throughout Bath—and he is as famous for his looks as for his musicality."

"What's all this," Selina said as she came to join Kitty and a group of ladies. "Did I hear Signor Allegretto's name?"

"Yes," Kitty said. "We would recommend him as a teacher, wouldn't we?"

"Oh yes. He has taught me for years now and has always been very patient and kind." Selina put a finger to her lips. "Especially on one particular occasion."

"And I can guess when that was," Kitty said. "I well remember how much I laughed to hear your account."

The group of ladies were excessively keen to hear all about the incident, and so Selina described the day she went to her music lesson in disguise, purely to see how Signor Allegretto would react.

"Of course, I was only around eleven years old," Selina explained. "Is that an excuse for thoughtless behavior? Well, let's just say it seemed so at the time. Anyway, Signor Allegretto was seated at the pianoforte in the withdrawing room of our home at Number 1, waiting for me to come for my lesson accompanied by my mama. I thought it would be funny to go to my lesson early, without waiting for Mama—and I had dressed as an urchin. We had a wonderful dressing up box in our nursery—we still do as a matter of fact, if any of you ladies fancy dressing up any time."

Many heads nodded at this point. The Templetons' dressing up box was famous amongst the families of Bath and had been a source of amusement for years, and not only for children—but that is another story.

"I came into the room wearing a torn pair of breeches, a stained, ragged shirt, and with my hair under a cap," Selina said. "I dared not risk addressing Signor Allegretto because I knew he would recognize my voice, so I made a growling noise, intending to surprise him."

"That was your biggest mistake," Kitty said. "The growling noise—and also coming up behind him when he didn't even realize you were in the room and putting your hand on his arm."

"Possibly." Selina grinned. "But how was I to know that he'd recently had his pocket picked by a young urchin in Stall Street?"

"You weren't to know—it must have given him a fright, though," Kitty said. "The whole upsetting incident must have leapt into his mind again in a most unwelcome fashion."

"How did he react?" one of the ladies asked.

"Yes. Do go on," another said. "Musicians can be rather temperamental—or so I have heard."

"Signor Allegretto is not a temperamental man," Selina said, "although he is very sensitive."

"I expect he was a little startled," the first lady said.

"Actually, he nearly jumped out of his skin," Selina admitted.

Kitty giggled. "I've heard this tale so many times and still find it funny."

"And once he'd got over being startled," Selina said, "he became rather cross with me, then spent ages apologizing because he said it wasn't my fault and he knew I had meant no harm. Then he calmed down and said it was all rather amusing, now he came to think of it."

"'Twas all right in the end," the second lady said.

"Not quite," Selina said, "because once he saw the funny side, he began laughing very loudly, almost hysterically. Then Mama came into the room, saying she had no idea where I was and gave Signor Allegretto a lecture about unseemly behavior. Apparently laughing like a drain is no way to behave in polite society."

"Didn't your mama tell you off for being dressed as an urchin?" one of the ladies asked.

"No! She didn't even realize I was there because I had immediately hidden behind a curtain. Signor Allegretto was such a good sport, he didn't give the game away, but merely apologized for being too loud. He said he'd been thinking of something excessively funny and got carried away—which was completely true."

The ladies all started talking at once then.

"This is quite a story!"

"And then?"

"Yes! Don't stop now."

"We have to know the next installment."

Selina beamed. There was nothing she enjoyed more than an appreciative audience, whether it was to hear her sing or to listen to one of her tales. And she freely admitted, to herself at least, that these tales grew taller with every rendition. For what was the point of life if one couldn't have a laugh now and then? And spin a story to make fun of the world.

"Once Mama had left the room," Selina continued, "I came out from behind the curtain and apologized again to Signor Allegretto. Then I ran off, managing to avoid seeing anyone on the stairs, changed into my normal clothes, found Mama and returned to my singing lesson. I behaved with the utmost decorum throughout the session—so much so that I began to worry that Mama might become suspicious and guess I had been up to no good."

Again, the ladies all spoke at once.

"Stop, I beg you!"

"Too, too funny."

"Selina! I am having to wipe tears from my eyes."

"Did your mama ever find out?"

"Yes, did you confess in the end?"

"The men are all looking at us and wondering what on earth we are talking about . . ."

"And ever since then," Selina said, raising her voice above the hubbub, "ever since then I have been very grateful to Signor Allegretto and very fond of him too. He's a decent sort of man, and a wonderful teacher and musician."

Everyone in the crowd agreed that Signor Allegretto did sound a most uncommon sort of fellow.

The ladies drifted away at that point, and a few other guests started playing cards in one corner of the room. After a few minutes, Selina was alone with Kitty in front of the fire.

"I am sorry that George did not seem the right match for you," Kitty said. "I hope you will not think too harshly of Henry and me; we were not trying to push you together. Or perhaps we were, a little—but you genuinely seemed so fond of each other. Are you sure there is no hope?"

Selina was silent. What could she say that she had not already said earlier? Sometimes it was better to close a chapter and move on with one's life. She had thought George was going to be hers—but then discovered aspects of his character that meant they were incompatible. They would never have been a good match, for physical attraction was not enough. Even when it was exceptionally strong.

Oh, why is it that my body is so out of step with my mind? For in the dark of every night I long for George to put his arms round me, to kiss me, to be one with me . . .

"Look around the room," Kitty said. "There are myriad other young men here, many of them most handsome and with lively personalities to match your own."

Selina flashed her a warning look.

"I understand," Kitty said, "and I will no longer interfere. 'Tis your concern, not mine, although I do hope you will find happiness with someone special ere long. I hate to see you in a state of melancholy."

"You know me," Selina said. "I'm never downcast for more than a short time, and of course I do not think of you and Henry harshly. I am thrilled and grateful to have been asked to this splendid party—but I do reserve the right to choose my own partner."

Lord! If only that partner had been able to be George, for when I look at him now, my heart spins round in a tizzy. My treacherous body betrays a weakness for his appearance, while at the same time my brain tells me that we have nothing in common.

"Excuse me a minute," Kitty said, "for I must wander amongst my guests. Mama always told me it was the duty of a good hostess to circulate as much as possible and make sure everyone is comfortable."

Selina smiled. "Your first dinner party has been a triumph. I only hope you will not be too tired tomorrow—you have spared no effort in making this a perfect occasion."

"Not quite perfect," Kitty whispered, "for I have not yet found you a husband."

"Go and see your other guests!"

Selina looked into the depths of the crackling fire. How comforting it was to feel the warmth. She looked around the withdrawing room—the room and indeed the whole house was strikingly similar to her own home with her parents and brother Edmund next door at Number 1 Royal Crescent. There were differences too, though, for Henry and Kitty had already stamped their own personalities on their new home in the short time they had been married—barely a month.

It had been very generous of Lord and Lady Templeton to buy Number 2 for the young couple, and Selina in particular was delighted because it meant she still lived close to her dear brother Henry—and to Kitty, her best friend from childhood. Perchance Selina's parents planned to populate more of the Royal Crescent with the Templeton family. When her brother Edmund chose a bride, would their papa buy another house in the Crescent, to keep Edward and his new wife close by? Not that Edmund had shown any signs of wanting to settle down.

Selina tried to crush the thoughts that were growing inside her. Would her papa buy a house for her when she got married? A house for her to live in with her husband and hopefully children? She imagined herself living in one of Bath's splendid terraced houses—Number 3 Royal Crescent, for instance, which Selina had recently heard was for sale. Would the view from her withdrawing room once married be onto the Crescent Lawn but from Number 3, not Number 1, as it had been so far all her life? Selina imagined herself talking to the housekeeper and cook, planning meals, organizing the household . . . soon she was running from room to room, wondering how long it would take to fill the nursery with a brood of children.

Then she imagined herself in the bed of her marital home, turning to her soulmate.

"I love you," he whispered.

Strong arms around her, soft lips brushing hers and a hard muscular body pressing against her . . . and the face—whose was it? Who would her husband be? Selina closed her eyes. Her treacherous body took over and supplied the details. The face of her soulmate was framed with bright blonde hair and had green glittering eyes. In her vision, George did not talk of logic, cards, or horses, but murmured soft endearments and nibbled her neck, telling her how ardently he loved her and wished to join with her . . .

"Miss Templeton?" Selina opened her eyes and spun round. George stood close by, his hands clasped behind his back. "A fine fire, is it not?"

"Are you particularly fond of fires?" Selina said, willing her heart to stop beating as fast as her favorite Scottish reel.

"As a matter fact, I am," George said. "Some of my happiest childhood memories are of when my father took me out riding; very often, we would then sit on the ground and light a fire."

"And no doubt you conversed about all sorts of things sitting round your campfire," Selina said.

George paused. "Mostly we did not talk at all, but stared into the depths. I do not always feel the need to chat. And I love being outside with nature, by an open fire. There is much to see within the flames—and much to ponder."

A long silence followed.

"Is that what we are doing now," Selina asked, "with both of us regarding the flames—are we pondering the deep meaning of life?"

George lifted his eyes, and Selina was transfixed by their unusually clear green depths. 'Twas like beholding a cold and heartless winter sea. She could drown in those eyes—and no one would be able to save her.

"Miss Templeton," George said, "I am not used to talking much with the fairer sex, however, this evening I wish to say . . ."

"Lord, Mr. Fitzgerald," Selina said, "I believe you have nothing to say to me. If you had, you would already have said it, for we sat together at dinner for a long time. I know you're a man of few words; indeed, you've just told me your favorite activity is sitting by a fire while totally silent."

Selina stopped suddenly when she saw an unusual expression

flit across George's face. What was it? Anguish? Selina was a little ashamed. She hardly knew the man and should not be talking to him in such a flippant manner. It was all very well to tease and torment her brother Henry with nonsense—why, she and Henry had sparred all their lives—but George was a guest in Henry's house, and he did not seem to appreciate her levity. Nor did he deserve her facetious comments. Perhaps he thought she was trying to belittle him in some way? In truth, Selina did not know why she was carrying on like this—or why George made her feel so on edge. He was one of the most enigmatic people she'd ever met, and she found him inexplicably irritating—like a splinter in her finger that she wanted to get rid of.

Yet sometimes, I feel the opposite, and want to keep George near for the rest of my life.

"Do you not want to join the card game over there in the corner?" Selina asked. "I know how much you like playing."

"No. But thank you for suggesting it. I have no wish to join in and am perfectly content here by the fire. Besides, it is not so much the game I like, more the patterns I see in the cards. And it's the same for me with music."

This was mighty odd. Selina had never heard of cards being linked with music before. Although now, on reflection, she could see there was a certain similarity—if one possessed a dry logical brain. And if one were a creature of habit who valued sequence and order above all else. In other words—if one were unimaginative.

Selina put her shoulders back. She was not like that. She preferred spontaneity and naturalness. When she married, Selina would choose a man she loved, one who acted on the spur of the moment and was full to the brim with ideas and lively thoughts—not one who stared into fires and muttered about logic. Where was the romance in that? The emotion? And love?

One thing is for sure: Mr. George Fitzgerald is the last person on earth I would ever want to marry.

Isn't he?

CHAPTER TWO

George

SHORTLY AFTERWARDS, THE party began to break up and guests took their leave.

As George stood in the entrance hall waiting to say goodbye to his hosts, Henry grasped his arm, whispering in his ear, "Do not leave yet, good friend. There is much I wish to say to you. Stay on awhile and have another drink with me."

"Are you sure?" George said. "You must be tired of guests after a long evening. Do you not wish to relax with your dear wife?"

Henry smiled. "Time enough for all that. I want to help a good friend—do not look so surprised, George. And Kitty and I are going away to London very soon for a few weeks, perhaps longer, so this might be the last chance for some time that we can chat privately. Please, do stay."

George nodded. "I thank you."

"Go and sit in the parlor," Henry said. "We will have a drink together—we will talk."

George slipped through the door, closed it, and sat down by the fire. Was Henry going to ask him what he thought of his sister, Selina? Try to find out how things were going? He was fairly sure Kitty had been talking to Selina about him earlier in the evening, for he had heard his name mentioned across the crowded room and had seen the two friends conversing earnestly.

Shaking his head sorrowfully, George leaned back in the chair. There was no romantic future for him and Selina—alas. Their last awkward conversation by the fire upstairs had put paid to any remaining hope he might still have harbored. George had desperately wanted to confide in Selina then, to explain that he was so distracted by her presence that he felt unable to be his normal self. Granted, he was generally somewhat of an introvert, yet he was more than able to hold forth on many topics in the right company, generally male.

But not when I'm facing the goddess of my dreams, the woman I want to marry and cherish forever—for then I seem unable to speak rationally.

'Twas regrettable that George's attempt to speak his mind had fallen flat. He suspected that Selina had also struggled to be true to herself, prattling on about George's love of fire and cards. Perhaps she had been attempting to tease him—possibly even to flirt? Who knew. But it came across as a touch brittle—almost as if she was trying to put him in his place. Could it have been due to nerves on her part? George knew all about nerves.

Selina had more or less dismissed him, suggesting he should go and play cards. He had then explained clearly to her that he was not a gambling addict, no, for his interest in cards was something quite different, and there was a link to his interest in music. Even as he had said those words, he'd sensed her withdrawing from him. She obviously found his conversation insufferably tedious, for not long after that she had looked a little distracted before making her excuses and moving swiftly to the far side of the room.

That was the second time she had walked away from him that evening. The first was when they had been sitting on the sofa. When he had closed his eyes to listen to the music, she had taken the chance to slip away. The writing on the wall was clear: Selina thought little of him and did not want to be in his company.

George heard muffled voices from the entrance hall as the front door finally closed.

"All our guests are now gone," Kitty said. "What a wonderful evening it has been, dearest—and now we will make our own sweet music, will we not?"

Henry shushed Kitty at this point, and there was silence for a few seconds followed by a giggle from Kitty.

"Not quite everyone has gone," Henry said in a lower, but still audible, voice. "One guest remains. George is in the parlor and I need to talk to him."

"I understand," Kitty said. "Selina told me . . . and he was very quiet—nervous? She can be hasty to judge. Do your best . . . be not too long, my dearest."

"I will fetch some Madeira from the tantalus in the dining room and have a chat with George. I promise I will not be too long, darling Kitty."

George shifted in his seat, feeling embarrassed that he had such good hearing—and a little guilty that Henry was not going to go upstairs with Kitty straight away. 'Twas thoughtful and kind of Henry to insist on a private meeting, but George resolved to try to make the conversation short, and then he would be away, galloping across the city on Trigger, homeward bound.

A few minutes later, Henry stepped into the room holding two glasses of Madeira—and came straight to the point.

"George, you must tell me what has happened with my sister. Kitty and I had such high hopes for the pair of you."

George dropped his head. "Your sister has indicated that she finds me the most insufferable bore in Bath, if not in the whole southwest of England."

Henry frowned. "To be honest, I thought as much, from her demeanor. But why? The two of you seemed so close before."

"I sincerely believe there was a strong physical connection between us."

There still is a strong physical attraction—on my side at least. There always will be.

"However," George continued, "we have never really had the chance to sit next to each other for any length of time until this evening. Now she knows me better, she likes me less."

"Yes, well, we sat you next to each other on purpose," Henry said. "The seating plan was meticulously organized."

"Thank you for that—you are both very kind. Sadly, the opportunity was ill used by me, for I felt so overcome sitting next to the object of my desire that I was unable to speak for most of the meal—I merely sat there like a stupid stuffed turkey. And I am not sure your sister approved of my clothes, either."

"Your clothes?"

"She stared at my breeches, which as you can see are a little dirty. There was a sudden rainstorm on the way here, and Trigger's hooves threw up quantities of mud."

"Selina cares not for appearances," Henry said. "If she noticed the mud on your breeches, she will have admired you for it because she would have thought you had been on a great adventure. She does not give two figs for the values of the *ton*; her main aim in life is to break free from the confines of polite society. I well remember the arguments she had with our mama about how she should dress—for Selina is reluctant to wear the usual trappings of femininity such as gloves, bonnets, and so on."

"Shoes?"

"Ah, yes," Henry said. "There were many arguments about shoes. When she was a small girl, as soon as she was out on the Crescent Lawn, she would toss her footwear aside and pull her stockings off. She loved the feel of the grass tickling her toes. The governess was always complaining."

"It's a wonderful sensation, to feel the ground through your feet," George said.

"There you are then. You have something in common."

George grinned. "My parents were always quite happy when I wanted to go barefoot in the garden."

"Interesting, especially as your father is a doctor. Perhaps there is some benefit in being close to nature that the rest of us don't know about."

"I am sure there is. Anyway, I prefer being outside. How I hate being cooped up in a house."

"Another thing that Selina used to fight for was to have the sun on her face," Henry said. "She would take off her bonnet and hold her face up to the sky, no matter how many times Mama scolded her for encouraging freckles."

George took a sip of his drink. "'Tis unfair that women have so few freedoms. No one has ever told me to cover the skin of my face in case I become tanned or have freckles."

"Yes, I hadn't thought of that. S'pose Selina does feel hemmed in somewhat. 'Tis a shame. And because Selina has a particularly bold and adventurous spirit, our parents have always tried to keep the firm hand of discipline upon her."

"I cannot believe Miss Templeton has ever have done something she needed to be disciplined about."

"You'd be surprised," Henry said. "Have I not told you about the incident on the parapet above Number 1 Royal Crescent?"

"No, you have not. What happened?"

"Oh, nothing very terrible. Only that Selina thought it would be a good idea when we were children to persuade me to climb out of the window of a servant's bedroom with her and stand on the roof next to the low parapet. Selina is very fond of birds and said we would be able to see as far as eagles. All I would need to do was follow her out of the window and along the ledge. As luck would have it, my father was on the Crescent Fields at the time and saw us make what he called 'the incredibly stupid decision to risk our lives.'"

George's eyebrows were almost up in his hair by now. He had been fond of tree climbing in his youth but had never dreamt of this sort of caper.

"Of course," Henry said, "as an adult, I can look back and see how dangerous and foolish the whole enterprise was, but at the time I felt compelled to do what Selina said. She can be very persuasive!"

"She is quite a character. I do admire that about her."

I admire everything about her—and always will.

"So why was it so hard to talk to her at dinner, if you admire her so much?"

"'Tis because I admire her that it was so difficult—I did not want to put a foot wrong. Sadly, this made me nervous, and I struggled to think of things that she might be interested in. Then eventually I remembered that night when we were all in the Octagon."

"Oh yes," Henry said. "The night you exposed Lord Steyne as a card shark. Who could forget? George, you were positively on fire that evening. I've never heard you so eloquent. I actually thought you should train to be a barrister because of your performance. Everyone was terribly impressed!"

"Well, I have no difficulty spouting forth when I know what I'm talking about, and also, although Miss Templeton was there, I did not realize it at the time, so I did not feel constrained or distracted by my feelings for her."

Henry narrowed his eyes. "You have been fond of my sister for a long time then, have you? For you, it is not merely a fleeting attraction of the last couple of months."

George was silent. How could he explain to Henry that he had spent years worshipping Selina from afar, ardently wishing he was the sort of man who found it possible to have an easy relationship with women. George had watched his friends flirting with ladies at balls, in the Pump Room, at musical gatherings, why, simply everywhere in Bath—whereas he himself found it difficult to speak lightly about trivial subjects, which seemed to be what was required. The usual conversational gambits of the *ton* had always been a closed book to him.

"Tell me," Henry said softly. "You can find the words."

"I, I cannot," George said. "It runs too deep."

"Do you love my sister?"

George nodded.

"And you have for years?"

Again, the nod.

Henry sighed. "Now, I wonder, what we can do about this?"

"There's nothing to be done. I've already ruined my chance this evening at dinner. After making the mistake of saying nothing, I then made the further mistake of saying far too much, droning on about cards and gambling." George clutched his head. "I may have come across as being rather boastful."

"And why not?" Henry said. "You have always been the best of our set at cards. Your skill and energy are boundless, and your brain must be the size of a planet to keep all those numbers and plans logically assembled. At Cambridge, you were universally admired for the brilliance of your mind. Not like the rest of us boneheads, the ones that went into the army."

"You are too kind. I'm sure I have no intelligence that is not common to all."

"And are you still sure you want to become a doctor?"

George's eyes lit up. "I am really enjoying being my father's apprentice and hope one day to be as fine a doctor as he is. He says I am all but ready to set up on my own, although I know I still have much to learn. Yesterday I accompanied him on his visits and saw firsthand how he alleviates the suffering of the poor."

"Your father treats both rich and poor?"

"He does. He treats anyone in need and often says how fortunate he is to have independent wealth so that he can afford to minister to the less well-off. Oh, Henry, if you could see how some have to live—the suffering . . ."

Henry's mouth formed a thin line. "I saw suffering aplenty when I was at war and on my long, long journey home."

"Of course," George said. "None of us will forget what you had to go through. But in this city of Bath, there are those in real need only a few steps away from all the elegance and prosperity. 'Tis a scandal, and there is much to be done. So many diseases could be prevented or relieved by basic medical care."

"Well, I am glad you find your work fulfilling. You must be

very busy."

"Medicine does not take all my energies. I also spend much time at my father's stables in Newton St Loe. My papa breeds a good many horses there, and there is always much to do."

"Quite a thriving business, I have heard," Henry said.

"'Tis always a hive of activity. I enjoy helping out there—for all horses deserve proper medical attention."

"I suppose they do. Certainly, the horses I knew at Waterloo were some of the bravest creatures I have ever encountered, and it was horrible to see their suffering. All that was available to treat them was a quick mercy killing."

"Did you have to do that?" George said.

Henry nodded. "'Twas not easy—but necessary."

"Indeed."

There was a silence, at the end of which Henry let out a long breath. "You will make a fine doctor, George, for you are a very good listener. You will make an excellent husband too. Therefore we must formulate a plan, for your affection for my sister runs deep. I am sure something can be done to help the situation between you and Selina."

"Perhaps. But I have taken up too much of your time." George tipped the remaining Madeira down his throat and stood up. "Many thanks, my friend, for the most wonderful evening. I will see you soon."

"Yes—and we will talk again."

"You must then tell me how your own affairs are going," George said. "You are still considering going into the law?"

"I am, though 'tis early days at the moment. A connection of my father has recommended many learned tomes for me to read which will take a deal of time, and of course I must not neglect Kitty, then there is our new home and our forthcoming jaunt to London . . . but yes, I think law will be the right step for me. I will not go back to the army—not after Waterloo."

"A wise decision, for life is too long to spend it doing something you do not enjoy."

"You are certainly right about that," Henry said. "By the way, when I return from London, I will be bringing Carter back with me."

"Carter? Your manservant, Carter? What the devil has he been doing in London?"

"He has been there for weeks. He left immediately after my wedding; he was called away suddenly on private business."

"You are a generous employer, to allow him so much time off."

Henry smiled. "Carter has another job as well as being my manservant."

"Another job?"

"A government job. I cannot tell you more."

"How mysterious!" George said.

"That's not the only mystery about him. I will tell you more on my return from London. Now, shall I walk you to the stable to collect Trigger? I could do with some air."

Outside, the night was crisp and clear. The two men turned left to walk to the end of the Crescent, stopping briefly outside Number 1.

"In all the time I lived here with my family," Henry said, "I never dreamt I would end up living right next door at Number 2 with Kitty."

"'Tis a very convenient arrangement," George said. "By Jove! What's that on the roof?"

"Where?"

"Oh, er, nothing; a shadow, perchance?"

"Or too much wine!"

"Doubtless," George replied. "Come! Let us hasten round to the stable. You can say hello to Trigger, for I know how fond of him you are."

I thought I saw someone on the roof—in fact I am sure I did. And if it is who I think it is, I will not betray her to her brother. Or anyone.

I would never betray Selina.

Selina

SELINA TOOK A step back from the parapet. It would not do to be found out. George had looked up, but she was confident he had not seen her, for why would he expect her to be out here?

When she was a little girl and had trespassed on the roof in the company of her brothers and Kitty, Selina had received such a reprimand from her parents that she did not attempt the adventure again for many years. Then, gradually, it became a habit of hers to creep out onto the roof, mostly at night, for during the day someone always wanted to know where she was. These days she chose to exit via the servant's room at the far end of the corridor, the tiniest room that was scarcely ever occupied unless the Templetons had a lot of guests staying. She was adept at creeping along the top corridor in the dead of night and highly skilled at avoiding the squeaky floorboards. Thus far, she was satisfied she had avoided detection from what the snobbiest members of the *ton* called the *lower orders*.

'Twas a risky procedure, for sure. There was the ever-present chance that she would be noticed by someone either inside or outside the house, but there had also been one or two dangerous moments when she had leaned a little too far over and nearly slipped. However, the adventure had been worth it for the exhilaration and freedom.

Sometimes, on a moonlit summer night, Selina took a book up to the roof and relaxed over the pages of a gothic thriller or a tender romance, the balmy breeze wafting over her. At other times, she had clung to the stones behind her as rain lashed down, looking over the Crescent Lawn to the Crescent Fields and beyond during an electrical storm. Then, she had felt truly alive, imagining herself at the prow of a mighty ship crashing through the waves on the high seas.

The one thing Selina had not dared to do—yet—was climb

over the ridge of stone until she reached Henry and Kitty's house, Number 2 Royal Crescent. That would be trespassing. And involve risking her neck. Although she could see that for an athletic and courageous person, if circumstances required, it would be possible to travel round the whole top of the Crescent. Perhaps one day . . .

Selina climbed back through the small sash window, closing it firmly behind her. 'Twas intriguing that George had stayed so long with Henry at Number 2. Henry must have wanted to have a private chat with him. Selina's cheeks flamed. Had they been discussing her? How dare they! She was heartily fed up with people poking their noses into her business. It had happened all her life. When she was but a girl, people had said,

"I wonder who you're going to marry?"

"What sort of gentleman do you think you want to settle down with?"

"You are bound to make an advantageous match with a face like yours—and your father's fortune."

As soon as Selina grew old enough to set foot in a ballroom, she had felt the male gaze on her, assessing her face, her figure, and her background. And heard with her own ears discussions of what certain young ladies were "worth" in terms of financial wealth. Really, sometimes Bath was no better than a cattle market. What were the chances that George had been asking Henry exactly how much her dowry was this very evening?

Ah no, that was a shameful thought. There was no need for George to choose his bride from an affluent family. His father, Doctor Fitzgerald, was very wealthy. Perhaps not as rich as Lord Templeton, Selina's father, but then few in Bath were. George had grown up with every advantage. The Fitzgerald home in Devonshire Buildings was a fine house, although it was outside the city, south of the river. Doctor Fitzgerald also owned farms and much land to the west, including a fine set of stables in Newton St. Loe.

There was a small country estate in Devon as well, but apparently the Fitzgeralds preferred to reside near Bath for the best part of the year, as most of Doctor Fitzgerald's medical work was in the city and surrounding areas. He was renowned in Bath for the excellence of his treatment and the passion with which he carried out his medical vocation. Doctor Fitzgerald was also a good friend and colleague of Doctor Jenkins, who attended the Templetons—in fact, Selina had found out about the admirable reputation of George's father from Doctor Jenkins. Well, not directly from him, but the information had come from Doctor Jenkins's lips while he was talking to Lord and Lady Templeton one day. Selina was lucky enough to be nearby—with her ear to the keyhole—and had heard everything.

Creeping along the corridor to her chamber, Selina bit her lip. Up until this evening, George's circumstances had been an ever-present thought in her mind, and she had frequently imagined herself calling upon George's parents in their house in Devonshire Buildings, visiting their farms and the stables at Newton St. Loe and squeezing in a visit to their country estate in Devon. Heavens! She had even speculated about which church they should marry in. Now these images made a rapid retreat—for Selina had discovered what George really was. A pompous, boastful bore.

Selina opened the door to her bedroom, thought better of it, and flew down the stairs to the entrance hall to collect her cloak. From thence she went down to the basement and slipped out of the back of the house. She would go round to the stable, for that was where George and Henry were bound; hopefully, she would be able to hear their conversation.

Running along Upper Church Street, Selina passed the backs of the Crescent houses. What a stark contrast the view was to the graceful elegance and symmetry of the street scene at the front by the Crescent Lawn. Here at the rear of the buildings, all was mismatched and individual, each house boasting a different design, with strange bulbous extensions scattered about the terrace. Was this not a little like George? For he had a flawless exterior; his beautiful visage boasted regular, pleasing features and handsome eyes. Yet his personality was a higgledy-piggledy mess—full of contradictions and unexpected behaviors.

Selina moved softly along Crescent Lane and found the stable used by the Templeton family. Success! She could hear Henry and George's low voices.

"What a fine creature you are, Trigger," Henry said.

"He's very fond of you," George said.

"As I am of him, for did he not help me rescue my Kitty from the clutches of Lord Steyne last December?"

The two voices dropped to a murmur, then suddenly the stable door opened and Selina moved quickly, pressing herself into a dark and shadowy recess some distance away. She would not risk being discovered—for there were no words she could have found to explain why she was standing outside the stable eavesdropping. Even she herself did not know why she was doing this.

"I am sorry about my sister," Henry said to George.

Sorry? Henry is "sorry" about me? How dare he speak of me in this way!

"She does not always know what is best for her," Henry continued, "and she can be hasty in her judgement."

"'Tis my fault entirely," George said, "for I made a mess of things. I think before tonight, she thought I was something I was not. She has no idea that I am . . ."

You are what? Speak up, man!

"I will speak to Kitty," Henry said. "She may know what can be done. And if it is not to be, then remember that Kitty knows many young ladies and can make introductions aplenty for you— there will be someone out there for you, George."

"Pray do not bother yourself over me. I am a lost cause, and 'tis my fate to be alone. I do not mind. In fact, I've always thought matrimony was rather overrated."

Henry punched George lightly on his shoulder. "You do not mean this, my good friend."

"I do! I assure you."

"And I assure you," Henry said, "that when you meet the right woman, you will long to be joined to her in matrimony with every fiber of your being."

Selina sighed loudly from her hiding place.

"What was that?" Henry said.

"I heard nothing," George said.

"It was like a breath."

"Ah, that will be one of the other horses in the stable. Or may have been Trigger here." George stroked the horse's nose. "Come on, my old fellow. Time I got you back to the comfort of your own stable. You need to rest."

"I've always thought it very odd," Henry said, "that horses can sleep standing up."

"Yes. They have a special joint in their back legs that allows them to do this. How useful this would be for humans."

"Indeed," Henry said. "And will Trigger really rest better in his own stable? Is a horse truly aware which stable he is in?"

"Of course," George said. "Trigger is a sentient being. He is totally aware of his surroundings. He likes to be in another stable and meet other horses, yet is happiest to return to his own home. I even believe he can sense whether I am sleeping in my bedchamber in Devonshire Buildings just across the way from his stable."

"'Tis almost as if he were a member of your family."

"He definitely is," George said, "and is very much loved by the whole household."

Merciful heavens! George has a soft heart, to be sure.

George ruffled Trigger's mane, then gave him a quick kiss on the side of his head.

Selina stifled the groan that was threatening to escape from her lips. She might not have thought much of George's behavior at dinner, but her whole body was desperate for his touch. If only George were running his hands through Selina's hair, if only he were kissing her cheek, her mouth, what a fine thing that would be . . .

"I wish you godspeed," Henry said as George mounted Trigger.

"Thank you. I will be home in no time at all," George said. "'Tis only a couple of miles."

"A steep climb, though."

"Indeed," George said, "but Trigger is up to it, are you not, my friend?" He stroked Trigger gently on the side of his neck.

How George loved that horse! He did not seem to have much trouble talking to animals—nor Henry. Was he simply not prepared to make the effort when he was talking to Selina? She must be very low in his estimation, beneath all the men—and animals—in the world.

Selina allowed a few minutes for George and Henry to go ahead around Crescent Lane to Upper Church Street and thence to the Royal Crescent, before she followed. She intended to enter Number 1 as she had left—by slipping in via the servants' entrance. Perhaps she should wait a little longer in case Henry was lingering in the street and saw her? Although 'twas not likely he would do this, for he would be keen to join Kitty. He must be racing up the main stairs of Number 2 to their chamber right now.

When Selina reached the servants' entrance, she was amazed to find she could still see George on the other side of the road. He had not galloped away as she had anticipated but had dismounted and was leading Trigger very slowly down the sloping path at the side of the Crescent Lawn.

Dare she? Was she brave enough to follow him? One heard of all sorts of people being abroad at this time of the night—cutthroats, beggars, and other undesirables. Selina looked around carefully. No one! And no faces appearing at the windows of the houses in Brock Street to make reports to her parents in the morning. Everyone must be fast asleep.

Selina pulled the hood of her cloak right over her face and moved softly across the cobbles, following George and Trigger down the path and left onto the Gravel Walk. She kept to the shadows, leaving a good space between her and George as she followed him along the portion of Gravel Walk that ran along the back of the gardens of Brock Street. The route then curved slightly as the gardens of Brock Street merged into those of The Circus.

Why was Selina doing this? Had she lost her sense of reason? Should she go back? Selina looked behind herself and felt a little nervous. The sensation was an unusual one for her.

For I do not usually go chasing after men in the middle of the night, risking my reputation . . .

'Twas not too late to simply turn and go back—indeed, that would be the sensible course of action, the one she should take.

Just as Selina had decided that her venture was over and she would return to the comfort of her bedchamber, George and Trigger stopped dead. And George's gorgeous voice murmured softly, "Now then, Trigger, there, there, boy. You are right; we should make for home. But first, there is something . . ."

No! What was George doing? He was turning around with Trigger and beginning to walk towards her. Selina pressed herself against the high wall at the side of the path and the rough stones pressed uncomfortably into her back. There was nowhere to hide! And George would soon discover her.

Selina pulled her hood right over her face. She would be fine, for he did not know she was following him. Of what consequence would it be if he saw a woman standing by a wall on the Gravel Walk in the middle of the night? Many women probably stood in such places in the night—waiting for men? Selina was a little hazy about what actually went on in the streets of Bath after dark, but she had been warned often enough by her mama *never* to be out alone, particularly at night.

"There are ladies of the night," her mother had said frequently. "There is an alternative society that flourishes in the streets, a society you do not belong to."

George was nearly upon her. Would he think she was a lady

of the night? Selina clenched her teeth. She was not so green, but she did not know what ladies of the night did. For her mother had explained that to her many years ago—when Selina had asked at the age of thirteen.

"The ladies of the night," Lady Templeton had said, "perform paid services for men, and this is something that you never need to think about again. And now, Selina, this conversation is most definitely at an end. It will not be repeated."

Selina was worried. If George thought she was a lady of the night, might he ask her to perform a service? For a fee? She trembled. This was not a situation in which she wished to find herself. She was *way* out of her depth. And she knew she would be in trouble with her parents if they ever found out. The sound of Trigger's hooves stopped and she heard the horse's gentle whinny beside her. What would happen now?

George cleared his throat. "I will escort you home, Miss Templeton."

George

THE ONLY REASON I am not galloping halfway up Beechen Cliff by now," George said, "is because all the time I have been fully conscious of your presence. I cannot leave you in the street, but instead must do the gentlemanly thing and make sure you get home safely to Number 1."

Selina threw back the hood of her cloak. "You knew it was me? Did you not think I was a lady of the night?"

"Of course I knew it was you, Miss Templeton, and of course I did not think you were a—lady of the night. I was aware of you outside the stable and then following us back to Number 1."

What an amazing woman Selina is! Bold and courageous, yet so innocent and in need of my protection. Heaven knows what would have happened to her all alone in the street if I had not lingered tonight.

"How did you know?" Selina asked. "I thought I had been careful enough to escape detection. And why did you not say anything at the time?"

"I did not want to betray you to your brother," George said. "That would have been most unfair."

"Did you realize I was listening to you and Henry talking?"

"I did not think we were close enough for you to hear us clearly."

"I heard snippets," Selina said.

There was a pause while George tried to recollect all he had said to Henry about Selina—hopefully not too much that was embarrassing.

"I certainly did not hear everything," Selina said, "although I did hear you say you did not want to be married."

That was a shame, for I didn't really mean it.

"Why did you turn around and walk back to me now?" Selina asked.

"I decided the charade had gone on long enough. 'Twas time I walked you home. I would never leave you here to make your own way back—you must know that. All sorts of dangers lurk for a young woman such as yourself. You should be more careful, Miss Templeton."

"You sound like Mama! She's always warning me to be more cautious—without being specific about what the danger is that I must avoid."

"The danger," George said, "comes from men, sadly. And your mama is right to urge you to look after yourself." Then he smiled. "Why were you following me, by the way? Most sensible young women are sound asleep at this time of night."

"Why was I following you?" Selina paused. "Why should I answer you, especially since you are determined to tease me by talking about sensible young women—for you must know by now that I am nothing of the sort."

"'Tis true, a fondness for wandering on a roof at night can scarcely be considered prudent—nor can an aversion to wearing shoes, nor . . ."

"Enough! You do not need to list my misdemeanors. I recollect them all quite clearly."

"You have not yet answered my question—why do you take such risks?"

"Why should I not?" Selina stamped her foot. "You can have no idea what 'tis like to be a woman in today's world. I have so little freedom and am constantly warned of dangers lurking everywhere if I set foot outside the house by myself, especially, heaven forbid, after dark. And yet young men of my age have complete liberty to do as they choose."

George nodded. "I see what you mean. And agree 'tis most unfair. But sometimes, we have to do our best to fit in with the world as it is—to protect ourselves."

"Is that what you do?"

George paused for a moment and then a slow smile spread across his face. "Why, I do believe that it is, Miss Templeton. How very perceptive you are."

And utterly, completely adorable.

"I will tell you one thing," George said. "I was quite well aware you were observing us from the parapet above Number 1."

"You were? Are none of my secrets safe?"

Selina's eyes shone with merriment in the gentle moonlight, and George took a step closer. How he longed to take her into his arms, to embrace her tenderly, allow his finger to trace the soft curve of her cheek, then lower his lips onto hers for their first delicate kiss, before allowing passion to sweep over them . . .

"George! I mean, Mr. Fitzgerald! Are you feeling quite yourself? You look a little strange."

"Feel free to call me George," he said. "And, and . . ."

Would she ask him to call her Selina? If she did, would it mean anything?

"Oh, yes, I am more than happy to call you George," Selina said. "And obviously you may call me Selina. I have always thought of you as George, not Mr. Fitzgerald."

"Have you? That's . . . that's . . ."

"Oh yes. I think of all of Henry's friends by their Christian names because that is so often how he refers to them. Also, I despise any sort of formality. 'Tis so unnecessary, do you not think?"

"Absolutely!"

"I am glad we are agreed on that, *George*. And now, I think you should tell me one of your secrets, since you know so many of mine. Go on! Tell me one of your most well-guarded secrets."

Shall I tell her how much I ardently love and admire her? How I worship her? How I long to be one with her? That would be putting formality aside in no uncertain terms.

"George! You are looking strange again. I was only teasing you."

George said nothing—and felt a little despondent.

I am trying to think of a suitable reply; sadly, it is beyond me. How I long to be able to match your quick wit, Selina—for then you might admire me. And love me?

Trigger blew softly through his nostrils, waiting patiently for his master.

"Yes, yes," George said. "I know; we must take Selina back now."

I have no trouble talking to animals.

As they walked along the chips of gravel, Selina stumbled slightly, and George took her arm to steady her. What exquisite torture! Was this the closest he would ever get to holding his love? He could smell her sweet perfume and feel her vital life force as they walked along.

Once they reached the end of the Gravel Walk, Selina pulled her arm free.

"Thank you, George. I do not need your support any longer and will be fine from here."

"I will walk you right up to the door. I insist."

If anything were to happen to Selina because of my neglect, I could never bear it.

"All right, if you think it necessary."

"I do," George said.

"I do!" How I long to say these words to my sweet Selina in an entirely different context.

Number 1 Royal Crescent was now in view, and they walked side by side until they reached the servants' entrance.

"Thank goodness," Selina said as she tried the door. "Still unlocked!"

"What would you have done if you had found the door bolted?" George asked.

"I would probably have gone round to the front of Number 2 and thrown gravel at Henry and Kitty's bedroom until they took pity on me and came down to let me in," Selina said. "Then I would either have stayed the night in their house, or perhaps I could have been very brave and used the rooftop route from their house to reach Number 1. Don't look so horrified, George! I am sure it would be quite possible—although I have not yet attempted it."

Then, with quick thanks and a wave of her hand, Selina disappeared into the servants' quarters.

George mounted his horse, and Trigger trotted along the Gravel Walk, down past the Theatre Royal and on towards the river. It was surprising how many people were wandering the streets at this hour, many the worse for wear. A group of rowdy drinkers greeted George as he passed, cordially inviting him to have a drink with them.

"Maybe another time," he called out.

Once he had crossed the River Avon, the pace slowed a little, as Holloway was a steep climb for Trigger.

"There, there. Are you thirsty, old boy?"

Pausing for a moment by the water trough, George dismounted and encouraged Trigger to drink. Suddenly, a movement in a nearby bush caught his attention.

"Who's there?" George said.

"Damn your eyes!" a voice answered.

George took no notice, mounted Trigger again and continued up the road.

"Devil take you, Fitzgerald!" he heard faintly in the distance. "You will pay for what you did. A curse upon your head . . ."

Fitzgerald? The unseen ruffian had used his name. He knew him! And the voice—had George heard it before? The timbre seemed familiar.

George wiped his brow, feeling suddenly weary. The man could be someone George had encountered when out on a visit with his father—possibly a patient with grudge? This seemed a credible possibility, for 'twas fair to say that medicine could not cure all, and although the majority of patients were grateful for their efforts, there were always those who blamed their doctors when things went wrong.

Now George felt sorry for the man who had shouted at him from the bush and wished he knew who he was. He tapped the side of his head—something was niggling him. Perchance the man was nothing to do with George's medical work. But who else would it have been? George had no enemies—as far as he knew.

Unlike Henry—for last year Captain Henry Templeton had been threatened by a mortal enemy, none other than the infamous Lord Steyne.

Henry always said how grateful he was to George for carrying out the final part of the defeat of Lord Steyne—his exposure as a card shark in the Octagon shortly before last Christmas.

Wait! 'Twas possible Lord Steyne still bore George a deal of ill will because of what had happened in the Octagon—and the voice from the bushes by the water trough had sounded familiar. Could the hidden person have been Lord Steyne?

No, the idea was both fanciful and preposterous, for after George had exposed him as a card shark, Lord Steyne had fled the city. There were rumors—and hopes—that he'd even left the country and traveled to the Continent, so deep was his disgrace in the eyes of the *ton*. It was inconceivable that Lord Steyne would be cowering the foothills of Beechen Cliff in the middle of the night.

Wasn't it?

Of course it was! George relaxed his shoulders. A foolish imagining—the consequence of too much Madeira with Henry.

George was on the top of Beechen Cliff now, and 'twas only a short journey onwards to Devonshire Buildings and his home. Selina would be tucked up in bed by now. Would she be fast asleep and dreaming of romance and love? Or would she be lying awake, thinking about the events of the evening and plotting another adventure?

Why had Selina been on the parapet? And why had she decided to follow Henry and George to the stable? A sudden whim—or could she possibly be harboring feelings for George? She had seemed attracted to him at Christmas time.

Who was he kidding?

There was no evidence that Selina had any feelings for George. She was lively and friendly, of course, but was she not like that with everyone? What George had hoped was a blossoming romance had proved this evening to be nothing of the sort. However, talking to Henry had been a comfort. Perhaps he would be able to help George further? Although Henry had said how busy he was with all the law books he had to read—and he would be away to London fairly soon for an extended visit.

Trigger snorted, and George stroked his mane.

"You are right, my old friend. I must change the situation, not rely on Henry. If I want my devotion to Selina to be returned with love, 'tis up to me to achieve this. I must make a plan—not give up at the first hurdle."

For I am determined to win Selina's heart—and then her hand in marriage. Though I have not the faintest idea how to go about it.

CHAPTER THREE
Selina

SELINA STOOD AT the window of the withdrawing room of Number 1 Royal Crescent, staring out at the depressingly gray and drizzly February skies.

"Selina, my dear," her mother Lady Templeton said. "I'm sorry to say that Signor Allegretto has sent a note of apology. He will not be able to give you your singing lesson this morning."

"Oh, what a shame," Selina said. "I was so looking forward to it. What is the reason?"

"The poor man is not well. His note says he had a high fever in the night and his doctor has advised him to stay at home for fear of contagion. He will spend the day resting quietly in his lodgings and says he hopes you will carry on learning the new Handel air you have been working on together, although not before you have done a proper warm up, including the recent vocal exercises he has taught you. Does that make sense? Will you be able to do that before your lesson next week?"

"It does—and I will certainly try," Selina said.

"Perhaps I could help you by running through the Handel tomorrow?" Lady Templeton said. "I know the accompaniment well, and it is such a pretty song; I would really enjoy playing for you."

"That would be splendid, Mama," Selina said.

But what was she going to do now? The morning stretched endlessly in front of her—the whole day, in fact. And at the moment, it was far too wet to go out for a walk, which was what she longed to do. If only Kitty were here in Bath, in her house right next door, instead of gadding about in London.

"You are missing dear Kitty, are you not?" Lady Templeton said.

"How well you know me, Mama. Yes, I have so much to talk to her about, but it will have to wait. And of course I am happy that she and Henry are having such a wonderful time in London. Look, here—another letter arrived this very morning with all their news. They have been to so many balls and parties. I believe Henry is very keen to show off his new wife and introduce her to his army friends, many of whom seem to reside in the capital."

"I am sure they are having a splendid time," Lady Templeton said. "Ah! What it is to be young and in love—and newly married."

Selina wrinkled her nose. She knew what was coming next.

"Selina! Now, my dear."

"Yes, Mama?" Selina used as innocent a tone as she could muster.

"We need to have a talk. Another one. You are nineteen now. Goodness, you will be twenty later this year. It is time for you to look around. Time for your thoughts to turn to matrimony. You see how happy your dear friend Kitty is with your brother Henry. Would you not like this situation for yourself?"

"No. I do not think I would."

Why am I lying? I think of nothing else but being married to George! However, I will not discuss this with my mama.

Lady Templeton cleared her throat. "I had thought there might be an understanding between you and Mr. Fitzgerald."

"Did you, Mama?" Selina raised her brows.

"Everyone did. You seemed very fond of him in December and January, right up to when you were both invited to Henry and Kitty's first dinner party. You seemed tired the day after that—and rather despondent. I did not like to say anything at the time, but I wondered, my dear, did you have a *disappointment?*"

"A *what?*"

"Was there something you thought was starting—that did not?"

"Possibly," Selina said. "Although George, I mean Mr. Fitzgerald, is nothing to me. Besides, I do not care."

Will God punish me for telling these terrible lies? For I still think of George with longing every day and every night . . . but sadly, it was not to be.

It had been three long weeks—and three days—since the dinner party at Number 2. A considerable time had passed since Selina and George had walked together on the Gravel Walk at night in very unusual circumstances. Why on earth had George not visited? He knew full well that Selina was not at liberty to organize her social life in the way a man could but must wait until an invitation was extended. How she longed to be able to initiate action, not to have to sit timidly at home waiting for someone to show an interest in her.

Lady Templeton smoothed a wayward lock from Selina's eyes. "I think you do care, my dear. These things happen. You need to keep busy—while you wait."

This was one of Lady Templeton's favorite pieces of advice. So many times, Selina's mother had tried to interest her in starting a new embroidery project to keep her busy, encouraged her to practice her singing, or taken her to a concert or shopping. And which of these activities would Lady Templeton recommend this morning?

"I did have in mind," Lady Templeton said, "that we might go shopping later on. I have a fancy to go to Smith's in Bath Street. I hear Mr. Smith has some fine new ribbons in his shop; would you care to peruse them? 'Twould be my pleasure to purchase a selection and help you trim one of your bonnets—you cannot be ready for the summer too early."

"Mama! 'Tis only February. Why would I need to prepare for

summer now?" Selina glanced at the windows, where rivulets of rain snaked down the panes. "It is also pouring, and although I do not mind going out in any weather, the wilder the better, I know that you do not consider it suitable to go out when the streets are running with water."

"February is a good time to buy ribbons," Lady Templeton said. "You don't want to leave it too late, only to find that the choicest ones have been snapped up. This can happen with men, too, as well as ribbons. However, you are right about the weather. Ah, wait! I see a glimpse in the clouds and believe it will not be long before we are able to visit the shops."

Lady Templeton could be very determined when she wanted to be. Indeed, Lord Templeton had been known to refer to his wife's "whim of iron."

"Now, Selina, why do you not read a book until it is time to go out? But first, please spend some time over your appearance. Standards, my dear. Standards!" Lady Templeton stared at Selina's hair. "Perhaps a little rearrangement?" Then her feet. "Put your shoes on, my dear."

"All right, Mama," Selina said. "I will do as you say."

I will make sure I look my best—for there is always the chance that if I go into the city, I might see George. Not that I will acknowledge him, for he means nothing to me.

Once Lady Templeton had left the room, Selina reached under a cushion and pulled out a pamphlet she had been reading about Elizabeth Fry.

The prison reformer, Elizabeth Fry, had occupied a great deal of Selina's thoughts this February. She had first heard about her at dinner with her parents when Kitty's parents, Mr. and Mrs. Honeyfield, had come to dine at Number 1 shortly after Henry and Kitty had left for London. The conversation over the main course had opened Selina's eyes to the appalling conditions those awaiting trial found themselves in while they were incarcerated in gaol.

Lady Templeton put her head round the door of the withdrawing room. "Selina! I thought you said you were going to get ready to go out before you read your book. And that is not a book! What do you have there?"

"A pamphlet."

Lady Templeton held her hand out, and Selina handed it over.

"Ah yes, I see. Elizabeth Fry. Yes, she is a good woman. A Quaker, I believe. Where did you get this?"

"Henry," Selina said. "I told him in a letter how interested I was in Elizabeth Fry and prison reform and you know how interested he is in justice—well, with his connections in London and his law studies, he is able to obtain all manner of reading material, and so he sent me this improving pamphlet to read."

"Are you really interested in prison reform?"

"Well, yes. I have been since the Honeyfields came to dinner—do you remember?"

"Ah, yes," Lady Templeton said. "I remember talk of the appalling conditions in gaol—although this is hardly a suitable subject for you to study, my dear."

"I feel sorry for the people who are locked up, and I wish things could be better for them. Is that not part of my Christian duty?"

Lady Templeton put her head on one side. "Possibly. Well, all right then, read your pamphlet instead of your book, for the rain is still lashing down. But promise me you will spend some time on your appearance before we go out."

"Promise."

"I must have a word with the housekeeper—and will be back directly."

Selina ran to the gilt mirror on the wall and stared at herself critically, turning her head from side to side. She could see what her mother meant; her hair could do with a tidy up. First she smoothed down the worst of the flyaways on the crown of her head, and coaxed the locks framing her face back into spiral curls with nimble fingers. Then she pinched her cheeks to increase her already healthy glow, and posed in several dramatic poses before flinging herself down on the sofa and resuming her reading. She would put her shoes on later.

"Good Lord!" Selina said to the empty room a few minutes later. "This pamphlet is interesting."

About half an hour later, Selina set out with Lady Templeton on the shopping trip. The sun was not exactly shining, nor had the clouds dispersed, but it was no longer actively raining, and the pavements were not too slippery as they walked down Milsom Street.

"Very fine," Lady Templeton said, peering into the window of a shop. "Would you like a new hat, my dear—to cheer you up?"

"Mama! I know you think I've had a disappointment—which I have not—but if I had, how would having a new hat make it seem any better?"

"If it were only a slight disappointment," Lady Templeton said, "the thought of a new hat might make you feel better. Now I can see that perhaps the disappointment has gone deeper. Do not worry. I will not say another word on the subject."

It was quite infuriating the way Selina's mama tried to find out what was going on in her mind—and was often successful, too.

"Tell me more about your pamphlet, my dear," Lady Templeton said. "What have you found out about Elizabeth Fry?"

"I have discovered details of her prison visits. She found very degrading conditions, particularly for women, and so she decided to do something about it."

"That is truly admirable," Lady Templeton murmured.

"And she started a school for the children of the prisoners. She taught lessons inside the gaol herself, too. Is that not a fine thing?"

"It certainly is. However, I do wonder how she bore it—being in a place full of criminals."

"Not everyone inside a prison is a criminal, Mama. Many are

waiting for their trial."

"Oh, yes, of course," Lady Templeton said. "There should be a presumption of innocence—until proved otherwise by trial."

"I agree with that," Selina said. "Anyway, Henry told me people sometimes have to wait for months and months because there are not enough officials and courts. If they are eventually found innocent of a crime, they have been locked up all that time for nothing, and there's never any recompense made."

"This does not seem at all fair."

"And another thing, apparently Elizabeth Fry wants to teach the women in prison how to make stockings, so that when they leave prison, having served their sentence, they have a respectable trade they can carry on and not need to do whatever it was they used to do before being arrested. Stealing. And . . ."

Selina's voice trailed off. Perhaps some of the women were ladies of the night?

"I do not think we need to talk about ladies in prison anymore," Lady Templeton said. "Nor speculate as to what crime they might have committed to end up there."

If Mama is trying to shut down the conversation, then it appears my supposition is correct about these unfortunate women. What lives they must lead! How desperate they must feel. No doubt some of them have children too. Perhaps they commit crimes because they do not have enough money to feed their children? Could this happen in a beautiful city like Bath?

The rest of the journey down the hill to Smith's in Bath Street was spent in silence.

"Well," Lady Templeton said as they arrived outside the milliner's shop with its pretty pair of matching bow windows. "Would you look at that fabulous display! Quite enchanting."

The swirls of color and myriad textures were undoubtedly attractive. Was it right, though, to enjoy such things, when some poor creatures were in gaol? Selina felt inside her reticule to check her pamphlet was there—she had brought it with her in case there was a chance to read a few more paragraphs.

As Selina and her mother went inside the shop, the bell on the door gave a high-pitched tinkle.

"Good morning, Lady Templeton," the shopkeeper said. "Miss Templeton. How may I assist you today?"

"We would like to look at some ribbons," Lady Templeton said. "We are thinking it is not too soon to trim our hats for the warmer weather to come, and have heard you have taken delivery of new stock."

"Excellent," the shopkeeper said. "Allow me to assist you. These are new and very fine. There are some delicate pastels here, or these patterned designs if that is what you prefer . . ."

Despite herself, Selina was fascinated with the range before her and eagerly inspected the wares.

"What about this?" Lady Templeton said to her daughter, holding up a shiny blue ribbon. "It matches your eyes perfectly."

"I prefer this one," Selina said.

"Ah, the green satin," the shopkeeper said. "A fine choice."

Yes—the green matches George's eyes and brings his dear face to my mind. I freely admit he is handsome, even though his personality leaves a lot to be desired.

After much discussion and holding lengths of ribbon up and exclaiming, Selina and her mother made many selections.

"We will have all these, please. And yes, pray wrap them for me," Lady Templeton said to the shopkeeper. "Thank you. Most kind."

As they left the shop, Lady Templeton turned to Selina. "Did you know there was quite a scandal about Smith's?"

"No!" Selina was amazed to think that anything scandalous could have happened in a milliner's shop at the lower end of Bath. "What happened?"

"You were but a tiny child at the time," Lady Templeton said. "There was a wealthy lady, Mrs. Leigh-Perrot, who was accused of stealing a card of lace worth one pound."

"I cannot believe it! Why have I not heard this tale before?"

"'Twas all hushed up, after she was found not guilty. Mrs.

Leigh-Perrot is a wealthy woman, and she lived in The Paragon with her husband at the time. They may live there still, for all I know."

"If she were wealthy," Selina said, "why would she have stolen some lace? She could have afforded any amount of it."

"It must have been a mistake," Lady Templeton said. "I do not know the details. The case has come back to my mind because of what we were talking about before—the time people spend in prison before a trial. Well, Mrs. Leigh-Perrot spent eight months in gaol awaiting trial, and when her trial eventually started, after ten minutes she was pronounced not guilty."

"Eight months in gaol—for nothing!" Selina's eyes were round as saucers. "That is very unfair. I will ask Henry about it when he comes back."

"Yes," Lady Templeton said. "It would be interesting to hear what he thinks. And I believe Mrs. Leigh-Perrot went to gaol in Ilchester."

"Is that because there is no prison here? What a shame for her to be away from her home city while she awaited trial."

"There is a gaol in Bath, but I do not know why she was not sent there—however, I have been told her devoted husband insisted on staying with her in Ilchester. Inside the prison!"

"Fancy that!" Selina marvelled. "Refusing to be parted from your spouse."

"Yes, and apparently he also said that if she were found guilty and transported to Australia, he would go with her."

True love indeed! I wonder if my husband would be that loyal. Would George—if we were married?

"Where is the gaol in Bath?" Selina asked. "I have not heard of it before."

A prison in Bath! How extraordinary.

Lady Templeton put her head on one side. "Do you know, I'm not entirely sure. 'Tis possibly in the Pulteney area."

'Twas worth investigating, was it not? If only to find out what conditions the poor prisoners were kept in. Would Elizabeth Fry's reforms have reached Bath?

"This is not altogether a suitable conversation, Selina," Lady Templeton said. "People might overhear us."

"Sorry, Mama. But oh, look! There are the Honeyfields! They have seen us—and are coming over. 'Tis wonderful to see Kitty's mother looking so much better."

"Yes, it is indeed." Lady Templeton said. "Especially since her illness was so very long."

And Mr. Honeyfield will know where the Bath gaol is.

"Ah, good morning to you both, my dears!" Lady Templeton greeted her friends warmly. In truth, they were more than friends now—they were family, ever since Henry and Kitty had married last Christmas. "How serendipitous our encounter is."

There followed a lively chat about how Henry and Kitty were getting on in London, the necessity of acquiring good hat ribbons and, much to Selina's joy, the whereabouts of Bath gaol.

"'Tis over Pulteney Bridge, Miss Templeton," Mr. Honeyfield said to Selina. "Take a sharp left down Grove Street, and after a little while you will see it on the right-hand side of the road. 'Tis an interesting building—not like the old-fashioned prisons of yesterday which look more like fortresses. However, I cannot quite see why you want to know—I do hope you are not thinking of ending up there."

Everyone laughed heartily at this witticism. And Selina had an idea.

Just then, her eye was caught by the flash of a red silk waist-coat. Signor Allegretto! He was but yards away. Their eyes met, and he grimaced, then held a finger to his lips before vanishing. The man was meant to be contagious! How surprising that he would risk both his health and that of others by appearing on the streets of Bath. Selina did not betray she had seen her singing teacher, but instead stored the information away to be inspected later. What a thrilling day this was turning out to be.

"We must bid you farewell," Mrs. Honeyfield said to Lady Templeton, "for we have promised to meet friends at the Pump

Room. Maybe you will join us there later?"

"Perhaps," Lady Templeton said. "Thank you."

With smiles and many promises to meet again soon, the Honeyfields took their leave. How wonderful to encounter pleasing and unexpected company in the street; Bath was such a sociable place. Perhaps they might chance upon someone else—George, for instance?

Selina closed her eyes briefly.

"Miss Templeton!"

That beautiful deep voice, like honey-strewn gravel . . . was her mind playing tricks? Could wishes come true? Selina opened her eyes to see a tall handsome figure standing before her, doffing his hat.

"George! I mean, Mr. Fitzgerald!"

George

MY GOD! SHE was so beautiful standing there in a dream with her lashes closed. I could not imagine a more beautiful sight—until she opened her eyes and I found myself gazing into their cerulean depths—for now I have a glimpse of heaven.

"Mr. Fitzgerald," Lady Templeton said. "What an unexpected pleasure!"

"Lady Templeton." George nodded his head. "The pleasure is all mine, I do assure you."

Selina looked around. "And where, pray, is Trigger? I cannot believe you have abandoned your horse to walk the city streets."

George smiled. "Trigger occasionally allows me to go out without him—and that is the case today."

"We are on our way to the Pump Room," Lady Templeton said.

"Are we, Mama?" Selina said.

"You know full well we are, my dear, for have not the

Honeyfields begged us to join them just five minutes past?" Lady Templeton turned to George. "We would be glad of your company."

"Very kind, I am sure, but first, I have an errand to complete in the town."

How I wish I had already completed this task.

"Well, we plan to be there for some time," Lady Templeton said, "and we would be delighted to see you there."

"Thank you," George said.

Ah! Fate is smiling upon me today!

"What sort of errand do you have to undertake?" Selina asked George.

"'Tis nothing of much importance—an appointment with a tailor. I have packages to pick up."

Should George tell Selina what he was collecting from the tailor? Describe the new items of clothing, all part of his plan to win her heart? Last month at Henry and Kitty's dinner party, Selina had stared at his muddy breeches, perchance with disapproval, and George had taken this as a message that it was time to smarten himself up. More recently, George had been taking advice from his valet about the sort of clothes one should wear to attract a lady—and today he was due to collect a new outfit.

George raised his hat again as Selina and her mother took their leave, then he sprinted up to Milsom Street.

"Good morning, Mr. Fitzgerald," the tailor said. "Your new clothes are ready to try. I do hope you will be pleased."

"Is that necessary? I could try the clothes on later at home."

"'Tis all part of the service, sir, and there are occasionally a few last-minute adjustments to be made—if, for example, a gentleman has put on weight . . ." The tailor coughed. "Not that this is the case here. You have a fine figure, Mr. Fitzgerald! Very fine indeed. And I for one cannot wait to see how this new outfit will enhance your already splendidly muscular appearance."

What is he talking about? This all seems a bit personal—and un-

necessary.

A while later, George stood in front of a full-length mirror while the tailor pulled at his jacket and smoothed his collar.

Lord! These breeches are tight! How do people walk in them, let alone ride?

"Are these breeches the right size?" George said. "They seem a little, er, constricting."

"They are not breeches, but pantaloons, and designed for standing in," the tailor explained. "They are much tighter than past fashions, granted, but look at the line. Superb!"

"I think I see what you mean," George said. "And I'll be careful to keep standing up and not attempt to sit."

"Very droll, Mr. Fitzgerald," the tailor said.

George turned his head, instantly regretting it when the point of one side of his high collar jabbed into his cheek.

"Is this collar meant to be so prominent?" he queried.

"Yes!" the tailor said. "'Tis the height of fashion—pun fully intended."

George's mother had often complained about being uncomfortable while forced to wear highly fashionable clothes when she was younger; George had never really known what she meant until today.

"The cravat . . ." George said.

The tailor sighed. "Is there anything wrong with the cravat?"

"Not at all. I like the look and feel very much. The jacket, too."

"I am relieved to hear it. Now, if I might make a suggestion? Would you allow me to attempt to change your appearance further?"

"What do you want to do?" George said.

The tailor produced a large tortoiseshell comb. "Might I suggest that you get into the habit of combing your hair forward and to the side like this, then back towards the first side . . . let's ruffle a few locks here, get some bounce into the coiffeur—that's better. And I think a touch of Pomade de Graffa to hold it all in place. No? As you wish."

"Good Lord!" George said, taking a step backwards. "I look as if I've fallen off my horse with my foot caught in the stirrup and have been dragged along the ground for some considerable distance. In fact, that happened to me once when my horse bolted—and this is exactly what I looked like."

"'Tis the latest style," the tailor said. "Your hair has been artfully disarranged. The style gives you a poetic look."

"I am not sure I want to look like a poet."

"The ladies demand it," the tailor said.

"I bow to your judgement."

They say one must make sacrifices for love, and I suppose these are mine.

"We could fabricate you a very fine greatcoat, if you wish," the tailor said, "with eight capes. Doubtless you have seen these being worn on the streets of Bath and admired them? No?"

"I don't think I have," George said. "There again, I have not looked at men's coats much."

Lord alive! Why would anyone need more than one cape on their greatcoat? Why do you need even one cape on a coat? Does not the greatcoat replace the cape?

George walked out of the shop in Milsom Street feeling like a different person, with his old clothes in a package tied with string under his arm. He was amazed to receive admiring glances from members of the *ton* passing by.

I wonder what Selina will think of this motley ensemble?

George's plan was to join Lady Templeton and Selina in the Pump Room, and he needed to hurry. To his dismay, he found that it was not possible to stride out as he usually did. He was forced to take smaller, mincing steps due to the tightness of his pantaloons. How did normal people cope with this? And why did they? Was it always to make an impression on the ladies?

George fervently hoped two things: one, that Selina would be impressed, and two, that once she had been impressed, there would be no further need for him to dress in this inane way. He could not wait to revert to his more comfortable clothes.

The Pump Room was more crowded than he had ever known it, and the sound of the orchestra, mixed with the hubbub of several hundred people chattering, was almost deafening. How would he find Selina in the crush?

Eventually, aided by his superior height, George spotted Selina in the distance and started making his way across the room; in his haste, he inadvertently trod on a footman's toes.

"Heartfelt apologies!" George said to the man. "I do beg your pardon."

"'Twas my fault entirely, sir—'tis very busy today," the footman said. "Perhaps you are seeking a restorative glass of water? If you continue to travel in this direction, you will soon reach the fountain."

George nodded his thanks and continued in his quest, waiting a few moments before muttering under his breath, "Not that I am particularly fond of the vile-tasting mineral water here."

"Mr. Fitzgerald!" Lady Templeton said. "We are so pleased to see you here. And I think you know Mr. and Mrs. Honeyfield, do you not? Good, good." She turned to Selina, whose eyes were sweeping over George.

Pray God she does not find my altered appearance too comical!

"Mr. Fitzgerald would no doubt like to sample the waters," Lady Templeton continued. "Why do you not go with him, Selina? I will be quite happy here with Mr. and Mrs. Honeyfield."

"A capital suggestion," George said. "I have much need of refreshment."

And soon my spirit will be refreshed, by virtue of being in the company of the prettiest and liveliest young lady in the room—ah, did I not say earlier that fate was kind to me today?

"Follow me," Selina said. "There is quite a throng around the fountain, but I'm sure we will be able to push in."

Once they were away from Lady Templeton and the Honeyfields, Selina turned to George.

"I know you do not think much of the waters," she said, "for I heard you describing them as 'vile' but a few moments ago."

"Miss Templeton!" George said. "I am shocked! Do you mean to tell me you have been eavesdropping again?"

Selina giggled.

This was more like it! She was teasing him, and he was teasing her back. After a bit of skilful maneuvering, George managed to secure two glasses of cloudy water with rather strange bits of who-knew-what floating in them, and he and Selina moved over to the large window overlooking the Roman Baths.

"Your mother is watching us," George said.

"Welcome to my world," Selina said. "My whole life is spent under observation; it can become a little wearisome."

George was silent.

Quick, man! Think of something witty to say!

George lowered his head—regretting the move instantly as his collar stabbed him in the cheek again.

"So," Selina said, "this is what you were collecting from your tailor. A completely new outfit."

"Indeed, it is."

Selina reached up and pulled the points of the collar down a little. "That will be more comfortable. I intend no criticism, but I do think perhaps your tailor has made the collar rather large."

"Damn right," George said, pulling at his collar to try to get comfortable. "I do beg your pardon. I mean *absolutely* right. My new tailor might know all about style, but he knows nothing about comfort. He says these breeches, or as he calls them, pantaloons, are made primarily for standing. I have not attempted to sit down in them yet—and seriously wonder if they contain enough fabric to allow a fellow to do that."

Selina looked at George's legs—and flushed pink.

"Do not say a word," George said. "I know they are unsuita-ble. I have been a muttonhead and allowed myself to be persuaded to wear something over-fashionable. In his defense, the tailor said they had a very good line."

Selina looked at the garment again. "They do have a very

good line."

Then she looked up at George. "And I rather like the new hairstyle."

"Really? Is this a jest? The tailor attacked me with a comb and then ran his fingers through my hair to finish it off. He tried to put some fragrant potion on, but I was having none of it. The sooner I manage to get my hair under control again and wear it in my usual way, the happier I will be."

"I disagree. I like this natural style. It suits you; you look as if you have been out galloping through a field with the wind in your hair. You look like yourself, George. Always be yourself."

Selina likes my hair! The collar is regrettable and the pantaloons make her blush, but she likes the hair. One out of three is not bad.

"It has been some time since I saw you at Henry and Kitty's dinner party," Selina said.

"Yes," George said. "And since then, have you been out on the parapet at night much?"

"Shush! Mama might hear you."

"Do not worry. I will keep your secret."

What could George say next? What topic of conversation would interest Selina? He wanted to tell her how sorry he was that he had not seen her for many weeks—ah, how he longed to tell her the reason, namely, that he had been busy trying to formulate a plan to win her heart.

The first step of his plan, phase one, had been the visit to the tailor. The second step, and all subsequent ones, George had yet to work out. However, he knew that they would involve change. He would definitely have to transform himself if Selina were to like him, for she did not seem much enamored of him as he was. Although, she had just told him to always be himself. Admittedly, she had only been referring to a hairstyle. Hadn't she?

"And how have you been," George said, "since I saw you last?"

"I have become interested in gaols."

"Gaols?"

"Well, more prison reform," Selina said. "I've been reading about Elizabeth Fry. In fact, Henry has sent me the most fascinating pamphlet."

Selina pulled the text out of her reticule, smoothing it straight before passing it to George.

"Interesting," George said as he scanned it through. "Mrs. Fry sounds a formidable woman."

"Yes. She is not afraid to do what is right—she simply gets on with things, regardless of what people think."

"Do you think that is good, not caring what people think?"

"I do," Selina said decisively.

Perhaps I should not care so much what people think. Although, if I do not care what Selina thinks, I will not be able to please her. How confusing.

"I have something to tell you," Selina said.

George's heart beat a little faster to hear this. Was she going to confide in him—about her feelings?

"I will simply burst if I do not tell someone," Selina said. "And I cannot tell my mama. 'Tis about my music teacher, Signor Allegretto."

Does she have feelings for Signor Allegretto? People say he is very good looking. Ye gods, please, no!

Selina leaned forward to whisper in George's ear that she had seen Signor Allegretto near Bath Street that very morning—after he had sent a message saying he was ill in bed with a fever and could not come to give her a singing lesson. "Do you not think that is strange?"

"Perhaps he did not want to teach you," George said. "Teaching singing can be rather monotonous, I believe."

He regretted the words as soon as they were out of his mouth, for the corners of Selina's mouth drooped. Then she searched her reticule for her handkerchief and dabbed gently at the side of her eye as if to wipe away a tear.

"I do beg your pardon." George was stricken to the core. "I meant no offense."

To his surprise, Selina then swatted him on the shoulder and started laughing. "I was teasing!"

Teasing? Will I ever understand this mercurial creature? Does this mean she likes me as a potential husband—or that she is treating me as she treats her brother Henry? How will I ever find out? I must be bold!

"I, I would like to see you again," George said. "I wonder if I might call on you at home . . . sometime?"

"Of course you may," Selina said. "We can discuss gaols again. And I will tease you. Now I must go, for Mama has been trying to catch my eye for a few minutes and is beckoning."

Hallelujah! Selina said I might call on her! Granted, the mention of discussing prisons again was not quite so romantic—but every love story has to start somewhere.

Selina

"HOW WAS IT?" Lady Templeton asked Selina as they walked across Queen Square and up the hill towards Number 1 Royal Crescent.

"How was what?" Selina asked.

She knew full well what her mother was referring to but was playing for time. Lady Templeton was asking how she had got on talking to George, the man otherwise known as her *disappointment*. And Selina did not have the faintest idea how to answer. She clenched her fists. Granted, there had been a little jesting and fun—they had got on with each other tolerably well—but how despondent she felt! She did not want a superficial friendship with George—nor did she want to tease him in quite the same way she teased her brother Henry.

I want so much more . . .

And George had seemed ill at ease for much of their conversation—perhaps because of his visit to the tailor? Why on earth had he felt the need to change his appearance?

"Selina!" Lady Templeton said. "I asked you a question."

"Sorry, Mama," Selina said. "There's nothing to report."

For how can I tell my own mother how much I enjoyed staring at George's fine legs, and yet feel downcast for I know that nothing will ever come of this attraction. Nothing will blossom as it should—for our personalities are incompatible.

The pace slowed as the two women walked up Gay Street towards The Circus.

"I do believe this hill gets steeper every time I attempt to climb it," Lady Templeton said.

Selina spun round at the top and looked down through the city and across to the wooded hills beyond. "A fine view, is it not?" she said.

I will never tire of looking towards where George lives.

"Did Mr. Fitzgerald express a wish to see you again?" Lady Templeton said.

"No," Selina said. "Oh, wait. He did ask if he could call to see me sometime."

Sometime. That does not mean soon, does it? Sometime is a very lukewarm sort of arrangement.

"Oh, that is good," Lady Templeton said. "And when did you say you would be at home?"

"I did not specify a day or a time," Selina said, "although I did say he could call and we could discuss prisons."

"Selina, that cannot be a very encouraging prospect for a young man such as Mr. Fitzgerald. You should have taken the chance to tell him exactly when it would be convenient for him to call by mentioning which mornings you would be at home. I believe he is a busy young man with all his medical work—far too busy to travel over to the Crescent without being sure you will be in."

"If he had wanted to see me again after Henry and Kitty's dinner party, he would have made more of an effort," Selina said. "Mr. Fitzgerald left it for over three weeks, and we have only just met by chance. He is not interested in me, Mama."

"Time will tell," Lady Templeton said. "You may be surprised."

I've messed everything up! Of course I want George to call on me, but I am still somewhat put out that he has not attempted to before. And how unfair it is that young women should sit at home waiting for gentlemen to pay their respects. Why cannot I go to Beechen Cliff and call on George? Not that I want to, of course.

By the time she got home, Selina had decided that she never wanted to see George again. Moreover, she was far too busy for romance, due to her burgeoning interest in prison reform. She would make something of her life—she would make a difference. Her mission could be to help unfortunate creatures, as Elizabeth Fry had found a way to make life less awful for the poor women locked away in gaol. Perhaps Selina should learn how to make stockings, so that she could go into prisons and teach the skill to the poor women incarcerated there?

"Your father and I will be going out after luncheon," Lady Templeton said. "And I believe your brother Edmund will not be back for ages. He said he would be out all day, I am not sure where, and possibly for the evening too. You will have plenty to do, Selina dear; there is your embroidery to finish, and of course you can practice the Handel air that you are learning with Signor Allegretto."

How come Edmund has complete freedom to go around doing whatever he wants, with no questions asked? Life is unfair.

"I wish I could go out this afternoon too, Mama," Selina said. "I feel like a good walk around Bath."

Lady Templeton narrowed her eyes. "You have just been for a long walk, Selina—and it looks as if it will rain again this afternoon. I tell you what: if you are determined to go out, why not accompany us? Your father and I have a few social visits to make."

Selina blanched. "No thank you, Mama. I'm very fond of all your friends but believe you are right. There is an opportunity this afternoon for me to get on with my embroidery and my music. Maybe I will undertake some reading as well—something suitable and improving."

"If you are sure, my dear," Lady Templeton said. "Now, I must go and see Cook and make sure that luncheon is ready."

Later that afternoon, after her parents had gone out, Selina lay shoeless on the sofa in the withdrawing room. She had opened all the sash windows to their fullest extent and was enjoying the invigorating air howling round the room.

"Miss Templeton? Excuse me," a voice said. "Will you be requiring tea?"

Selina looked up from her daybed to see a maid standing near the door. "Yes, please! And if Cook has any of those special biscuits, I'm starving!"

The maid smiled. "I'll bring a tray directly. And would you like me to close the windows? 'Tis rather chilly in here."

"I like chilly."

"Very well, Miss Templeton."

On the maid's return, Selina was delighted to see that Cook had filled a plate with biscuits and added a couple of slices of cake too. She must feel sorry for Selina, confined to the house when everyone else was out.

Everyone else was out—ah! An opportunity not to be missed. Selina could do whatever she wanted.

"Thank you for bringing this tray," Selina said to the maid. "I will enjoy the tea, and then I do believe I will go and lie down in my bed for a while to rest. I do not quite feel myself."

"Are you unwell?" the maid asked. "Should I have a message sent to Doctor Jenkins?"

"Certainly not," Selina said. "I am not ill—I have just had a tiring morning. And I did not sleep well last night. A rest will be most beneficial."

"Very well—if you are sure?"

"Quite sure. And 'tis most important that I am not disturbed."
The maid nodded.

"Please pass this message onto the rest of the staff," Selina said. "No one need trouble themselves to try and find me this afternoon, for I will be fast asleep on my bed. Maybe in my bed."

Once alone again, Selina sat up on the sofa and hugged her knees in excitement.

Now is the time for me to put my plan into action!

Inspired by the account of Elizabeth Fry's prison visits, Selina intended to visit Bath City Gaol and see how she might help the prisoners. She would go in disguise, for it would not do if news reached her parents of a visit.

Selina drank a cup of scalding hot tea, wrapped the biscuits and slice of cake in a napkin, and took the stairs to the old nursery at the top of the house two at a time. She was soon rifling through the dressing up box. Excellent! Everything she needed was there.

Very soon, Selina was dressed in an ancient cloak and old-fashioned bonnet; in her hand she carried a drawstring bag bulging with biscuits and cake. No one would recognize her but instead would think she was a much older woman—not a young lady at all. She tiptoed down the stairs and opened the front door as quietly as possible. 'Twas imperative not to alert the servants.

Threading through the city via less crowded back streets, Selina soon arrived at Pulteney Bridge, which was thronged with shoppers. She put her head down when she saw one or two acquaintances; luckily, no one seemed to recognize her.

At the end of the bridge, Selina turned into Grove Street and inched down a slippery damp slope, drawing closer to the level of the river. Where exactly was the prison? Mr. Honeyfield had said this morning that the gaol did not look like a fortress but was an interesting building. Selina stood on the pavement looking around. There was something indefinably different about this area. She felt as if she had opened a door to another world—yet she was only a stone's throw from the elegant shops on Pulteney Bridge.

Selina kept on walking. Ah! There was one building larger than the rest on the right-hand side—four stories high with a stone balustrade around the top. The black front door had a central round knob and was studded with huge black nails. This must be the gaol! Selina shivered. Had coming here been a mistake? She could always hasten home directly—the sensible choice.

No! If Elizabeth Fry is not afraid to mix with unfortunate souls, then neither am I.

Perhaps it would be a good idea to investigate the perimeter of the building before she attempted to gain entry? Selina went down an alley at the side and found that there was an enormous rough stone wall enclosing an area at the back. It would not be a garden—perhaps a yard of some sort, where the prisoners might be allowed to have a little fresh air occasionally?

Not that the air is fresh here—I can smell dampness and rotten decay.

Selina went back to the front of the gaol, which certainly had a much more pleasing appearance than the strange area at the back.

Just then, a man passing by snatched the bonnet from her head and ran off with it down the street. Selina knew that clothes had a second-hand value—however, she did not expect her bonnet to be stolen in broad daylight. And in Bath!

Unfortunately, now that Selina was hatless, she was revealed to be a young lady, not a more mature female, and that attracted interest from two other men loitering in the street.

"All on your own?"

"What you doin' here?"

"Yeah, go back to the fancy streets what you came from . . ."

"Lost your hat, have you?"

Selina assumed the haughtiest expression she could muster and pulled the hood of her cloak over her hair before pulling the bell beside the front door of the gaol. To her relief, the men in the street ran off.

She rang the bell again—for longer—and a gaoler with a particularly lugubrious face appeared. "Your business here?"

"I—I have come to see the prisoners."

"Ain't visiting hours," the man said as he tried to close the door.

Selina pressed forward. "I have not come to see any particular person. I have come to see all the prisoners because I want to make their lives easier. 'Tis not right that you give inmates so little access to bathing facilities and keep them short of drinking water."

The gaoler gurned. "Do-gooder, are you? Plenty of water here. We get flooded regular like, on account of being so near the river."

"That is not what I meant, and you know it!" Selina snapped. "I wish to speak to the governor of the prison."

"He's out," the man said. "Only comes in occasionally."

Selina tried to peek behind the gaoler's back to see inside the building, but all she could glimpse was a large entrance hall.

"Who exactly is in there?" she demanded. "How many prisoners do you have?"

"Only about forty at the moment."

"How many of these prisoners are awaiting trial?" Selina asked. "And how many will be set free after their trial, meaning they should never have been in gaol at all—like Mrs. Leigh-Perrot? Have you heard of her?"

"Can't say that I have," the gaoler said. "What is she? Some sort of vagrant? Got a few of those in 'ere. And debtors. Owe money, did she?"

Selina turned away in despair, and the man slammed the door. How on earth did Elizabeth Fry manage to remain calm and do her good works? Selina hadn't really thought this through. She stamped her foot. Would she have to return with a man in order to be taken seriously? It was a man's world, when all was said and done.

The thief who had earlier made off with her bonnet reappeared in the street with a couple of companions—none other than the men who had been so impertinent before.

"Want your hat back, love?" the thief said.

"I would like it back, actually," Selina said. "Please return it."

"You can have it back. Ain't worth nothing," the man said. "Tried to sell it, but no one wanted it because it's so old."

He put the bonnet on his head and affected what he must have thought was a ladylike walk, swinging his hips from side to side, up and down the pavement. Suddenly, he took the bonnet off his head and threw it high in the air.

"Have to catch it if you want it back!"

Selina leapt in the air, but she was not tall enough to catch the bonnet before one of the man's companions snatched it. This second man then proceeded to throw the bonnet over Selina's head to the third man.

"Catch it, catch it," they jeered.

This went on for some time, back and forth between the three men, until Selina was so exhausted from leaping about that she was on the point of giving up. Then, as she was turning to leave, one of the men held his foot out, and she tripped and went flying.

"How dare you," she screamed. "You did that on purpose."

The men advanced on Selina as she lay on the ground—she was totally surrounded.

"Get away from her, you villains!" a voice roared as a man thundered down Grove Street. "How dare you treat a young lady in this way? You will live to regret your actions, mark my words!"

'Tis George! George has come to my rescue!

George took on the three men in one go, lashing out with his fists, kicking with incredible strength and vigor—and using language the like of which Selina had never heard in her life.

CHAPTER FOUR

George

V ERY SOON, THE men were defeated and had no option but to
flee the scene.

"Selina! My darling Selina! Are you all right? Did they harm
you?" George knelt down in the gutter and tenderly stroked
Selina's face.

"Why are you here?" Selina said. "How did you know I was at
the gaol?"

"Time enough to explain all that. First, let me see how you
are. Can you stand?"

George helped Selina to her feet, and she dusted herself
down. What a relief! It seemed that the most injured part of her
was her pride.

"How dare those men fight you," Selina said. "Three against
one! 'Tis not sportsmanlike. And you would not believe how rude
the gaoler in the prison was."

"What! You have been inside the gaol?"

Does she have no idea what these places are like?

"No, not exactly inside," Selina admitted, "for the gaoler
would not allow me to enter. I explained my purpose clearly—
that I wanted to reform the prison conditions here—but I'm sad
to say I achieved precisely nothing." She scowled. "This always
makes me angry—when I am not taken seriously."

George picked up Selina's bag and handed it to her.

"Ah, good," she said, looking inside. "The cake is not too squashed, although some of the biscuits are broken."

"You brought cake and biscuits?"

"I did, for we have so much at home, and I fully intended to pass the food on to the prisoners to enhance their meager diet. However, the man at the prison door was so disagreeable that I did not get a chance to hand anything over."

George glanced around and saw that a small crowd had gathered on the other side of the road and were observing them.

"Let's go somewhere quieter and more civilized," he said. "I should take you home."

"Must we go straightaway?" Selina said. "Could we not walk, maybe in Sydney Gardens? 'Tis not far."

"I think I should take you home. But are you sure you are up to the walk? I could find a sedan chair."

"Of course I am fine walking," Selina said. "And I have a bag full of cake and biscuits to give us energy. Can I tempt you with something to eat?"

You could tempt me with many things.

"Maybe later," George said. "For the biscuits and cake, I mean."

Within a few minutes, the pair were walking back over Pulteney Bridge, bound for Selina's home.

"Thank you for rescuing me," Selina said, "although I still don't understand why you were there."

"I went to Number 1 to pay you a visit," George said.

Selina stared at him.

"You look surprised," George said. "Did I misunderstand you when you said that I might call on you?"

"No, but you used the word 'sometime' when you asked. Therefore I did not think it would be today."

She is being tactful—she must have thought I asked if I could call merely to seem polite—with no intention of actually turning up. And perhaps she only said yes out of good manners—whereas in fact she did not want me to call. How confusing society is. Why do people not say what they mean?

"As I was still in Bath," George said, "I thought it would be a good opportunity to walk up to the Crescent and see you."

Because I longed to gaze into your beautiful eyes once more . . .

"What happened when you went to Number 1?" Selina suddenly stopped walking. "Oh dear! I do believe I might be in trouble with my mama, for I expect the servants found I was no longer in the house."

"Well, at first they said you were not able to receive visitors because you were not feeling quite yourself. And then the maid said she would step upstairs to check, in case you were feeling better. She came running down a few minutes later in a panic to say she had searched every room and you were nowhere to be found in the whole house. Once I had established both your parents and Edmund were also out but that you were not with them, I began to be worried too."

Worried is an understatement. I thought my heart would explode!

"And then you wondered if I had gone to visit the gaol?"

"Yes," George said. "After what you had told me this morning about Elizabeth Fry, and knowing how determined you were to help, I thought it was exactly where you might have gone."

"Lord! I shall be in hot water with Mama when I get back. I cannot remember how many times she has drummed into me that I may not leave the house on my own."

Especially to visit a gaol, Selina! A building that houses dangerous criminals. Do you truthfully have no idea how unwise this whole enterprise was?

"Your mama is right," George said, "for women need to be escorted when they are out."

"And whose fault is that?" Selina said. "Why cannot men behave properly, so that women may have the freedom to walk on the streets without fear of having their bonnet stolen or being tormented by a group of ruffians?"

""Tis a fair point. I apologize on behalf of all men. And your bonnet is very fine. You must have been furious when it was stolen. But I see they returned it."

"They said it was too old to sell. And there is no need to describe the bonnet as fine—for you know it is nothing of the sort. It is the oldest and most ramshackle bonnet from our dressing up box, and I wore it on purpose to be anonymous in the street. The same with the cloak."

I do not care what you wear—you always look beautiful to me.

"Would you like a biscuit now?" Selina said. "It is quite tiring, walking up this hill."

"I would, as a matter of fact, because I have not had much to eat today, however . . ."

"Before you say it, I already know young women are not meant to eat in the street. Something else Mama constantly reminds me of."

"'Tis a foolish rule," George said.

"How glad I am that you agree with me. And rules are meant . . ."

". . . to be broken?" George finished.

"Yes, like a biscuit as you bite into it. And if anyone reprimands me or reports me to my parents, I will say I felt faint after my adventure and had to eat something immediately—before I passed out."

Selina handed George a sugar biscuit.

"Delightful!" he said, little bits of sugar dropping off onto the high points of his collar.

Selina stood on tiptoe to brush them off.

"You do not look quite as smart as you did this morning," she said, "and I fear your new clothes are quite spoiled after fighting in the street."

"No matter." George looked down at his pantaloons which, embarrassingly, seemed to have a large rip in the side. "I fully intend never to wear these clothes again. They are far too uncomfortable."

"Where are your other clothes? You had them wrapped in a

package when I saw you this morning in the Pump Room. And where have you been since then?"

"I went for a wander around the city after you left the Pump Room, for I had one or two things on my mind. Then later, I went to Number 1 to visit you and took the liberty of leaving my old clothes with your servants. I thought I would be able to reach you faster if unencumbered."

"Good thinking," Selina said. "Make sure you collect the parcel when we reach my home—otherwise I will sweep the clothes into our dressing up box."

"I will remember, and I might ask your parents' permission to quickly change into my old clothes before I go back to Devonshire Buildings. I feel such a ninny dressed like this."

Especially with the embarrassing rip in my pantaloons.

"At least your hairstyle is intact," Selina said.

"Yes. A massive advantage of the windswept look the tailor recommended is that after fighting in the street, my hair is just as artfully disarranged as it was before."

Selina is smiling—she did say before that she liked my new hairstyle.

"Another biscuit?" Selina said. "Or a slice of cake?"

"Don't mind if I do." George accepted a large, very squashed slice of fruit cake. "I am feeling hungry, all of a sudden."

"You are impressively skilled at fighting. I hadn't expected that."

"I used to box at school."

"Boxing? Oh yes, Henry used to box at school too. But the kicking—where did that come from?"

"I am ashamed to say that we used to do free fighting at school," George said. "No rules—no holds barred."

"Why would you do that? Surely not for entertainment?"

"'Twas not for fun—but out of necessity," George said. "Some of the older boys at my school used to pick on the younger ones for no reason, and I thought it my duty to teach them a lesson."

How glad I am that I built up my fighting skills.

"I see," Selina said. "I do wish that they taught girls how to fight at school."

"Girls do not wish to fight," George said. "'Tis not natural for them."

"Girls fight all the time—but our weapons are usually words, often behind people's backs. I think that if girls were allowed to indulge in a bit of fisticuffs, there would not be so much unpleasantness. All would be sorted and forgotten. Whereas insults and rumors have a nasty habit of lingering."

"What an interesting point of view! I am sure there is much truth in what you say."

"Ah, we are nearly home," Selina said as they walked along Brock Street.

George had no doubt that both Selina's parents would be mightily relieved to see their daughter safe and well, but he also knew that the relief would be tinged with other emotions. Lord and Lady Templeton would not be pleased that Selina had chosen to leave her home unchaperoned, especially to visit a gaol—an outing that was bound to end badly.

The door was flung open long before Selina and George had even put a foot on the flight of steps.

"Selina, thank heavens," Lady Templeton cried. "And what are you wearing? I have been nearly out of my mind with worry."

"Inside, inside," Lord Templeton said. "People are watching."

In the entrance hall, it was as George had predicted. There were tears of joy that Selina had been found, profuse thanks offered to George—and then the recriminations started.

"You know I have told you never to go out alone," Lady Templeton said to Selina.

"How could you do this to your mother?" Lord Templeton said. "She has been crying and wailing this past half hour, ever since we came home to discover you were absent."

"I am so sorry! I see now I have done wrong." Selina hung her head—very dramatically. "But I was frantically keen to do some good in this world. I find I have so little freedom to do anything at all, save embroidery and singing."

This comment stopped her parents in their tracks—and no doubt gave them food for thought.

"Pardon me, Lord Templeton," George said. "Might I be permitted to retrieve my package of clothing? I am desirous of changing my apparel before I walk home."

"Of course, my dear young man," Lord Templeton said. "You're welcome to change upstairs in my dressing room. My valet will assist you. And may I say again how very grateful we are to you for bringing Selina home safely. We were so pleased when the servants were able to report that you were determined to find her—and thought you knew where to look."

"I echo my husband's thanks," Lady Templeton said, "and am horrified to see the state of your clothes after fighting off those ruffians. I do hope you will allow us . . ."

"No need," George said. "I had already planned to put these clothes into the rag bag by the end of the day."

One of the servants showed George up to Lord Templeton's dressing room, and he started changing. After a few minutes, the valet appeared at the door.

"Thank you, but I can manage," George said.

I have no wish to compound my embarrassment my allowing Lord Templeton's valet a close look at my torn pantaloons and ruined jacket.

"As you wish, sir."

When George went downstairs, Selina was alone in the entrance hall.

"Mama and Papa are in the parlor," she said. "I wanted to catch you before you left and thank you one more time for saving me. I am more grateful than I can express."

And I will never be able to express how fearful I was when I saw you lying on the ground encircled by those vultures. If I have done one good thing in my life, it was today, when I was able to rescue you.

"'Twas nothing," George said. "I am glad to have been of assistance."

"You are too modest," Selina said. "And oh, George, I realize now I will have to give up my plans to reform the gaol. The task is beyond me."

"For your safety, I am pleased to hear it," George said. "I'm sure your tremendous drive and talents could be put to use in other ways. And I am not talking about embroidery."

"Exactly what I was thinking," Selina said. "As it happens, I am very interested in the question of slavery—as I believe we all should be."

"Slavery?" George said. "'Tis shameful, doubtless, but I am not sure how, in your position, you will be able to do very much."

"I am resolved to try," Selina said. "As a start, I will to write to Henry this evening to see if he can send me another pamphlet, this time about the evils of slavery."

Ye gods! Am I going to have to rescue Selina again on some future occasion? At least there is no sugar plantation worked by slaves in the city of Bath, or indeed in England, so she cannot get herself into such a pickle as she has done at the city gaol.

"There is to be a gathering in the Quaker meeting house soon—March the 7th—to discuss the full abolition of slavery. Would you like to come with me?"

"You should be escorted, most definitely," George said.

Selina took a step closer. "Thank you again for rescuing me."

She had never looked more beautiful. Sparkling eyes, a soft smile, hair disarranged from all that had happened . . .

"Selina!" George said hoarsely. "If anything had happened to you today, if you had been harmed . . . well, it does not bear thinking of. Promise me you will take proper care of yourself—always."

"I have just had the same lecture from my parents while you were upstairs changing. They said 'tis only because I mean the world to them."

How could George show Selina how much she meant to him? He had already rescued her from danger today, restored her to her family, and given her his best advice. George sighed. The danger was passed. And he felt so much more like himself, back in his comfortable old clothes again.

Selina gazed up at George, her mouth delicately curving into the sweetest smile imaginable, and her eyes glistening in the most distracting manner. He bent his head towards Selina's until his lips were hovering but a few inches above hers.

George would show Selina exactly how much she meant to him—he would show her what was in his heart. Lowering his lips to hers, he . . .

Selina

THE DOOR TO the parlor opened and Selina took a swift step backwards, away from George—and temptation.

"Mr. Fitzgerald," Lord Templeton said, "how glad I am to see you are still here, for I wanted to thank you once more for the responsible and protective way in which you acted this afternoon; we will be forever in your debt."

"Yes," Lady Templeton said, joining her husband. "I echo that sentiment."

Were her mama and papa conscious of what had been about to happen? How mortifying that would have been. Selina held her hands to her flaming cheeks.

"My dear Selina," Lady Templeton said, "I fear this whole regrettable episode is catching up with you. We must get you upstairs—something to eat, maybe?"

"I am fine, Mama—thanks to Mr. Fitzgerald."

"You have proved yourself a fine young man today," Lord Templeton said to George. "Responsible, capable—and strong."

Selina had always believed in striking while the iron was hot, and today was no exception.

"As it happens," she said, "I'm looking for someone to escort me to a meeting on March 7th at the Quaker Meeting House in the city. Someone responsible, capable—and strong."

And divinely handsome . . .

"The Quaker Meeting House?" Lady Templeton said. "What is all this about?"

"Not more prison reform, I hope?" Lord Templeton said. "'Tis not because it isn't a good cause, mind you, but thinking purely of your safety."

"I have realized the error of my ways now," Selina said, "and know I have to be more careful. In fact, I have just been conversing with George, I mean Mr. Fitzgerald, about that very topic."

"I am glad to hear it," Lord Templeton said.

"From henceforth, I will be leaving prison reform to Elizabeth Fry and her group of reformers," Selina said, "although I will be cheering them on from the sidelines. And to be honest, I believe it is in the big cities like London where the most reform is needed. The gaol in Bath is quite a fine building."

"The street is a little rough," George said, "and despite the gaol looking like a fine building, I do not doubt that the conditions inside are not what we should expect from the modern age."

"Yes," Lord Templeton said, "much change is needed. There is often a long wait behind bars before trial, which is undeserved by the innocent. Then, when the accused come to trial, sentences can be very harsh. The law needs to be reformed—'tis a frequent topic of conversation after dinner."

"I have never heard this discussed," Selina said. "It sounds most interesting."

"We wait until the fairer sex have withdrawn after the meal," Lord Templeton explained. "'Tis not quite suitable."

How unjust! Why must we women always be left out when anything interesting is being discussed?

"I would love to hear all about trials and sentencing," Selina said. "I can only imagine how much reform is needed in the law, for poor people can be executed or transported for the most petty of crimes, but those who have access to a good barrister, well . . ."

"You are right, Selina," Lord Templeton said. "Those who are wealthy can usually get themselves out of trouble."

"We were discussing this earlier this morning," Lady Templeton said. "You remember, Selina—about Mrs. Leigh-Perrot?"

"Ah, yes," Selina said.

"I have heard of the case," George said. "Mrs. Leigh-Perrot was accused of taking some lace, was she not?"

"We do not believe she took it," Lady Templeton said.

"Yes," Selina said. "I am convinced she was accused unfairly by the shopkeeper. It could have been some sort of blackmail—perhaps they hoped she would pay them to drop the case?"

"Perchance," George said, "she did take the lace but was not quite responsible for her actions."

"She was not deranged," Selina said, "surely?"

"That is not quite what I meant," George said. "It is possible to fall victim to strange compulsions—in fact I have come across a case of this recently when working with my father. I cannot give details, but suffice to say there is a lady he treated who felt a need to take objects she did not need. She was in all other aspects a rational creature—and yet could not seem to help herself. This cannot be described as stealing."

"How strange," Lady Templeton said.

What is strange is that we are standing in the entrance hall discussing Mrs. Leigh-Perrot and stealing, when my mind is occupied with hoping against hope that neither Mama nor Papa saw that George had been about to kiss me but minutes ago . . .

"Selina, you're looking tired," Lady Templeton said. "I insist you come upstairs with me. You need to eat. I will send a message to the kitchen and have a tray sent up."

"Yes, Mama," Selina said, "but might I ask what you think of my request about going to a meeting in March? 'Tis not to do with prison reform or Elizabeth Fry."

"Ah yes," Lord Templeton said. "The Quaker Meeting House. What is due to be discussed at this meeting?"

"Slavery," Selina said.

Lady Templeton nodded and smiled—an encouraging sign. She was herself passionate and vocal about the evils of slavery and slave ownership.

"Hmm," Lord Templeton said. "The decision as to whether I allow you to attend that meeting will be made on another day."

"But if I was allowed to attend," Selina said, "might I ask if you would be willing to allow Mr. Fitzgerald to escort me?"

"Selina!" Lady Templeton said. "Upstairs! I will leave your father to discuss that with Mr. Fitzgerald."

As Selina followed her mother up the staircase, she tried to imagine what would have happened if her parents had not chosen that particular moment to move from the parlor to the entrance hall. She would have been kissed by a young man—her first romantic kiss. What would it have been like? Would it have lived up to her dreams? Possibly not, for in her dreams her first kiss always took place in an enchanted forest, or on a moonlit lawn— or the high seas . . . definitely somewhere where she was surrounded by dramatic scenery, with nature all around.

I am not entirely happy that George felt moved to kiss me in a mundane entrance hall after he had rescued me. Apart from the lack of romance in the domestic surroundings, the kiss would almost have been like a payment for services rendered.

Selina stifled a giggle. Payment for services rendered was sounding perilously close to being a lady of the night.

Lady Templeton rang the bell as they reached the withdrawing room.

"Please sit down on the sofa, Selina," she said. "You seem a little agitated. Amused one minute, then as if you have the cares of the world on your shoulders the next. You must be very overtired. Is there anything in particular worrying you?"

"Everything!" Selina said. "There is so much that needs reforming in this world of ours. Sometimes it preys on my mind, and I find it troubling."

"You are a young woman," Lady Templeton said, "and you

should be having fun and socializing. You have many freedoms now that you will not have when you are married with a family. Make the most of this time."

"But I feel I have no power to change anything."

Lady Templeton put her hand over Selina's. "I know how you feel."

"You do?"

"Of course!" Lady Templeton said. "When you are young, you want to make things better, change the world—you are quick to see the defects in how we live. However, you must learn to be realistic. Learn to see the value of all the good things that happen—the things that work. Be pragmatic."

"But then nothing will change," Selina said.

"Not true," her mother said, "for when you look at the world with clear eyes, you will see that every little thing you do makes a difference. The way you speak to people, the way you help people . . ."

A maid came into the room.

"Ah!" Lady Templeton said. "Please would you ask Cook to send up some tea and cake—and biscuits—for poor Miss Templeton has had quite a shock this afternoon."

"I will ask," the maid said, "although I do not believe there is any cake or biscuits left, for . . ."

"Oh, Mama," Selina said, "Cook sent up a generous plate of cake and biscuits this afternoon when you were out—and I'm afraid I took it all to the gaol. I was intending to feed the prisoners, but in the end it was not possible, and George, I mean Mr. Fitzgerald, and I ate it on the journey home. He seemed very hungry."

Lady Templeton smiled. "Maybe some bread and butter?" she said to the maid. "Does Cook have plenty of bread?"

"She does," the maid said. "I will bring a tray directly."

"Where were we?" Lady Templeton said once the maid had departed.

"You were saying that every little thing I do in my life has an impact."

"Yes, that's right," Lady Templeton said. "I like to think that every good deed we do starts a ripple in the ocean, and then together, we can build up mighty waves."

"I begin to see what you mean," Selina said, "and I do try to be polite to people but feel I need more opportunities to make the ripples count."

"I have been thinking about that," Lady Templeton said, "and I have a suggestion to make which I hope you will think is a good idea."

Oh, please let the suggestion not involve either needlework or singing. I want to do something real—something outside Number 1 Royal Crescent.

"You may be aware that I know the lady who runs the Sunday school at church," Lady Templeton said. "Mrs. Godwin is a good soul who has helped many children. She also says there is much work still to be done; if she had extra help, she would be able to bring more light into the children's lives, not just on Sundays. Ideally, she is looking for someone to help her take the children out for walks and maybe help them with their reading and suchlike. She has oft asked me if I have time, but my busy schedule simply won't allow it. Would you be interested in helping her?"

"I think I would," Selina said.

This is like a door opening in front of me—and I am determined to seize the opportunity.

"I know it is not as big a project as you had hoped to be involved in," Lady Templeton said. "You will not be reforming the prisons or abolishing slavery worldwide. However, everything comes from small beginnings, and if you can help educate a child, why, you can change the future."

Change the future—I like the sound of this.

The deep thud of the front door closing floated upstairs, and Selina ran over to the window to watch George leaving.

She turned her head to say to her mama, "Do you think Papa

has agreed to let me go to the Quaker Meeting House in March?"

"We will have to wait and see," Lady Templeton said from the sofa. "I hope so—for it sounds very interesting. I might even consider coming with you myself. And Henry and Kitty should be back from London by then—perchance they will want to attend."

Selina smiled and looked out of the window again. George was now on the far side of the road, his parcel of clothes under his arm, facing the Crescent Lawn. He turned and looked up at the window, catching Selina's eye. She waved her farewell—and in response, he blew her a kiss.

George

HOW WONDERFUL IT would have been if that kiss had been a real one on Selina's beautiful lips.

George waited until Selina had disappeared from the window, then turned to take the path that led to Queen Square at the side of the Crescent Lawn. Time to get home. It would be a long walk, but one George would enjoy.

For I have much to think about.

Maybe one day all the tiresome difficulties between him and Selina would be swept away? If only George could find the courage to speak out more in Selina's presence and behave more naturally—and Selina, if only she could . . .

George struggled to think of anything about Selina that was not already perfect. He did not blame her for not being in love with him—for that was not a fault, more a completely understandable situation. The lively and beautiful Miss Templeton of Number 1 Royal Crescent could choose anyone she wanted. George was a shy nobody, dull of wit and of indifferent appearance. He was but the son of a doctor, living south of the city.

George looked at the ground, willing himself to be positive. Had he forgotten about his plan to win the hand and heart of Miss

Selina Templeton? He had tried his best with the first phase of the plan, but sadly, his aim to change his appearance by purchasing a new outfit from a highly fashionable tailor in Milsom Street had not been entirely successful.

In truth, it had not been an unmitigated disaster either, for Selina had liked his new hairstyle in the Pump Room, and although his pantaloons had made her blush, she had admitted they had a very good line—whatever that meant. George shook his head. There was no way he would ever be able to wear pantaloons that tight for the rest of his life, even if it meant Selina could admire their line. It simply wasn't his style. His future wife—pray God that would be Selina—would have to accept him as he was. Slightly dishevelled, comfortably dressed, caring not one jot about fashion—Mr. George Fitzgerald of Devonshire Buildings was an outdoors sort of person. But what if he were to make more of an effort to change? What if . . .

Suddenly, a small person appeared as if from nowhere and cannoned into George. He felt his knees give way, then tumbled to the ground, his package slipping from his fingers.

"What the devil?" George leapt to his feet and saw a young girl standing in front of him.

"Begging your pardon, sir," she said. "I am that sorry I didn't see you."

George smiled. "I apologize for my language. There is no harm done."

"But your parcel!"

The brown paper had torn open, and George's outfit was languishing in a pile of mud.

"Please don't worry," George said.

The young girl bent down and retrieved the clothes, rolling them into a makeshift bundle, which she handed over.

"Thank you," George said. "But are you all right? That was quite a collision—and entirely my fault. My mind was miles away. A thousand apologies."

"I was running really fast," the girl said. "I've been on an errand for Cook and have to get back to the kitchen quickly."

George scrutinized the girl carefully. "I have seen you before, earlier today. You work at Number 1, do you not?"

"I do," the girl said. "I am Martha."

She seemed pleased that George had recognized her—understandably, for many did not notice the faces of those from below stairs.

"Ah! So you are the famous Martha?"

"Yes, sir. Lady Templeton was kind enough to bring me to work for her after all the trouble before Christmas."

"I remember everything now," George said. "I saw you outside the Cottage Crescent before Christmas when you were a servant of Lord Steyne's. Everyone will be eternally grateful to you for the part you played in saving Miss Kitty Honeyfield from his clutches."

"That was a strange occasion, and no mistake," Martha said. "And now Miss Honeyfield is Mrs. Henry Templeton."

"Indeed!" George said. "And very happy they are, too. Well, Martha, I expect you find your work at Number 1 much more pleasant than working for Lord Steyne."

"That I do," Martha said. "Lady Templeton is the kindest employer in the world, and I'm lucky to be here. The food's much better at Number 1 than at the Cottage Crescent, too."

"And do you look after Miss Selina Templeton sometimes?" George asked.

"I mostly work in the kitchen, but I have seen Miss Templeton around the house, and she always says hello to me and asks if I am happy and if everyone is being kind to me downstairs."

How typical of Selina! She cares for everyone. Correction, almost everyone—for I am not yet convinced she cares for me.

George's pantaloons slipped free from the bundle he was holding and fell to the ground.

"Oh dear," Martha said, picking them up and inspecting them. "These seem to be torn. I am so sorry, sir. Please, let me take them. I will have them mended and returned to you. My mother is a needle woman and will be able to repair them invisibly—you will never see the damage. I would be so grateful if you would allow me to do this for you—I would not wish a report of my carelessness to reach Lord Templeton."

"The pantaloons were torn well before they fell to the ground," George said. "The honest truth is that this parcel of nonsense is destined for the rag bag. I bought the outfit only today, mistakenly thinking it would enhance my appearance; then sadly, found I was not suited to such a fashionable outfit."

"Not suited?" Martha said. "But you are a gentleman."

"I could scarcely walk in those pantaloons," George said. "I will spare you the details of the high collar. And the jacket hasn't looked the same after I fell into a fight in the street. I intend to dispose of the lot."

Martha looked at George with big eyes. What the devil was she trying to say?

Finally, George understood.

"You say your mother is a needle woman," he said gently. "Would she perchance be interested in having these clothes? She may do whatever she wants with them, for I never want to see them again."

Martha opened her mouth as if to speak, but no sound came out, and she continued staring. George would have to be more direct.

"I do not want the clothes," George said. "I do not want any payment for them, but am very happy to give them to you and your mama. Would you like them?"

"We would, sir," Martha whispered. "Mr. Fitzgerald, you cannot know what this means to us. These are fine clothes, and my mother will be able to repair and launder them, and then . . ."

"Then you can do with them as you wish," George said, handing the bundle over. "If your mother wants to sell them, she's at complete liberty to do so. If you want your father to wear them, that is fine. Or do you perhaps have older brothers?"

"My mother is a widow," Martha said, "and, and the rest of

my family would not . . ."

How foolish I am! No one in Martha's family would want to wear these clothes. Only a fashionable dandy in the ton *would desire to be seen in such a bizarre outfit. And the clothes have a monetary value that will surely help the family.*

"I understand," George said. "You should sell the clothes, and you're welcome to whatever you can get for them. Now, do not let me keep you, for you said you were in a rush to get back to Cook."

Martha thanked George profusely several more times before racing towards the back of Number 1 with her bundle.

George resumed his journey with a lighter heart, thankful to have gotten rid of the clothes in a way that benefitted those less fortunate than himself. It was wonderful to hear that Martha had settled in so well at Number 1. At George's home in Devonshire Buildings, his parents had always been very keen on the welfare of the servants, and George had been brought up to be polite and thoughtful on all occasions to those who worked in the house.

There were many other households where this was not the case, where servants were exploited and even on occasions abused. The move for young Martha from one of Lord Steyne's households to a vastly superior home with the Templetons was fortuitous. George shuddered. How would Martha have been treated by Lord Steyne as she had grown older and entered womanhood?

George strolled through the city streets, heading for home. What a joy it was to be able to stride out in comfortable breeches again instead of those outlandish pantaloons! He came across several dandies struggling to walk normally, such was the tightness of their garments.

And to think I was one of them earlier this morning. What a buffoon I must have looked! How embarrassing it is to realize Selina was probably trying her hardest to be kind to me about my ludicrous outfit. The only things she criticized were the high points of my collar.

Ah! Selina. Time to continue formulating a plan to win her

heart. George's spirits had picked up somewhat after colliding with Martha. He no longer felt sorry for himself but appreciated his very fortunate position in society. He would continue his campaign to win Selina's heart. What would the next step be? Did she not mention that she would like him to go to the Quaker meeting with her? And before he left Number 1, while Selina was upstairs with her mama, Lord Templeton had given his approval for the plan. The date was already seared into George's mind— March 7th. He might have to miss a few house visits to patients with his father that day, but George was certain he would be excused his normal duties to attend such a worthy event as a talk about slavery.

But how to get ready for this meeting? The obvious thing was to find out as much about slavery as possible. Perhaps George should write to Henry and ask him to send some pamphlets from London, as Selina was going to do? Or debate slavery with his father, which would be very useful preparation. George remembered the thrill of speaking out in the Octagon before Christmas when he had revealed to the assembled masses that Lord Steyne was a cheat and a liar.

For when I am fired up, I find I can be articulate; I am resolved to speak out in the Quaker Meeting House and make Selina proud of me. Show her who I really am.

George was racing up Holloway now, his long legs taking the steep hill with ease. He had a quick look behind the bushes near the water trough, remembering the man who had shouted at him after Henry's dinner party in January. No one there, thank the Lord. Although, even if there had been a man shouting insults at him again, George did not believe he would have been bothered by it today, for he was on a mission. He was going to research the topic of slavery more thoroughly than even William Wilberforce himself. He was going to deliver such an impassioned speech at the meeting that Selina would fall instantly in love with him and want to be his wife more than anything in the whole world.

On his arrival home, George went straight to his father's

library. Doctor Fitzgerald was seated at his desk writing notes.

"George! Have you had a good day?"

"Outstanding, thank you, Papa."

"I am surprised you were so long in the city," his father said. "Weren't you going to collect some new outfit from your tailor?"

"Yes," George said. "Then one thing led to another. I visited the Pump Room, and went on a long walk all round the city while I mulled a few things over. Later, I called on the Templetons and had an adventure. All in all, 'twas quite an eventful day."

"Good, good, glad to hear it," Doctor Fitzgerald said. "You deserve a day off from your studies and from trailing round with me on my doctor's visits."

George started scanning the library shelves.

"Are you looking for anything in particular?" his father said.

"Yes. I would like to know more about slavery."

"Ah!" Doctor Fitzgerald said, standing up. "Now, I happen to have a few interesting books about slavery. Bother! I can't quite reach. Would you try, George? You're so much taller than I am."

"Gladly." George tried to reach the highest shelf. "Actually, I believe I need to get the ladder."

Once at the top of the steps, George found a very dusty collection of books and pamphlets that appeared to have lain undisturbed for many a year.

"What is the reason for the sudden interest?" Doctor Fitzgerald asked.

"Someone mentioned there is to be a talk at the Quaker Meeting House next month. I thought I would find out more about the topic before I attended."

"Ah!" Doctor Fitzgerald said. "A lady is involved."

"I did not mention a lady."

"You did not need to. You are my son, and I know you better than you think. Besides, your hair looks different. This always means a lady is involved."

George came down the ladder with his pile of reading material. "Thank you, Papa. I will take this to my room."

"And whoever the lady is," Doctor Fitzgerald said, "she is a very lucky person to have your heart."

George blushed and fled up the stairs. Once in his chamber, he set the books down on a small table beside his bed, then sat at his writing desk and started devising the second phase of his plan. There were sixteen days between now and the seventh of March, so sixteen squares to be drawn on a sheet of paper. He wrote an aim for each day, factoring in his reading schedule, discussions with his father—and maybe a trip to the library in Milsom Street could be squeezed in too? Also, 'twas important to have a little flexibility built into the calendar towards the end, for one never knew what might turn up.

And there it was! George sat back and surveyed his perfect plan with great satisfaction. By the evening of the sixth of March, he would become an expert on the subject of slavery. And on the seventh of March, he would escort Selina to the Quaker Meeting House, listen carefully to all that was said, and then deliver such a withering condemnation of the evils of slavery that she would fall into his arms. It would be easy.

Wouldn't it?

CHAPTER FIVE
Selina

"SELINA!" LADY TEMPLETON said. "Come away from the window. Mr. Fitzgerald will be here soon enough."

It was Thursday March 7th, and Selina was in the parlor with her mother, awaiting George's arrival. Lord Templeton had given his blessing for the outing to the Quaker Meeting House, and Henry and Kitty, newly returned from London, would be joining them too.

"What makes you think I'm anxious to see Mr. Fitzgerald?" Selina said. "My main interest in looking out of the window is to watch the wind blowing the trees around."

"If you say that is your main interest, I will have to believe you," Lady Templeton said, "although perhaps you have a secondary interest in noting when Mr. Fitzgerald arrives?"

"Perhaps," Selina said. "Perhaps not."

I see Mama is smothering a smile in that irritating way she has when she thinks she has discovered a secret.

Selina had not seen George since the day he had rescued her from outside the gaol in Grove Street. It was a little surprising that he had not come to call or sent an invitation to a concert or suchlike. Selina sat down and dug the nails of one hand into the palm of the other. He must think she was nothing but a foolish young girl to have gotten herself into such a predicament.

Dressing up in old clothes? Taking biscuits and cake to give to the prisoners? 'Twas not exactly the behavior of a mature and rational young woman. Selina had done a lot of thinking since her escapade in Grove Street, and she could now appreciate how foolish she had been—and what a narrow escape she'd had.

"Thanks to George," she murmured.

"Did you say something?" Lady Templeton asked.

"No," Selina said.

George was a few years older than she was, the same as her brother Henry. Therefore he might be thinking it was high time he was settled with a wife and a home of his own. Yes, that must be the reason he had not been in contact—he had been too busy searching the ballrooms of Bath for his future wife. No wonder George hadn't bothered to try and see Selina again.

"How are you enjoying working with the children from the Sunday school?" Lady Templeton said. "I have heard very good reports from Mrs. Godwin."

Selina brightened up a little. "I am enjoying it immensely."

"The task has certainly kept you busy over these past weeks," Lady Templeton said, "and it has been good to see you eager to get up in the mornings, with plenty to look forward to."

Selina had indeed discovered a new sense of purpose since helping to educate the children. At first, she had lent a hand to Mrs. Godwin at Sunday school, reading Bible stories and helping with craft work, but now her help had been sought on other days too, taking the children for walks on the Crescent Fields, showing them how to identify different types of leaves, and supervising games. Occasionally she had done some singing with them in one of the rooms at the back of the church.

"Yes," Lady Templeton said, "it has been good to see you busy, and I hope you feel you are contributing something worthwhile."

"I do, Mama—and fear not. I have not tried to go and visit the gaol again."

"That I know for sure," Lady Templeton said, "for I have

been keeping an eye on you."

This was certainly true. Selina had felt her every move had been scrutinized by her parents following the rather frightening events outside the prison last month. She'd even struggled to find time for her usual rooftop jaunts at night because her mama was constantly popping in and out of her chamber at bedtime on some pretext or another. She would ask to borrow a comb, or make sure Selina had a good book to read in bed and that she had a glass of water.

Why, I have only once in the past week been up on the roof! Luckily it was a beautifully clear night and I was able to view the stars . . . how I love gazing up at the heavens.

Voices in the entrance hall! Henry and Kitty had arrived. They had been back home in Bath for over a week now, and so far, Selina had met up with Kitty every day. How wonderful it was to have her best friend next door again.

"Hello, hello," Henry said, coming into the parlor. "I have just seen George striding along Brock Street on his way here."

George would be with them within minutes. Maybe seconds! Selina smoothed the skirt of her dress and steadied her breath. 'Twas important she made a good impression as a sensible young woman—not the impulsive, wilful creature George must think her. And if he had news that he was engaged to be married to a young lady of the *ton,* then Selina would show from her demeanor how thrilled she was for him and offer hearty congratulations.

What! Must I behave like this? For if George is engaged to be married, I shall want to run to the roof and fling myself off . . . or at least be very unhappy for an exceptionally long time.

"Selina," Henry said, "have you finished reading the pamphlet about slavery I sent you from London?"

"I've read it several times," Selina said. "'Tis very interesting. I know a lot about the subject now—although I am not so sure how things could be improved, for all is tied up so much with finances."

"Ah! Mr. Fitzgerald," Lady Templeton said as George stepped

into the parlor. "Now the party is complete, and I will leave you young people to make your way to Lower Borough Walls. I hope you find the meeting fascinating, and I look forward to hearing all about it."

"Are you sure you do not want to come with us, Mama?" Henry said.

"Perchance another time," Lady Templeton said. "I have much to do here, and your father and I have an engagement this afternoon as well. Besides, with three companions, I do believe that Selina will be safely supervised."

"Why, Mama!" Selina said. "I am no longer a child."

"I know," Lady Templeton said. "However, you need protecting from danger—and from your own impulses."

How can Mama talk to me like this in public—in front of George?

"Do not forget to take your cloak, Selina," Lady Templeton said, "for 'tis cold outside."

"Yes," Henry said, "and make it your normal everyday cloak, not one of those strange garments you like to wear from the dressing up box. We have all heard how you were dressed when you went to the gaol."

Selina swatted Henry on the shoulder. "Enough! If I am to behave, then you must not provoke me, Henry."

"See what I have to put up with, George?" Henry said as they set off for the Meeting House. "My sister has been attacking me on a daily basis since infancy."

George opened his mouth as if to say something—then closed it again with a grin.

"Come, George," Henry said. "Walk beside me, and we will leave Kitty and Selina to gossip behind us."

"How was your singing lesson this morning?" Kitty said to Selina. "I know how much you enjoy your time with Signor Allegretto."

"We had a good lesson," Selina said. "We always have fun, and he's so knowledgeable about music—although today he was more subdued than normal. And there was something rather strange—he was sporting a black eye."

"I don't think I've ever seen anyone with a black eye," Kitty said. "I've read about it in books, after people have been fighting or maybe fallen off a steep cliff."

"Dear Kitty," Selina said, "you love your reading so much, do you not? I believe you see the whole of life through the prism of literature."

"I confess that sometimes I have found a book more exciting than real life," Kitty said, "though that was in the past—not now that I'm married to dear Henry."

"So being married to Henry is like living inside the pages of a novel?" Selina said. "I can scarce believe that!"

The two friends started giggling.

"What are you two talking about?" Henry said, turning round. "Did I perchance hear my name mentioned?"

"We were discussing books," Selina said.

"Is this true?" Henry asked Kitty.

"Oh yes," she said. "We were definitely discussing books."

Henry laughed and turned back to George. "My wife is very fond of reading—but not very fond of telling me what she talks to Selina about. 'Twas ever thus!"

"Go on," Kitty said to Selina, "tell me more about Signor Allegretto's black eye."

"Well, of course I asked him how he got it," Selina said, "but he did not seem to like me mentioning it. He is very particular about his appearance."

"Did he have no explanation to give you?" Kitty said.

"Some silly story about tripping over his shoes in the dark at home," Selina said. "I did not believe a word of it."

"I remember you said you saw him in the street a few weeks ago when he was meant to be teaching you," Kitty said. "Did you ever ask him about that?"

"I tried to," Selina said, "the next time I saw him at my lesson. Again, he didn't wish to talk about it. There was the same embarrassment—and a touch of indignation."

"He must have something else going on in his life that we know not of," Kitty said.

"I am sure you are right."

"Oh no!" Kitty said. "I know that look. You are planning to find out what it is."

"I am quite determined," Selina said.

Once the four young people reached Lower Borough Walls, they joined the queue of people waiting to go into the Meeting House.

"I had no idea it would be this popular," George said to Selina.

"And why would it not be?" she said, "for there must be many in Bath who are concerned about a serious subject like this. I am so pleased to see there are lots of ladies here, for many consider we females have feathers in our heads instead of brains. We are more than capable of considering deep matters."

"Yes, yes, of course. I, I did not mean . . ." George's voice trailed away, and he looked a little downcast.

Why does George not understand when I tease him? And why do I always want to goad him?

Once inside the building, they found seats on the narrow benches facing into the middle of the room. Henry sat next to his wife, and Selina sat beside her—and next to George.

The men have sandwiched us ladies between them—to protect us or to make sure we behave ourselves? I would not like to hazard a guess as to which is the correct assumption.

A plainly dressed man welcomed everyone there and told them they were going to hear some things that might upset them but that were nevertheless of great significance. They were lucky enough to have a special speaker that day—Mr. John Freedman, a gentleman from the other side of the world who was making it his life's work to travel all over England to bear witness to what was being suffered abroad. At the end of Mr. Freedman's speech, there would be plenty of time for other individuals to speak, and for questions to be taken.

How thrilling! Selina could not wait to see the main speaker. She, along with many members of the crowd, gasped with astonishment as a gentleman of middle years entered the chamber to talk to them.

"Ladies and gentlemen . . ." Mr. Freedman began. "I am an escaped slave and am here to tell you my life story—to describe what it is like to be born into slavery on a plantation in the West Indies, to grow up a slave, to be taken from your parents and spend your life doing the bidding of others. To have children, only to be separated from them . . ."

This is indeed shocking! I already knew everything he is telling us in theory—but how much more vivid is his personal testimony.

The atmosphere in the chamber was extremely quiet and attentive. No one interrupted the gentleman or made any comments to their neighbor. All sat in rapt attention.

At the end of his speech, thunderous applause broke out.

"Bravo!" Henry shouted, echoed by many around the chamber, and then one by one, everyone got their feet and cheered the man.

The plainly dressed man who had introduced Mr. Freedman then stood up again.

"You may think that we in England have already done enough, for was not the slave trade outlawed nine years ago? But my friends, I tell you, slavery continues in British colonies unchecked, and stories such as we have just heard are depressingly commonplace. There is still much to do before this evil is wiped off the face of the Earth. We need to make it our goal to eradicate slave ownership. We must look to our territories abroad."

"Hear, hear!"

"Bravo!"

"This must be done!"

"Now," the man said, "please raise your hand if you wish to speak."

George's hand shot up so suddenly that Selina was forced to

move slightly to the side as his strong arm whooshed past her ear.

"Yes, you sir," the man said, pointing at George. "Please, stand and start our discussion. The floor is yours."

I cannot wait to hear George's words.

George

GEORGE STARTED BY catching the eyes of the people in front of him, then slowly turned all the way round until he had surveyed every single soul in the room. 'Twas important to keep them waiting because then what he said would have more impact—wasn't that what his papa had told him?

"Make your words count," Doctor Fitzgerald had counselled. "And remember, there could be people there in the chamber whose finances are tied up with slavery—you must convince them we have a duty to our brothers and sisters all over the world that transcends the hunger to accumulate more wealth."

"Ladies and gentlemen," George began.

I will not look directly at Selina during my speech, but must endeavour to think of the greater good—for then I will not be nervous.

"In our society, you will often hear people say they do not have the freedom to do what they want. They may want to purchase a field—but find it is not for sale, or the price is too high. They may want to travel to London quickly—but find the weather is against them or their horses are too tired and a change of steed is not immediately available. They may wish to buy some strawberries—but find they are not in season . . ."

There were a few smiles at the thought of people's desire to consume strawberries being thwarted.

"Yes, ladies and gentlemen, we do not always have the freedom to do what we want in this life, and this can be a source of irritation and an occasion for grumbling. And yet I tell you, it is my firm belief that most of us here today have precious little idea what a loss of freedom really means. Specifically, what a loss of freedom means to an enslaved African."

I need to listen to myself! None of us here save Mr. Freedman have any idea what this loss of freedom means.

George crumpled his carefully prepared notes in his hands and allowed them to drop to the floor.

"I was intending to outline the indignities, sufferings and hardships experienced on a daily basis in the plantations, but what right have I to do so? Today, we have had the absolute privilege of hearing a firsthand account from our esteemed colleague, Mr. Freedman, who is seated here amongst us."

A spontaneous round of heartfelt applause filled the chamber, with many getting to their feet to honor Mr. Freedman.

"I commend you, sir, for your bravery in speaking out and for devoting your energies to educating the public. You are our brother, and your testimony is vital. Thank you for your determination to make the world a better place, a world where all men—and women—have an equal value and opportunities . . ."

What is that tapping sound? Ah! Selina is stamping her foot. I know how much she would like to improve conditions for women in particular. The percussive sound at least means she is still wearing her shoes.

". . . and where no person is deprived of their liberty and kept in servitude in order to gratify the greed of others. We should all strive to move towards full abolition. Pray God 'twill come soon, and I thank you for listening."

Several ladies dabbed their eyes with pocket handkerchiefs at the mention of other human souls being kept in servitude. At least, George hoped that was what it was. Heaven forfend they were thinking of how much money their families would lose if full abolition were to be passed in law.

George allowed himself one look at Selina as he sat down and nearly overbalanced.

Lord! The way she's gazing at me. She looks so disappointed. Perchance she was expecting a longer speech? She must think I had not prepared properly for the occasion, which is so far from the truth. But I

*have made the right decision. I could not deliver my planned words—
'twould have been insensitive and wrong. Thank God I realized in time.*

George then felt a sting of guilt about his reasons for writing the speech in the first place. Selina no doubt thought he had been motivated to speak out purely for reasons of justice and fairness, but the truth was, he had spent hours and hours studying and composing his speech because he wanted to impress Selina. After all, his oration in the Quaker Meeting House was to be phase two of the plan to capture her heart.

"Well done, George," Henry said, leaning over Kitty and Selina. "Sound words."

"Short," Selina said, "but to the point."

She held up George's discarded crumpled speech.

"And I intend to read the full version just as soon as I can."

"Anyone else who wishes to share their views, please raise your hand," the plainly dressed man said. "We will be pleased to listen."

"Please, do not read my speech, Selina," George whispered. "'Tis pompous and idiotic. I see that now."

Selina stuffed the speech into her reticule and then put her finger to her lips as another person stood up to address the room.

The afternoon continued, with speaker after speaker adding details of the appalling conditions that slaves endured and resolving that this practice must end. Many had sensible suggestions for how to educate the public; some offered to write pamphlets, while others were keen to help distribute the literature and debate with people in the street. Many also pledged to do their best to rely less on imports from the West Indies, in order that pressure might be applied to the finances of the slave owners.

"Well, that has given us much food for thought," Henry said as they came out of the Meeting House and started to walk back to the Crescent. "What do you think, Selina?"

"All very interesting," she replied. "But I am wondering what I can personally do to help."

To George's consternation, she then reached into her reticule and pulled out his speech, smoothing down the crumpled sheets.

"Perhaps I will find ideas in your full speech, George? The one you unaccountably decided not to deliver?"

"That is harsh, Selina," Henry said. "George will have had very good reasons for deciding to censor his own words."

"Exactly what were these reasons?" Selina asked George.

"Well, after I had heard John Freedman speak, I no longer felt qualified," George mumbled.

"But I am left short of information!" Selina's eyes danced—did this signify amusement—possibly at George's expense? Or was she merely exasperated?

"How am I to help the cause, Mr. Fitzgerald, if I do not have the full facts?"

Zounds! Mr. Fitzgerald. So formal again.

"Wait! Let me see—ah! I think I have the answer." Selina pointed to a page. "This is intriguing. 'Tis about the Anti-Saccharites. I will read this section aloud."

"Only with George's permission," Henry said.

George nodded. Who was he to refuse Selina anything?

Selina grinned broadly and stood as if delivering a speech in Parliament.

"I would remind you of the Anti-Saccharites who did so much to support abolition at the end of the last century. For those who know not of what I speak, the Anti-Saccharites drastically reduced their use of sugar—for sugar is produced by slaves. The Anti-Saccharites stopped taking sugar in their tea, and in cooked dishes, no doubt finding the sweetness of the argument against slavery was enough to sustain them. They gave up the freedom of enjoying sugar to try to help others find their own freedom."

"Wise words," Henry said.

"Yes, indeed," echoed Kitty.

"This gives me an idea!" Selina held the pages of George's speech high in the air, like a soldier bearing a flag into battle.

"Oh no!" Henry said. "You are already hatching one of your

plots. Let me see. Are you to revive the Anti-Saccharite movement? Demand that we should forgo puddings made with plantation sugar?"

"Mm, I am not sure about puddings," Selina said. "Are they not nutritious? As well as delicious? George, help me. As a medical man, do you consider puddings to be good for us?"

"Not especially," George said. "Many people eat very healthily without them."

"Are you to take the sugar from my tea?" Henry asked Selina.

"I think even you could manage to give up sugar in your tea," she retorted. "Ah, what I wouldn't give for a cup of tea right now."

"I tell you what," George said, "why don't we go to Hunter's? My treat. 'Tis very near—but a stone's throw from the abbey."

"A capital idea," Henry said. "Oh, Kitty—are you all right? What is the matter, my dear?"

Kitty was holding a handkerchief to her mouth. "The thought of tea—ah! I think I need to sit down."

"Let us hasten to Hunter's," Henry said. "A refreshing cup of tea will do you good, and I have heard their ices and mousses are divine."

Poor Kitty had gone quite green by now. "No, Henry, you misunderstand me. I cannot bear the idea of tea and certainly do not want to go to Hunter's and smell it—let alone drink it."

"Of course. What a thoughtless, blundering idiot I am," Henry said. "Would you like me to take you home, dearest Kitty?"

She nodded. "I am sorry to be such a nuisance," she said to George and Selina, "it's just that, er . . ."

With his medical training, George knew exactly why Kitty could not bear the smell or taste of tea. Earlier, in the Meeting House, she had looked a little drawn, and now she seemed to feel nauseous. There was no doubting the reason—Henry and Kitty must have exciting news that they had not yet shared: their family was to increase.

"Do not let us spoil your fun," Henry said to George. "You

and Selina should continue to Hunter's. I will walk Kitty home. In fact, I think I will call for a sedan chair."

"There is no need," Kitty said. "I am not an invalid! I am perfectly able to walk—and would prefer it."

"If you are sure," Henry said, taking his wife by the arm. "Lean on me, my dearest. And goodbye, George! Do not be a stranger. Selina, doubtless we will see you tomorrow, as we do every day. Goodbye, goodbye . . ."

"The fresh air will do Kitty good," George said.

"Yes," Selina said. "'Tis far more refreshing than being shut in a stuffy sedan chair in her condition."

"You knew?" George said.

"No," Selina said. "I suspected, then had my suspicions confirmed. I will have a lot to talk to Kitty about when we meet tomorrow. By the way, do I have your permission to borrow your speech? I have been much struck with the portion about the Anti-Saccharites and would like to read through the full prose."

"Of course you may borrow it—and keep it if it interests you, for I have another copy at home."

George and Selina walked the short distance to Hunter's Tea Shop and sat at a table in the window.

"I think you will want tea with no sugar," George said to Selina. "Will you allow yourself to have an ice? Or perhaps a fruit tart? I believe they contain sugar as well."

"Do not tease me, Mr. Fitzgerald!" Selina said. "I am not in the mood. However, you are right, we need to be conscious of all we consume and have in our homes that comes from across the seas. And for that reason, perhaps I will have a piece of bread and butter with my tea."

"A fine idea," George said, "and we did have rather a lot of cake and biscuits on our return from the gaol last month. We have both been well fed with sugar."

"Indeed!"

Ten minutes later, George and Selina were enjoying cups of tea—with no sugar—together with wafer-thin triangles of buttered bread.

"What have you been doing with yourself since last I saw you?" George said.

This simple question lit a fire beneath Selina, and she talked animatedly and at length about Mrs. Godwin, the children she had been helping, and what fun it had been.

"I take them for long walks across the Crescent Fields," she said. "I know every tree and ditch there, for I have been running around that glorious space since infancy. 'Tis a joy to help the children enjoy nature."

How beautiful she looks! She has thrown herself life and soul into helping these children.

"One of the boys has a bad leg," Selina said, "and sometimes struggles to keep up. Yesterday I ended up giving him a lift on my back, which was rather tiring, I can tell you. A pony would have been useful! Come to think of it, it would be wonderful to give them all riding lessons."

Riding lessons for the children? An interesting idea.

"I told you it was Mama's suggestion, didn't I?" Selina said. "Helping out with the children, I mean?"

"Yes."

"She's trying to keep a close eye on me now after, well, you know, after how silly I was about visiting the gaol. I'm sorry about that, by the way. You went considerably beyond the call of duty and were such a hero when you rescued me that day."

"I only did what anyone would've done," George said.

"You did more than that, and you know it," Selina said. "I am truly sorry I put you in that position. Your clothes were quite ruined."

"Ah! Those clothes," George said. "I did not want to wear them again."

"I know all about that," Selina said, "for as soon as Martha got back to Number 1, she told everyone downstairs about how wonderfully generous you had been; the news filtered upstairs very quickly. That was a fine thing you did and meant a lot to

Martha and her mother."

"I was glad to be able to help them."

Selina smiled warmly. George opened his mouth—then closed it again. There was so much more he wanted to say to her. He longed to explain why he had not tried to see her since that day at the gaol, to tell her how busy he had been, spending almost every waking hour either undertaking his medical work, or studying the various books and pamphlets he had about slavery and discussing them with his father, so determined was he to make his speech the very best he could.

So why was George not saying it? What was preventing him? George clenched his fists into angry balls. The truth was, he wanted Selina to think he had managed to do his fine speech without all that preparation. He wanted her to think he had a brilliant mind, to admire him—and then love him.

But he must not be downcast! He had completed phase two of his plan to woo her, and it hadn't gone too badly, especially in contrast with phase one, trying to change his appearance with new clothes. That had been both embarrassing and undignified. Even now, when George thought of those ripped pantaloons, he winced. No, there was plenty of room for optimism. Onward and upward! Phase three of his plan would be starting soon.

When I have managed to work out what it should be . . .

"We had better be getting back soon," George said, "for your mama might become anxious."

Without warning, the heavens opened and there was a sudden squall outside in the street. Rain lashed the panes of the window and made it difficult to hear.

"Ah! We cannot leave now," George said, raising his voice, "or you will be wet through by the time we get home."

"I do not mind a little rain," Selina said. "In fact, I love to feel its freshness on my face."

"This is not a little rain," George said. "This is a torrent! You will be drenched."

A sudden, intimate vision of Selina wearing one of her delightful white muslin frocks while dancing in the rain sprang to mind. George swallowed nervously.

"We should wait another five minutes or so," he said. "Let the weather settle."

"'Tis not much of a spring we are having, is it?" Selina said. "We must hope for better when the summer months come."

A figure rushed past Hunter's window, splashing awkwardly in the puddles. No! Surely not? It couldn't be . . .

"What is wrong?" Selina said.

"Oh, nothing. Excuse me a minute." George dashed away, causing the bell to tinkle alarmingly as he flung the entrance door open and looked up and down the street. There was no one there. Perhaps it was his imagination? Or had the person already gone round the corner?

George went inside and sat down again.

"I thought I recognized someone. However, visibility is poor out there in the rainstorm and I could easily have been mistaken."

George decided he would mention this to Lord Templeton when he returned with Selina to Number 1—and he could ask him to tell Henry discreetly as well. There was no need to alarm the ladies at this point.

For unless I am very much mistaken, I have just seen the most unwelcome figure of Lord Steyne passing by.

Selina

"GEORGE! WHO WAS it? This person you thought you recognized?" Selina said.

Who could be so important that George felt compelled to run into the street in a rainstorm?

Interesting—how I love a mystery!

George ran his fingers through his damp hair. This new hairstyle suited him so much better—and was enhanced by a few drops of rain and a bit of ruffling. How Selina longed to run her hands through his locks . . .

George looks so romantic! Like a poet.

"'Twas no one important," George said, "if it even were him."

Clear as mud—I see George is determined not to take me into his confidence about whoever it was he saw—or didn't see.

"Now, shall I order more tea?" George suggested. "We will not be able to leave quite yet, on account of the weather."

"Yes please," Selina said. "And—oh, dear me. How tempting."

If only I had not thought to give up sugar, for I see little pastry tarts being eaten all around us, and they look so delicious.

George smiled. "I expect you're wondering how much sugar is in a pastry tart."

"Indeed I am," Selina said, "and you know full well why. For if 'tis only a few grains, my conscience might allow me to eat one, but alas, if there are a few teaspoons in each tart, that is a different matter. For then I will have to stick to my resolve not to consume sugar—all for the greater good, the total eradication of slavery."

"If something is wrong, it is wrong," George said. "Whether it be a few grains or a few teaspoons, the crime is the same, surely? For if someone picks your pocket and steals a sixpence in the street, they can be punished in the same manner as someone who takes a great deal more in a house burglary."

Ah! George is terribly handsome when he is passionate about a subject. Would it not be wonderful to be in his arms right now and have him loose that passion on me?

The door to the teashop flung open at that point, rudely interrupting Selina's blissful imaginings, and a man ran through to the very back of the shop and seated himself at a table in a shadowy corner.

"'Tis Signor Allegretto!" Selina clasped her hands together. "How nice to see him here."

"Signor Allegretto?" George said. "Your singing teacher?"

"Yes, the very person. But why would he rush through to the back of the shop at such a pace? You think he would look around to see if there was anyone he knew. He could have come to sit at our table—'twould have been perfectly acceptable."

"Possibly he wants some time on his own. People do, sometimes."

"Well, you might like being solitary," Selina said, "but I cannot believe that of Signor Allegretto. He is the most gregarious man I have ever known—always laughing and joking and definitely happiest in company. In fact, he's oft told me that when he goes home at night, he can be quite lonely in his lodgings and he longs for a lady to share his life."

George raised an eyebrow, and Selina giggled.

"Oh dear," she said, "that came out all wrong. I am sure he used different words—I did not mean to imply that Signor Allegretto said anything improper."

"I should hope not," George said, the corners of his mouth twitching.

"I have decided. I am going to go and speak to Signor Allegretto and ask him to join us at our table."

"Do you think that is wise? I'm not sure . . ."

Selina rattled her teacup in its saucer.

Lord! Cannot a woman even walk across a room on her own and ask someone if they want to share a pot of tea?

"If you do not think it is wise for me to ask on my own," she said, "you will have to come with me while I issue the invitation."

George followed Selina to the back of the room, and they greeted Signor Allegretto and asked if he would like to join them at their table in the window. He sprang to his feet and seemed very surprised to see them, so it was obviously not a deliberate act to fail to greet them when he had come in.

"I do not wish to appear rude," Signor Allegretto said. "'Tis just that I am much more comfortable sitting at the back of the shop. I am, of course, very happy to take tea with you—but do not want to sit in the window for passers-by to gawp at."

"Well," Selina said, "we could join you at your table."

"I would be honored." Signor Allegretto gave a deep bow and, with a flourish, indicated a chair for Selina at his table.

"I will order fresh tea," George said, "and let it be known to the staff that we have moved tables."

While George was busy doing that on the other side of the room, Selina decided to take matters into her own hands. After all, there was an intriguing mystery to solve. Possibly several mysteries.

"Signor Allegretto!" Selina whispered. "Please, confide in me. I think you are in some sort of trouble."

"Why do you think that?"

Was Selina going to have to spell it out?

"First, you have a black eye—I know you gave me an explanation for that this morning, but I was not entirely convinced. And, some time ago, you said you could not teach me because you had a fever, however on the same day I saw you on the streets of Bath. Do not think I will give up asking you about that! You were out, walking around, on the very day you were apparently contagious. Now you are cowering at the back of Hunter's, not wanting to be seen. Are you afraid of someone? Oh, pray tell me what is going on."

"I cannot," Signor Allegretto said, "for I do not want to put you in danger."

"Danger?" George said as he sat down. "If Miss Templeton is in danger, it is your solemn duty to tell me what is going on."

Signor Allegretto covered his face with his hands. "'Tis to protect her that I am doing this. Everything is such a mess! I know not what to do."

"Is this danger to do with a certain member of the *ton?*" George said.

"Yes," Signor Allegretto said. "How the devil . . . ?"

George's voice shrank to a whisper.

"I believe I saw the gentleman concerned just now in the street. He looked far scruffier than I have ever known him—he was completely unkempt. And there was an incident back in January when a man threatened me. I was not sure then, but now . . ."

"So that's why you ran out of the door?" Selina said. "Why didn't you explain before? I have a right to know these things."

Danger? George is in danger? This is not good news.

"So that we are clear," Signor Allegretto said, "are you talking about a certain lord whose name begins with *S*?'"

"Lord Steyne," George whispered.

Selina realized that this was a serious matter, of course she did, and yet she could not help feeling quietly thrilled. So little ever happened in her life, and certainly nothing to do with black eyes, threats, or people hiding at the back of Hunter's. She leant forward eagerly.

"When were you threatened, George?" she asked.

"After Henry and Kitty's dinner party, when I was traveling up Holloway on my way home. I stopped for Trigger to drink from the trough, and someone cursed me. I could not see them because they were concealed behind a bush, but I thought I recognized the voice as Lord Steyne's. That was puzzling though, for everyone said he had fled abroad, so I more or less dismissed the suspicion. However, now that I am convinced I have seen him here, outside in the street a mere ten minutes ago, I feel sure it was also him I heard on Holloway that evening."

"When you say someone cursed you from behind a bush," Selina said, "what exactly did he say?"

"I cannot repeat his words in front of a lady."

"Fiddlesticks! I assure you, growing up with my two brothers Henry and Edmund, I probably know every swear word there is in the English language."

Although when George fought those ruffians outside the gaol to save me, I believe my vocabulary increased somewhat. I was amazed to hear the phrases he used and am not sure I actually know what all of them mean.

"You must take this threat seriously," Signor Allegretto said to Selina. "'Tis no laughing matter. Perhaps if I explain to you what has happened to me, it will fill in the missing pieces of the puzzle for you."

Then he turned to George.

"Mr. Fitzgerald, will that be all right? Do I have your permission to speak freely in front of Miss Templeton—or would it be more proper if we talked man-to-man?"

What? Am I to be left out of all the excitement—as usual?

"I think we can proceed as we are," George said, "for I do not believe Miss Templeton frightens easily."

"True," Signor Allegretto said. "She has the courage of a lioness."

A compliment, I suppose. Although it does annoy me that men think women are such tender creatures that we are to be kept in the dark most of the time.

Signor Allegretto then started detailing every move Lord Steyne had made against him.

"It was back in January," he said, "when I first began to be aware that I was being followed. I would turn round suddenly in the street, convinced that someone was on my heels—but there was never anyone there. I do not mind admitting it made me feel very uneasy."

This situation went on for some time until one day, two ruffians forced Signor Allegretto down a narrow alley and he came face-to-face with Lord Steyne.

"I could not believe my eyes," Signor Allegretto said, "for everyone thought this man had gone abroad after all the trouble."

George's mouth set in a grim line.

"Lord Steyne mentioned your name," Signor Allegretto said to George. "He has quite a grudge against you."

"Why?" Selina said. "What has George, I mean Mr. Fitzgerald, ever done to Lord Steyne . . . oh, wait. It is because of what happened in the Octagon, is it not?"

Signor Allegretto nodded, turned to George, and said, "Lord Steyne cannot forgive you for that. He's done many, many bad things—everyone knows that—but the one thing that destroyed his reputation forever with the *ton* was being exposed as a card cheat. That was the end for him. You managed to push him over the precipice, and he moved from being a pampered member of Bath society to a virtual nobody. Regardless of how much money he has, no one wants to socialize with him now that you have destroyed his reputation."

"I still don't understand," Selina said. "Lord Steyne is angry with George—so why was he having *you* followed, Signor Allegretto?"

"I am coming to that. Lord Steyne said that I could be useful to him as I visit Number 1 to teach you, Miss Templeton, and he thought I would be able to find out all sorts of things and pass on details—let him know if and when Mr. Fitzgerald came to visit, and so on. This is all part of an extremely unpleasant scheme he is dreaming up."

Signor Allegretto's story got even more complicated at this point, and Selina found it hard to follow, but she understood that Lord Steyne had not left the country as everyone had thought after his disgrace. He had instead hidden out in one of his properties in the countryside around Bath, while making frequent—secret—trips into the city.

"He is determined to get me to act as a spy for him," Signor Allegretto said, "and that I will never do."

"Bravo!" Selina said. "And this is the reason for the strange happenings, is it?"

"Yes," Signor Allegretto said, "for the day I said I had a contagious fever and could not teach you, it was because Lord Steyne said I had to meet him down by the river. He tried again to force me to work for him—I said no."

"And later," Selina said, "the black eye?"

"Lord Steyne set his ruffians upon me, but I was not to be persuaded by violence. I am immovable and will never spy for such a man—I will never betray any family I work for, particularly the Templeton family, which I hold in such high regard."

"I can understand that Lord Steyne has a grudge against me," George said, "but what has the Templeton family got to do with this?"

"How better to punish someone, than to harm the person they love," Signor Allegretto said.

"What on earth do you mean?" George said.

Yes—what is he talking about? The person you love . . .oh! Could it be . . . ?

Signor Allegretto stared at George and then at Selina for quite some time.

"Why, Lord Steyne means to spoil things between you two," he said at last. "Do the pair of you not realize you are in love with each other? I apologize for talking in such a direct way—I am Italian and cannot help it. We wear our hearts on our sleeves. It is plain to everyone that you, Miss Templeton, and you, Mr. Fitzgerald, belong together. You love each other—and have done so since before Christmas. You are both looking shocked. One day I will be proved right, mark my words."

Well, really! I am attracted to George—sometimes—but that is not love. And I think he used to be attracted to me, although alas, he has not shown the same signs more recently, for he seems reluctant to see me very often. But love? George, in love—with me? Arrant nonsense!

Isn't it?

CHAPTER SIX

George

I S SIGNOR ALLEGRETTO the most perceptive person I have ever met? Or the most imaginatively mistaken, at least about Selina's feelings?

"Why have you waited until now to tell us about Lord Steyne, Signor Allegretto?" George said. "Did you not realize that Miss Templeton could have been in danger?"

"That was my dilemma," Signor Allegretto said, "for Lord Steyne told me that if I confided in anyone, if I breathed a single word, he would first of all slit my throat, and then he would carry out his plan to spoil the beautiful romance between you two. He would make sure you were never happy together—the ultimate revenge on the man who had destroyed his reputation. Do you see my problem? If I told someone, I could have made things worse."

And you could have had your throat cut. A sobering thought.

"And yet you have told us today," George said. "A brave decision."

"Thank you for understanding," Signor Allegretto said. "I do not consider myself a brave man. In fact, when I leave Hunter's, I will do so by the back door, for fear of encountering my enemy."

He glanced towards the window.

"Ah! I see the rain has stopped. This has been a very pleasant interlude, however now, alas, I must bid you farewell. And Miss

Templeton, do not forget I will expect you to be note perfect in the Mozart aria by the time of your lesson next week."

George shook Signor Allegretto's hand warmly, and Selina bade him farewell. They watched as he disappeared into the kitchen area, obviously still intent on making an unobtrusive exit through the back door.

"And now I believe we should set off for Number 1," George said. "We will leave by the front door."

"Your word is my command," Selina said.

George took her arm and they walked past the Abbey and Pump Room, towards Milsom Street. A watery sun came out, struggling to cast its beams through the lowering skies.

"Which way should we go now?" George said. "Carry on up Milsom Street, then past the Upper Rooms? Or would you prefer to go through Queen Square and into the Crescent Fields? 'Tis wet underfoot."

"Oh, I would much prefer to go via the Crescent Fields, regardless of how wet 'tis underfoot. Mama will probably scold me for ruining my shoes, but I care not."

"If you are sure," George said. "I do not wish to be the cause of friction between you and Lady Templeton."

"I am used to being scolded by Mama. She does not really mean all the things she says. Besides, I have plenty more shoes, most of them in very good condition."

"Because you so rarely wear them?"

"'Tis true I am happiest without."

The pair walked in companionable silence until deep into the Crescent Fields. There was hardly anyone about, most people being far too sensible as the sky was threatening rain again. There were plenty of sheep, though.

Eventually Selina tackled the subject George had been dreading. "I suppose we'll have to tell my parents what Signor Allegretto said."

"Tell them everything?"

"Well, not everything," Selina said. "Everything we know to

be true. Not all the idiocy about the pair of us being in love with each other—which is nonsense."

"I agree, 'tis absolute balderdash," George said in a subdued voice, feeling the agonizing twist of a knife deep in his heart to hear Selina's words. She sounded so certain!

"Perchance Signor Allegretto really did have a contagious fever," he continued, "and he has somehow imagined the whole scenario, due to a high temperature."

"'Tis possible" Selina said. "He is very excitable—a true musician."

"But he could not have made up the part about Lord Steyne, the ruffians, and his black eye. That chimes with what we already know about Lord Steyne. No, on the whole I believe him—apart from . . ."

"I know exactly what you mean, and think the truth of the matter must be that Lord Steyne simply wanted someone to keep an eye on Number 1—and probably Number 2—in case you visited my parents, Edmund, or Henry. Have you considered that Lord Steyne might have had people watching you at other times, or even been shadowing you himself? Maybe that was why he was hiding behind the water trough on Holloway—for that is on the way to your home in Devonshire Buildings. You need to be careful, George. I would not like any harm to come to you."

She would not like any harm to come to me. Is this significant? Or merely the concern of a friend? Or acquaintance.

"Moreover, Signor Allegretto is a fanciful man," Selina said.

"I believe you are right, for he imagines love where none exists."

Although Signor Allegretto is not mistaken about the love that exists on my side, for I worship Selina. I truly believe I am in love with her—ah, how I long for her to be my wife.

"We two know the truth," Selina said. "We are friends—good friends—but will never be anything more, for our characters are too different. Why can people not see that?"

A sudden thought struck George—and caused him to feel

frightened for Selina's sake. "You say people cannot see the truth—that means . . . oh, 'tis no matter."

"George, you cannot start saying something to pique my curiosity and then not finish your sentence. Please, go on!"

"I have no wish to alarm you, however, what if Signor Allegretto is right? What if everyone in Bath, save ourselves, really does think we are in love? That means Lord Steyne also mistakenly thinks we are in love. He wishes to harm me—and therefore 'tis probable he wants to harm you as well."

"If I were in danger, there would be evidence of it—and there is none."

"There is! What was all that on Grove Street outside the gaol? Is it possible those ruffians could have followed you? The one that stole your hat and his two companions? You rarely go out alone—but that day was an exception. Perhaps Lord Steyne set a watch upon your home—then had you followed to the prison, since you were leaving alone."

"I suppose you could be right, for I was surprised to meet such strange creatures, even though I was near a gaol. Certainly I did not expect to be set upon by three men."

"Yes, 'twas unusual for the area," George said. "Grove Street is not a highly fashionable street by any stretch of the imagination. However, I cannot say I have ever heard of trouble like this—in broad daylight, too. I thought at the time you were unlucky; now I'm not so convinced. Maybe the whole attack was organized by Lord Steyne."

What in God's name would have happened if I had not arrived in time? Would Selina have been abducted? Lord Steyne is guilty of treating young ladies shamefully in the past.

"This casts a different light on the situation," Selina said. "Perhaps we should tell my parents, and Henry too, everything that Signor Allegretto has revealed—making it clear he is totally mistaken, as is everyone else, about any possible mutual feeling between us."

"Possibly we should tell them," George said. "But are you

sure? Absolutely sure? I mean, about the mutual affection part not being real?"

George stared at Selina, willing her to say the words that would make his dreams come true—and trying desperately to pluck up the courage to declare his undying love.

"Of course I am sure," Selina said.

She looks anything but sure! My love is twisting her fingers together and has such a wistful look in her eyes . . .

Selina waited a few moments before continuing, "For if we two were madly in love with each other and we found ourselves alone on the Crescent Fields, it would be natural for us to embrace, would it not?"

"Natural, yes," George said, "although probably not the proper thing to do, for people might see. Besides, even though we might be madly in love, unless we were actually promised to one another, it would not be right. I could not compromise a lady."

A pitter patter of gentle raindrops started.

"Quick!" Selina said. "We can make for that clump of trees over there. There is an ancient yew in the middle that will shelter us; it has a large space inside once you push through the branches."

George raced after her, and very soon they were nestled behind a thick curtain of dense branches with needle-like leaves; not a drop of rain was able to penetrate.

Selina drew her cloak around her.

"Are you cold?" George said. "Let us go closer to the trunk."

Maybe huddle together? Purely to keep warm . . .

Selina leaned against the tree trunk and looked up at George. She was heartbreakingly beautiful in the half-light. She and George were in their own private world, one where normal rules did not apply, a beautiful, innocent world like the Garden of Eden. George took a step closer to Selina and she lifted her face to his.

"George," she murmured, her lips softly parting.

Did she feel it too? The magnetic pull? Would it be wrong to kiss her?

Is this the beginning of phase three of my plan to woo Selina?

George tilted his head sideways and lowered his lips onto hers, brushing them softly with a delicate kiss.

"We would do this," he said, "if we were in love—which of course we have agreed we are not."

"Yes," Selina said, "and then I would put my arms on your shoulders and . . ."

Gently, Selina's fingers crept round to the back of George's head, and her fingers entwined themselves in the hair at the base of his neck. Then she pulled him towards her.

This time the kiss was deeper. More intense. Heavenly!

"Selina, Selina . . ." George moaned softly.

If only she knew how much I want her, how much I love her. But she is convinced there's nothing between us. Oh, what are we doing?

"Perhaps we should not kiss," Selina said, "as we are not lovers, only friends."

"Friends may hug," George said, putting his arms around her and feeling the softness of her tiny waist. Selina put her head on his shoulder, and they stood like that for a long, long while.

"And now I believe the rain has stopped," George said. "We must go to your parents, and you must receive a scolding for ruining your shoes."

Selina looked down at her feet. "I think I deserve it this time. So much mud!"

They walked in silence until they reached the door of Number 1 and a servant let them in.

"Goodness!" Lady Templeton said, bustling into the entrance hall. "You two certainly got caught in the rain coming back from Hunter's, didn't you? And Selina. Your shoes! If you both take your outer layers off, I will have them dried by the fire in the kitchen. Henry and Kitty came back some while ago—and Henry came round to tell us that Kitty is lying down in her chamber. She, er . . ."

"We know, Mama," Selina said.

"I thought you would have guessed," Lady Templeton said. "'Tis wonderful news, but very early days, of course, and I know you will keep this to yourselves. Discretion is so important in these matters."

George took off his greatcoat and Selina her cloak, handing them to a waiting servant.

"Mama," Selina said, "we must speak with you and Papa, for something has happened."

Lady Templeton looked absolutely delighted to hear this.

No! Does she think, along with the rest of Bath, that Selina and I are in love with each other? Perhaps think that I have declared myself? However, this would not be possible, for I would have had to talk to Lord Templeton first. Wouldn't I?

"It is about Signor Allegretto," Selina said. "Come, let us go into the parlor, and we will tell you all about it."

Did Lady Templeton perhaps look a little disappointed?

George followed Selina and her mother into the parlor, apologizing profusely for the state of his boots. Lord Templeton was already seated beside the fire.

Selina very rapidly outlined to her parents an edited version of how Signor Allegretto had been suffering at the hands of Lord Steyne. Naturally, Lord and Lady Templeton were both shocked and worried at the turn of events.

"I thought we'd seen the last of that odious creature," Lord Templeton said. "We have to be very careful from now on. I do not believe the man would dare come into this house, but you must be accompanied at all times when away from home, Selina. And no more running off down to the gaol or silly nonsense like that. Do I have your word?"

"Yes, Papa. Although I am sure I am in no danger whatsoever."

"Nevertheless, please take care, Selina," Lord Templeton said. "And you'll stay to dinner, Mr. Fitzgerald? I will see if Henry is able to come over later, as long as Kitty can spare him. 'Twould be good for us men to work out what to do next over a bottle of port—and I happen to have rather a fine vintage in the cellar. Now, Selina, tell us all about the talk at the Quaker Meeting House. We are keen to hear how it went."

Selina started giving a very full account of all that had been said by the visiting speaker—the former slave. George found his attention wandering as memories flooded back of his time spent with Selina under the yew tree on the Crescent Fields.

A tiny slice of heaven fell from the sky today and bound us tightly together. What bliss! I will treasure Selina's kisses for the rest of my life. Now I need to work out what to do next to win her heart.

Selina

GEORGE STAYED TO dinner at Number 1. Selina sat opposite him and listened carefully as he answered all Lord Templeton's questions, first about his medical work and then about his ideas for the eradication of slavery.

'Tis almost as if Papa is interviewing him for a position in his household.

Possibly Lord Templeton was one of the many people in Bath who thought that George would be a suitable husband for Selina? He was wrong, of course, for Selina had very little in common with George. He was far too different from her. Sometimes very eloquent, but mostly reserved—almost pathologically shy. He did not feel things as passionately as his appearance would suggest— for he looked like a wild poet, yet behaved in a considered, restrained, and rational manner. Mostly. To be fair, some said that those who possess a quiet personality often have hidden depths and fire running through their veins. Didn't they?

George did not hesitate to fight the ruffians outside the gaol—and there was certainly much passion evident under the tree on the Crescent Fields . . .

"You are not eating much, Selina," Lady Templeton said. "Do

you feel unwell?"

"No, Mama—I find my appetite has deserted me."

I cannot eat when my mind is full of George . . .

Lady Templeton pursued her lips. She often became anxious when any of her children displayed a lessening of appetite.

"You must eat," Lady Templeton urged her daughter. "A good appetite is a sign of health."

I want no food. But I do feel hungry when I look across the table to see George looking so dazzling—hungry for his kisses. Oh, how confusing this all is.

George seemed to have no problem with his appetite and was tucking in to all the dishes on the table.

"Please, Mr. Fitzgerald," Lady Templeton said. "Have some more beef."

"Yes," Lord Templeton said. "A fine young man like you needs sustenance. Do not stand on ceremony. Eat as much as you like."

This was further proof, if needed, that George had a very steady character. Kissing Selina under a tree on the Crescent Fields seemed to have made little impression on him, whereas Selina felt all at sixes and sevens whenever she thought of his lips upon hers.

My first romantic kiss! And how glorious—outside, under a tree, with nature all around us. Perfection!

Then Selina frowned. Perchance for George, kissing a young lady was an everyday occurrence. The evidence was plain to see—for there was precious little change to his demeanor. Could George be one of those men described as rakes? Henry had told Selina about such people—in fact, he had warned her against them. And Lady Templeton had advised Selina many a time to avoid being alone with a young man at a ball, especially one she did not know well.

"For some unscrupulous men will ask you to go outside with them," Lady Templeton had oft said. "They will always have an excuse; perhaps it is too hot in the ballroom, too noisy, or too crowded. Maybe you look as if you are going to faint and they wish to revive you. But once you're outside, they may try to take advantage of you by kissing you, possibly to compromise you so that they must marry you. Remember Selina, your father is a rich man, and many so-called gentlemen are mere fortune hunters. You are their prey."

Could this have been George's motivation for kissing Selina? Of course not—for there had been no one around to see them. So did that mean George was a rake and made a habit of kissing young women whenever he could—whenever no one was looking?

There is a third explanation—that he loves me and felt a magnetic pull towards me as I did to him—but does this not seem unlikely? For he made no effort to see me after my visit to the gaol until we went to the Quaker Meeting House today. And he did not declare himself . . .

Once the meal was over, Henry arrived to share a glass of port with George and Lord Templeton.

"Is Edmund not here this evening?" Henry said as he came into the dining room.

"I believe Edmund is at his club," Lady Templeton said. "I do hope he's having a good evening."

"If I know Edmund, he will be," Henry said.

Selina frowned.

'Tis all right for my brother to be out at all hours unchaperoned, whereas I cannot even open the front door without being told I must have someone with me. And why are clubs only for men?

"How is Kitty faring?" Selina asked Henry.

"Fine," Henry said. "Thank you for asking. She's spending the evening quietly at home but will be happy to see you tomorrow, I know."

"Excellent news," Lord Templeton said. "Now, 'tis time for you ladies to withdraw, for we men have much to discuss."

"I brought Carter with me too," Henry said. "He's pleased to be back at Number 2—his new home."

"Where is he?" Lord Templeton asked.

"In the servants' hall," Henry said. "He insisted on going down to see everyone there. I asked him to come and sit with us as soon as he can. He will be very useful when we formulate our plan to defeat Lord Steyne."

"Quite so," Lord Templeton said. "I am glad he has come back from London—and hope his business went well? I know he won't be allowed to tell us about it. 'Tis top secret, as always. Ah, yes. Carter is always welcome at my table. We owe him such a great debt of gratitude for how he looked after you, Henry, bringing you home safely after Waterloo, against all the odds. I will never forget his loyalty to this family."

"About that," Henry said. "'Tis time I told George a little more about Carter and his connection with our family—if that is acceptable to you, Mama? Papa?"

"Yes, do explain to Mr. Fitzgerald the special place Carter holds in our hearts," Lady Templeton said as she stood at the door ready to go upstairs with Selina.

Lord Templeton nodded. "I agree. I know you will be discreet, Mr. Fitzgerald. We need Carter's help to defeat Lord Steyne—again—and 'tis best you know the truth, otherwise you will be forever wondering why Carter is invited to sit with us at table."

"Why must we be banished?" Selina said to Lady Templeton once they were settled in the withdrawing room with a pot of tea. "Why are women not allowed to stay in the dining room?"

"Do not pout, dear," Lady Templeton said. "'Tis most unattractive and will lead to lines on the face. As for being 'banished,' that is not at all how I think of it. It might surprise you to know that sometimes the men would far rather be relaxing on the sofas upstairs in the drawing room, but instead they are obliged to talk about manly things and keep drinking when they have already had enough."

"I know you are trying to make me feel better," Selina said, "but the fact remains that the men are downstairs making plans and trying to sort out how they can defeat Lord Steyne. Do they think we have nothing to say about this? No opinions of our own?"

Lady Templeton smiled. "Sometimes the men do not get as much settled as they think when they have their sessions after dinner, particularly if the bottle of port goes around many times. Do you not think the ladies of Bath have many interesting discussions in their drawing rooms—and make many wise decisions?"

"This has not been my experience," Selina said. "I have been privy to many discussions about embroidery stitches and how to trim a bonnet, but not so many about slavery or prison reform— or how to deal with unsavory members of the aristocracy."

"Well, there is a serious conversation I would like to have with you now," Lady Templeton said.

"Really? Is it about votes for women? That is a cause dear to my heart. Hardly anyone else seems to have even considered it, but wouldn't it be grand if we could vote? And what if we could become Members of Parliament too? I think I would enjoy that."

"I do not want to talk about anything political," Lady Templeton said. "My topic of conversation is Mr. Fitzgerald."

"What about Mr. Fitzgerald?"

Oh no! Mama means to probe and find out what my feelings are for George. I shall tell her the truth—that I have none.

"Do you think he would make a good husband?" Lady Templeton said. "Do you think he would suit you? Because it is very, very important to choose someone to marry that you can be friends with—for the rest of your life. Romance is all very well— and important up to a point—but life can be hard in a way you cannot yet imagine, and you need a reliable, loyal person at your side. Do you think Mr. Fitzgerald could be that person?"

"We are friends," Selina said, "certainly, we are friends. But you mention reliability and loyalty. I wonder if Mr. Fitzgerald would be a loyal husband. Do you think he takes liberties with young women? How do you know what a person is truly like? Could he be a rake, do you think? You have warned me about rakes many times, Mama."

Lady Templeton coughed. "Yes, I have. However, sometimes men make mistakes. And we should forgive people who err. As you know, my own father made a mistake in his youth and a child resulted . . . although in the end, something beautiful resulted."

Selina put her hand on Lady Templeton's to comfort her. Everyone in the family knew the story of how Lady Templeton's father, as a young unmarried man, had seduced a maid in his parents' house, who then gave birth to a son. And that son grew up to be William Carter.

As an adult, Lady Templeton spent much time seeking out her half-brother and finally succeeded in drawing him into their family in an unusual and discreet way. Carter was already a government agent when Lady Templeton found him, and then he also became Henry's manservant. This was an unusual combination of occupations, but one that worked well, for being a manservant served as a useful cloak to his work as a spy. Carter was, of course, part of the Templeton family too, being Lady Templeton's half-brother and Henry, Edmund, and Selina's uncle. This knowledge was confined to family, a few close friends, and trusted servants.

As well as being related to the Templetons, William Carter was their most loyal defender and friend—and had saved Henry's life after Waterloo. Carter occupied a unique position, first in Lord and Lady Templeton's household, and now in Henry's. He was the only person who was truly free to move between upstairs and downstairs in both Number 1 and Number 2 Royal Crescent.

"What if a man goes on making mistakes?" Selina said. "I am not talking of a person like your father who saw the error of his ways and later made a good marriage. What if a rake is unre-formed?"

Lady Templeton regarded her daughter closely. "You will have to be more specific. What exactly are you saying? Have you heard something about Mr. Fitzgerald?"

"'Tis not because of something I have heard, Mama."

Lady Templeton sat bolt upright. "Has Mr. Fitzgerald made advances? Improper advances? Was it a mistake for Henry to allow him to escort you back from Bath this afternoon?"

What is an improper advance, for heaven's sake? What happened between us was the most natural thing in the world. There was nothing improper about it. My only concern is that George might be in the habit of kissing many ladies. And I want to be the only one.

"George has not been improper," Selina said. "At least, not with me. It was just something I was wondering about. Please forget I said anything—I have no wish to besmirch George's name."

How urgently I need to speak to Kitty! I will seek her company as soon as possible for I am in dire need of advice from a young woman of my own age.

"I will make sure you are chaperoned on every occasion from now on," Lady Templeton said. "You cannot be too careful. Even a whiff of scandal can spoil your chances of marriage. Selina? Are you listening to me? You look rather pale. Perhaps you should retire?"

"I have the beginnings of a megrim, Mama," Selina said.

Truly, my head is throbbing—and I so desperately want to be alone.

"I will go to my chamber now and will be fine by the morning. Goodnight, Mama."

What bliss it will be to lie on my bed while I think about George's kisses . . . and I intend to finish reading his speech too, before kissing it and placing it under my pillow. Perhaps later, if the coast is clear, I will go to the roof and watch him as he leaves.

George

WILLIAM CARTER SEEMED an interesting man—with an exceptionally unusual background and occupation. George was sitting next to him at the dining table. The bottle of port had made several journeys round the table by this point, and Carter had refused it every time.

"Not drinking, Carter?" Lord Templeton said.

"No—I had some ale in the servants' hall," Carter said, "and I want to keep a clear head, for we must formulate a plan."

"Yes, indeed," Henry said. "I must say, I never thought Lord Steyne would be bold enough to show his face in Bath again. We should have been more severe with him at the time—arrested him and reported him to the Constable."

"Hindsight is a wonderful thing," Lord Templeton said, "but I agree with you. We must locate the man."

"Then destroy him," Carter said.

"I'll drink to that," Henry said.

"Me too," George said.

For I will not have any danger near Selina . . .

"Tell me more about when you saw Lord Steyne near Hunter's," Carter said to George. "Was there anyone with him? One of his followers, maybe?"

"As far as I could see, the man was entirely alone," George said. "He looked scruffier than he had before Christmas, not like a member of the *ton*."

"It sounds as if he's down on his luck," Carter said. "I suspect his servants have deserted him, along with much of his gang—although doubtless there are still a few roughnecks in Bath who will do his bidding for the right price."

"'Tis a crying shame the episode in the Octagon did not finish him off as we had hoped," George said to Carter.

"I am sure the damage you did to Lord Steyne's reputation has wounded him grievously," Carter said. "We were all very grateful for what you did that day."

"'Twas a victory in battle," George said. "Now, we need to win the war."

"Precisely," Carter said. "I see we understand each other. And can you tell me more about the attack on Miss Templeton outside the gaol? I have heard some talk of it—perhaps you might fill me in with further details?"

"Gladly," George said. "Do you also suspect the whole event was orchestrated by Lord Steyne?"

"I think it is possible, yes."

Carter listened intently while George outlined the main events as he saw them, culminating in how Selina had managed to escape from the ruffians.

"Well done, sir, for fighting the attackers off," Carter said. "I note you have been very modest about your own part in the proceedings—luckily Selina has already told the Templetons what a hero you were, and Henry has given me a full account."

I would fight those creatures every day if I had to, to keep my dear Selina safe.

"I must say," Carter began, "perhaps this is tactless of me, but I was, ahem, a little surprised."

"You did not think I had it in me?" George said. "You doubted my ability to brawl in the street like a common man?"

"Something like that," Carter said. "No disrespect intended, but you look like a fine young gentleman, and in my experience fine young gentlemen are not often good at fighting—more's the pity."

"I had plenty of practice when I was at school," George said. "I could not abide the way bullies prayed on the younger boys, and so I stood up for them whenever I could."

"I will butt into your conversation here," Henry said, "because I can confirm that when we were at university together, I once saw George in a fight. He used all sorts of incredible techniques. High kicks, hair pulling, arm twisting, grabbing the fellow by the throat . . . the rest of us were in awe of the sheer inventiveness of his aggression."

"Henry! You make me sound like some sort of lowlife," George said.

"I do not mean to," Henry said. "I admire you for your fighting skills—especially because you only use them on the side of right."

"If you're ever in need of an occupation," Carter said to George, "you're welcome to work for me."

Henry grinned. "You think Carter does not mean it, George. He does! I wish I had been taught to fight properly before I went to Waterloo—the tricks of the trade, as it were. They gave us a pistol and a sword, put us on a horse—and that was that. It always amazes me that we won that day last summer."

"Possibly the French were trained no better," Carter said. "And the atrocious weather did not favor the French, as it hampered their communications more than ours."

"Let us not talk of Waterloo," Lord Templeton said. "Our dear Henry returned in the end—all thanks to you, Carter."

"Hear, hear," George said, raising his glass. "But what are we going to do about Lord Steyne? We should have a plan."

"I will put a few things into motion," Carter said. "There are men I know who can be our eyes and ears around the city and surrounding area. 'Tis imperative to find out where Lord Steyne is before we can make a move. Leave it with me for now, and I will report back."

"Perchance he's staying incognito at his house in the Cottage Crescent?" Henry said. "'Tis far enough away from the city that he would not be seen much."

"Possibly," Carter said. "'Tis definitely worth a look."

"If he were staying there," Lord Templeton said, "surely there would be some tittle tattle? Servants can be bribed to give information."

"Judging from what Mr. Fitzgerald said about Lord Steyne looking bedraggled," Carter said, "Lord Steyne is probably having to manage on his own."

"Yes," George said. "The man looked as if he'd been sleeping in a cave."

"Would the other residents in Cottage Crescent not notice him?" Henry said. "It is, after all, a terraced property."

"What if he has been living in the cellar?" Carter said. "Granted, he would have the possibility of being seen as he left the building, but it is the end house and less overlooked."

"There is also quite a large stable at the back," George said. "He could have been sheltering there. A stable is warmer than a cellar."

"How would he be getting his food?" Lord Templeton said.

Carter grinned. "With difficulty!"

"He is probably reduced to foraging in the hedgerows," Henry said.

"There's not much there at this time of year," Carter said.

"If he has had to live like this," Lord Templeton said, "it is not surprising he bears a massive grudge against you, Mr. Fitzgerald."

"What worries me," George said, "is the thought that Miss Templeton is in danger from Lord Steyne—because of me. You already know what Signor Allegretto said to us in Hunter's. Apparently there are silly rumors flying around."

"Rumors that you are in love with my sister, as she is with you," Henry said, "and one day you will be married to each other."

George turned puce. "Mere gossip, I assure you."

"These rumors must be publicly denied for the sake of Selina's safety," Lord Templeton said. "What do you think, Carter?"

"I agree," Carter said. "It must be as if there is a wall of ice between Mr. Fitzgerald and Miss Templeton."

"'Tis harsh—but necessary," Henry said.

"Indeed," Carter said. "None of us can afford to make the mistake of underestimating Lord Steyne—he is a wicked, unprincipled man."

"What say you, George?" Henry asked. "You must have an opinion on this matter—after all, 'tis personal. Will you be able to conceal your true feelings until Lord Steyne is under lock and key?"

What could George say? If a wall of ice were to be placed between him and Selina, 'twould be better for George to deny his feelings clearly to her family—now. The Templeton servants were presumably loyal to Lord and Lady Templeton—yet one could not be too sure. There were no staff in the room at the moment, but they might be waiting outside, within earshot. Anything was possible.

No, George would not take a risk. Selina would never be harmed because of him.

"I do not need to conceal my true feelings—for I have none," George said in a loud, bold voice. "I utterly deny there is anything between Miss Templeton and myself; we are friends, that is all. I accompanied Selina, ahem, Miss Templeton, to the Quaker Meeting House today, but as for the rumors of any romantic attachment between us, I assure you they are entirely—and completely—false."

Three pairs of eyes regarded George. Henry smiled. Lord Templeton put his head on one side. And Carter leant forward to say, "We none of us believe you, Mr. Fitzgerald—although we admire you for the stand you are taking, for you are putting Miss Templeton's safety above your own feelings."

Shortly after that, George bid his farewells, for 'twas high time he went home. As he opened the door of the dining room, he was surprised to see the servant girl, Martha, scurrying away. How extraordinary that such a young girl should still be awake at this hour.

Henry followed George out of the dining room. "I must be getting back to see how Kitty is. My papa and Carter will sit a while longer, no doubt. They love to put the world to rights!"

"At least we have made a plan of sorts," George said.

"Ah, yes. We will find Lord Steyne and squash the rumors. But you do not have to pretend with me, George."

"What do you mean?"

"You do not have to pretend you're not in love with Selina," Henry said. "Though heaven knows why you would be, for she's such an aggravating person. I would have thought she'd be the last person on Earth anyone would want to marry."

"She's not aggravating," George snapped. "Well, not very

often. She's a fine person—clever, beautiful, and lively. Why, any man in England would be proud to call her his wife."

Henry laughed. "'Tis true, then. You do still have feelings for her. Let us hope it is not too long before Lord Steyne is defeated, and then you will finally be able to declare yourself—and I will be proud to call you brother. I think you two are a perfect match."

"But we are so different," George said.

"Have you not heard the saying, 'opposites attract'? And if you had the same thoughts on everything, what would you have to talk about in your lives together?"

"True," George murmured.

"And do not worry about Lord Templeton," Henry said, "for I know that my papa would be honored to welcome you into the family, for he has told me so himself."

Ye gods! All falls into place—but for that fiend, Lord Steyne. Although I am still confused about Selina, for despite our kiss on the Crescent Fields, I know not what her true feelings are. She feels a physical attraction, certainly, but that does not always mean love.

Henry and George left Number 1 together, then Henry bade George goodnight and set off to walk the short distance to Number 2 to be with his beloved wife.

How I envy Henry his wonderful partnership with Kitty. I wonder if I will ever be lucky enough to enjoy that with dear Selina.

George crossed the road and stood for a few moments surveying the Crescent. As his eyes adjusted to the dark night sky, he glimpsed what he'd been hoping to see—a small figure clad in white behind the parapet of Number 1. George could see that Selina's hair was loose around her shoulders. How he longed for another kiss, to feel her soft body yielding to him as he put his arms around her.

Was it his imagination? She was some distance away. No, it was certain—she was raising her hand in greeting. George looked around him fearfully. There were a couple of shadowy figures at the far side of the Crescent—and he had no idea who they were. Could they be henchmen reporting back to Lord Steyne? Would they be able to give evidence of a bond between George and Selina if he waved back?

George groaned. However hard it was, he must do the right thing—for had he not given his word that there would be a wall of ice between him and Selina—at least until the danger of Lord Steyne's obnoxious presence had passed?

George did not return Selina's greeting, but instead affected a sullen look and deliberately turned his back on her before marching stiffly away. As he had been discussing with Carter so recently, there was a hard battle to be fought if they were to win the war.

CHAPTER SEVEN

Selina

G EORGE TURNED HIS *back on me! And after kissing me on the Crescent Fields so gloriously. He is a rake, for sure. He has used me!*

Hot tears poured down Selina's face as she climbed back into the empty servants' bedroom she used as an exit onto the roof of Number 1.

Wait! She was being ridiculous. There were many other reasons why George might not have returned her greeting. He might be a little short sighted—although he had never mentioned it. Perchance he was too shy to say? For he seemed reluctant to talk about himself much. His father wore spectacles. Perhaps short sight could be inherited? For one could inherit all manner of things from one's parents. Fine green eyes, silky blonde hair . . .

Besides, having read George's speech earlier on first retiring to her room, she could scarcely believe that a man capable of writing such fine sentiments could also be a rake.

On her way to her chamber, Selina saw a small figure at the top of the servants' stairs.

"Martha! What are you doing up so late?"

"I cannot sleep," Martha said, "and besides, I have something to tell you."

"What is it?"

"I do not know if I should speak—except you did once say you would be pleased if I passed on anything of interest I discovered while working in your father's house."

"I always like to know what is going on," Selina said. "Please, Martha. Don't be shy. Just tell me. I promise I will not be angry—whatever it is. Would you like to come to my room for a few minutes? Would that make it easier?"

Martha nodded, and Selina took her by the hand to her own chamber, opening the door very carefully so as not to disturb her mama in her room nearby. Lady Templeton was an annoyingly light sleeper.

"Now, what is it?" Selina said. "What has upset you so?"

"I was downstairs in the entrance hall," Martha said. "Sometimes I prowl around the house at night when I cannot sleep. Anyway, I overheard something said in the dining room. I was not exactly listening to the conversation, but one portion came through loud and clear when I was near the, er, the . . ."

"Keyhole?" Selina suggested.

"Yes," Martha said. "I was near the keyhole."

Selina chuckled. "Don't worry, Martha, I spent a large part of my childhood in this house listening at that keyhole, and many other keyholes too. No one would tell me anything, and I was determined to take matters into my hands and find out things myself. If people are not keeping you informed, it is never wrong to listen at keyholes."

"If you say so, Miss Templeton," Martha said.

The poor mite looks relieved—and I am all agog to learn what was said after the ladies had withdrawn from the dining room.

"Now then," Selina said. "Tell me precisely what it was that you heard. Try to be exact."

"'Twas about you. Something Mr. Fitzgerald said."

How marvellous! Martha is about to reveal another part of the puzzle. Did George confide in either Henry or Carter of his feelings for me? Or did Papa ask him what his intentions were?

"Mr. Fitzgerald said you and he were friends," Martha said.

"That is true," Selina said, smiling.

"He also totally denied there was anything else between you. And said he did not have any feelings."

"Are you quite sure?"

"Yes," Martha said, "for Mr. Fitzgerald spoke very loudly."

"Anything else?" Selina croaked.

"He said the rumors of a romantic attachment between you were entirely—and completely—false."

"Did Mr. Fitzgerald say anything else after that? Did the others say anything?"

"Nothing that I could hear," Martha said. "Shortly after that I heard steps across the room and thought someone was going to open the door, so I fled. Oh, Miss Templeton! I am sorry that I have upset you. I knew I should not have told you."

"You did exactly the right thing, Martha, and I thank you. You're not in any trouble, I do assure you. But now you must go. There are not many hours left before you have to get up again, my child. Hurry back to your bed—and thank you for having the courage to tell me the truth."

They say the truth hurts—but this truth will be better for me in the long run. 'Tis far better for me to know that George is a rake, rather than pin my hopes on him.

I was not sure whether he had seen me when he turned his back on me while I was on the rooftop—now, however, I know he did notice me and turned away deliberately to show his indifference.

He has made a declaration this evening—sadly, not the declaration my heart was hoping for, although 'twas a declaration, nevertheless— that he cares not for me and denies there is any romantic feeling between us. And he dared to utter this travesty after we had kissed so passionately under the yew tree but a few hours before! The man is a scoundrel.

The tears Selina had shed earlier on the parapet were nothing to the torrent of weeping that now overwhelmed her. She lay on her bed with her face pressed into the pillow, screaming into the feathery depths. Then she beat her blankets with clenched fists and thrashed the mattress with stiff legs, only stopping when her entire pillow was wet with tears.

Belatedly remembering about George's speech, Selina reached under her pillow and rescued the soggy sheets from their hiding place; she briefly thought about tearing his words to pieces and throwing the fragments into the fire, but changed her mind and laid the damp sheets to dry on the mantlepiece. She might be angry with the author, but she was still able to appreciate the reasoned arguments of a good piece of prose.

Then, tears spent, Selina lay on her bed, totally exhausted, staring up at the ceiling.

'Tis only now I fully realize how much I love George—now that I know for certain he does not want me. How cruel life can be.

BY THE TIME she got up the next day, Selina had resolved to accept her fate. She would never marry—because the only person she wanted to marry was George. Despite the fact that he was a rake and had turned his back on her, she still loved him and wanted to spend the rest of her life with him. She yearned for his touch. Oh, how she longed for him . . .

At least I know the truth now; George's intentions were not honorable.

In the middle of the night, Selina had briefly considered entering a nunnery, such was her dark distress—however, now she was up and about, she thought this would not be necessary. Instead, she would remain unmarried for the rest of her life—and she would never reveal to a living soul the tale of her tragic disappointment.

Selina had decided to devote herself to good works—like furthering the cause of women who strove to become Members of Parliament. Or perhaps she could reform the social structure of England? Selina wrinkled her nose. Mmm. These were hard, perhaps impossible, tasks. For now, she would carry on with her work helping the local children. In fact, she was due to take some of them for a walk on the Crescent Fields with Mrs. Godwin today. They were going to learn about nature, examining all the trees they could find and studying the shapes of different clouds.

Selina glanced out of the window. Ideal weather! There were plenty of clouds scudding about, many gray and threatening rain. She could not have borne it if today had dawned with clear skies and bright sunshine. A blustery March day with plenty of drizzle was exactly what her present mood demanded.

As she washed and dressed herself, her limbs felt heavy and her head woozy. Everything was such an effort! Her abigail came in to help her, but Selina snapped, "No need! I can manage perfectly well, thank you."

She was going to have to manage on her own for the rest of her life—therefore, she might as well start now.

Why is it that the hardest thing in life is to keep going and pretend that all is well—when in truth your heart is breaking?

Her hair decided to be difficult this morning, refusing to be coaxed into its usual style, and Selina burst into a fresh storm of weeping. There was a timid knock at the door, and the abigail put her head round.

"Are you sure I cannot help you, Miss Templeton?"

Selina gulped back her tears and gave a crooked smile. "I think I do need your help after all."

The abigail twisted Selina's locks around her fingers and deftly secured them with a ribbon. There! The job was done.

"You look very fine, Miss Templeton."

"Thank you," Selina said, "and I am sorry for my rudeness earlier."

The abigail looked at Selina in the mirror as she stood behind her, smiled, and then placed her hand on Selina's shoulder for a few seconds.

"Whatever the matter is, all will come right in the end," the abigail whispered. "Don't you worry."

"Thank you," Selina murmured.

There could not be a bigger contrast between Selina's life and that of the abigail. Selina was a wealthy young woman living in a beautiful house in one of the most elegant cities in England, surrounded by a loving and attentive family. She did not have to work to earn her living and could have any clothes she wanted. People treated her with civility wherever she went in polite society, greeting her as "Miss Templeton." Furthermore, she had access to a fine pianoforte, delicious meals were served to her every day, and she had an abigail to help her dress and do her hair. The poor abigail had no such luxuries and would have to work hard all her life.

And I do not even use her name but call her "the abigail." How ashamed I feel.

Selina walked down to the parlor to have her breakfast, full to the brim with a determination to be positive. For the first time in her life, she felt like a true grown-up. She would be grateful for what she had in life, instead of bemoaning the fact that she could not marry the man she wanted. In some ways she'd had a lucky escape, for George had shown himself to be fickle—and unprincipled.

Plenty of people are unlucky in love. I will learn to cope.

When Lady Templeton came and sat down at the table, Selina gave her a bright smile.

"Did you sleep well, my dear?" Lady Templeton said. "You look a little tired. Should you stay at home today?"

"'Tis nothing—a trick of the light, I assure you," Selina said. "I am well rested and fully resolved to get on with my work with the children today."

"Your papa is a trifle under the weather this morning," Lady Templeton said, "and will breakfast in his room. I believe he sat up with the other men 'til the early hours."

By midway through her breakfast, Selina's cheeks were aching from the effort of controlling the full, unrelenting smile she had plastered on her face. How tiring it was, pretending to be cheerful.

I feel like Mama's favorite clock on the mantelpiece—the one with the glass front. 'Twill be my fate for the rest of my life to go round with a sheet of glass between my inner thoughts and the rest of the world. I must present my best face, despite being trapped in unhappiness.

Perchance the glass will shield me from further damage—as a carapace protects a crab. Although this barrier will prevent me from being able to love again, for my feelings are now buried so deep, they cannot be accessed.

Lady Templeton scrutinized Selina closely. "I am thinking of accompanying you when you go to the Crescent Fields this morning. I have a few errands to run but can easily put them aside for another day."

"There is no need," Selina said, "for I will be accompanied by Mrs. Godwin."

"Nevertheless," Lady Templeton said, "I will come with you. We cannot be too careful with *the danger* all around. Also, my dear, I think you did not sleep quite as well as you said, for you look a little pale. Are you sure you feel up to going out today?"

"Absolutely," Selina said. "I must get outside."

I long to feel the wind in my hair—although this will not be possible if Mama accompanies me, for she is never keen for me to remove my bonnet.

"I say, anything left for breakfast?" Edmund crashed through the door.

"Edmund!" Lady Templeton said. "How delightful to see you. Did you have a pleasant evening at your club?"

"Very fine, thank you, Mama," he said.

"And what are your plans for today?" Lady Templeton said.

"Nothing much. I might see my friends again later. And Papa wants to talk over some estate business this morning. He is planning to buy another house in the Crescent, I believe. I am not awfully keen to hear about estate matters, to tell the truth. Papa does go on so about every last detail."

"'Tis important for you to learn how to run the family estate, Edmund," Lady Templeton said. "After all, one day you will inherit."

Selina's fingernails raked the tablecloth.

Why is it always the eldest male who inherits? 'Tis so unfair on Henry, and of course on me. As a mere female, I would never be trusted with running an estate whether I was the youngest or oldest in the family.

"Mama thinks I need an extra person to chaperone me on the Crescent Fields," Selina said to Edmund. "Would you like to come with me while I take the children for a walk this morning?"

"Rather," Edmund said. "I am sure Papa will be able to tell me about the estate business some other time."

"Good," Selina said. "And that leaves you free to do your errands, Mama."

"Well, yes, I suppose that would be most acceptable, Edmund, if you could accompany your sister," Lady Templeton said. "Mind you keep an eye on her, though. There is *the danger* to consider. We have had some information from Signor Allegretto about Lord Steyne—and it is imperative that Selina is kept safe."

"I'm entirely trustworthy, as you know, Mama," Edmund said. "By the way, when you say *the danger* like that, it does sound frightfully exciting."

"Oh, Edmund! You are incorrigible," Lady Templeton said.

"What exactly is *the danger*, Mama?" Edmund asked.

"I am not entirely sure," Lady Templeton said. "I believe the men formulated some sort of plan late last night—Carter was here, and he is an expert on all things dangerous. Your father told me this morning that it is better to keep the information within a tight circle, by which I think he means only the men who were here yesterday—that is, your father, Henry, Mr. Fitzgerald, and Carter."

How unreasonable! After all, I was with George when Signor Allegretto told us all about Lord Steyne.

Edmund took a large bite of his toast and crunched noisily.

"When I eat like that, you reprimand me," Selina complained to Lady Templeton.

She gave an indulgent smile. "I am not minded to scold this morning. Edmund's presence at the breakfast table is very infrequent these days, and I do not wish to cast a cloud over the meal."

My mind is full of clouds, mostly very dark. And I fear they will stay there forever.

George

THE SAME DAY, George skipped breakfast and decided to take Trigger for a gallop over the hills. He had gotten home very late the night before and not slept at all well.

I need to clear my head after all the excitement of yesterday.

George was finding it hard to come to terms with the fact that he must keep his distance from Selina. How was he ever going to put phase four of his plan to woo her into action? And what was phase four anyway? Phase three had been giving in to his impulse to kiss Selina under the tree. How beautiful that had been, how soft and tender her lips—how much he had wanted it to continue.

At the very top of Beechen Cliff, looking out over the city, George could see Selina's house at the end of the Royal Crescent, with the Crescent Fields in front—where only yesterday Selina had been in his arms. Trigger neighed and tossed his head.

"What's that, old boy?" George said to the horse. "Do you want to go there again? We have time, for Papa does not require my services until this afternoon on his visits."

George felt an urgent need to be in exactly the same place that he had been yesterday—safely hidden under the branches of the old yew tree. He must, of course, be conscious of the wall of ice Carter had said must spring up between him and Selina. This was the best way to protect Selina from Lord Steyne—although it was going to be hard. For what if George saw Selina on the Fields today? What then? Would he have to turn his back on her, as he had when she'd waved at him last night? Or could he risk a polite "hello?" George sighed. He would deal with this scenario if and when it occurred.

Very soon, George was traveling down Holloway with Trigger. A few acquaintances greeted him as he crossed the city, and he smiled without stopping. Occasionally, he looked warily behind himself to see if he was being followed—but thankfully saw no ruffians.

As he passed the Theatre Royal, George remembered that later that evening he had promised to accompany his mama to a play—there was a new production lately come down from London she was wild to see.

Hopefully the show will be a welcome distraction from thinking about Selina and the danger.

On George went until he reached the Crescent Fields. When he found the vast yew tree, he dismounted from Trigger and pushed through the curtain of branches, gently leading his horse.

"There, there, Trigger. You'll be fine. Head down! That's it. See! There's a big space inside, plenty of room for a man and a horse.

And plenty of room for a man to kiss the sweetest young woman in the world.

Trigger pawed at the ground and snorted.

"Yes, I know," George said. "You have had enough and would much rather be back on Beechen Cliff galloping around. However, indulge me for a moment. Let me have my memories—for I wish to be here for a few moments longer, here where I kissed my love for the very first time."

And if we never embrace again, I will have a beautiful memory to carry me through life to my grave. If I cannot marry Selina, I will resign myself to a single life, no matter how much my parents tell me it is my responsibility to wed.

However, I must endeavor to be positive. The wall of ice is there between Selina and me for a very good reason—but, in the end, ice melts, and hopefully, in the fullness of time, all will be well between us. I must be patient and trust that Carter will find Lord Steyne and defeat him.

Suddenly, George heard approaching voices and peeped through the branches. To his shock, he saw Edmund, Selina, a middle-aged lady he did not know, and a group of children approaching the very tree he was sheltering under.

"This is a yew tree," Selina said. "A very dense, fine, evergreen tree."

"It's massively tall," said one of the children.

"What does 'evergreen' mean?" another asked.

"Evergreen," Selina said, "means that it does not lose its leaves in the autumn and have to wait until the spring for them to grow back again. Have a look around you, children. You can see that many other trees have bare branches and will not get their full cloak of leaves until the summer."

"The trees are frightening when they do not have their leaves," a child said.

"Yes!" another said. "They look like skeletons."

Trigger gave a soft whinny, and the children became very excited.

"There is something inside the yew tree!"

"Could be a dragon?"

"It sounds like a horse."

"I'm going in!"

"Me too!"

Very soon the group of ten children was right in the middle of the tree with George and Trigger.

"There's a man in here!"

"Who is he?"

"These leaves are weird—like needles."

What am I supposed to do now? What will Selina think of me, hiding away like a criminal? And I must remember I am not allowed to act in a friendly manner—I must think of the wall of ice.

"Come out at once, children," Selina said, "or I will have to come in and get you."

"Leave it to me, Selina," Edmund said as he flung himself through the branches into the middle of the tree.

"George!" he said. "Good Lord! What are you doing here? 'Tis a rum sort of place to be."

"I thought it might rain," George said, "for it did look cloudy, and Trigger does not like the rain."

"He is a horse," Edmund said, "and has no business either liking or disliking the weather. But George, 'tis very good to see you. And Trigger! Come outside and see Selina—she's with Mrs. Godwin, who is in charge of all these little ones." Edmund smiled and patted the heads of the nearest children. "Come on— everybody out. And try not to touch anything. You need to be careful with yew trees, for they are frightfully poisonous."

Selina was looking even more beautiful than ever, wearing a scarlet cloak, her bonnet clasped by her side and soft tendrils of hair escaping around her face.

"Mr. Fitzgerald," she hissed. "What on earth are you doing here? Er, I mean, allow me to present Mrs. Godwin. She runs the Sunday school at church, and I've been helping her take the children out on outings to broaden their education—and have some fun."

George nodded. "I believe you have mentioned your work with the children before. Good morning, Mrs. Godwin."

"Good morning, sir," Mrs. Godwin answered. "Miss Templeton has been invaluable in helping with the children. Now I have another pair of hands, we are able to give them all sorts of extra opportunities to study. There is so much to see at this time of year when spring is beginning its magic."

Selina was grimacing at George now—then she curled her lip and looked away. No doubt she had been told about the wall of ice that must be between them for her own protection.

George should act in the same manner. A deep furrow appeared between his brows—followed by a most unpleasant glare. No one passing by would think he had any interest whatsoever in Miss Selina Templeton.

I have to hand it to Selina; she is the consummate actress. From her demeanor, one would never guess that we are friends—or that we kissed so recently under this tree. She is pretending most convincingly that she finds my company both unwelcome and abhorrent.

"May I pat your horse?" one of the children said.

"Of course," George said. "His name is Trigger. Shall I lift you up? That's it. Ruffle his mane. He likes that."

"Might I sit on his back?" a boy asked.

"If Mrs. Godwin thinks that is all right, of course you may."

"A fine idea—thank you, Mr. Fitzgerald," Mrs. Godwin said. Then she turned to the boy and said, "Pass me your crutch, dear, for you will not need that to sit astride a horse."

The poor child has a bad leg—ah yes, I believe Selina mentioned him before, when we had tea in Hunter's. How wonderful it will be for him to be atop a horse and have another creature do the work of moving for him. I wonder what exactly is wrong with the leg—I shall have to ask my papa what I can do to help the child.

George lifted the little boy onto Trigger's back as gently as he could.

"Shall we walk once round the yew tree?" he asked the boy.

"Yes please, sir!" The boy looked so proud sitting on top of Trigger; the horse behaved impeccably, walking very slowly and carefully.

"Can you make Trigger gallop?" the little boy said.

"I fear that would not be ideal," George said. "Maybe when you have more skill and horse-riding technique? Now, would the other children like to sit on Trigger's back? I'm very happy to walk them a few steps around the Fields."

"Mr. Fitzgerald," Mrs. Godwin said, "we cannot put you to that trouble."

"'Tis no trouble, I assure you," George said. "'Twould be my pleasure."

The children took turns to ride around on Trigger. And throughout the whole procedure, Selina turned her back and stared at the houses of the Crescent, seemingly fascinated by a sight she saw every day of her life. Not once did she look at George or acknowledge his presence.

There were quite a few other people on the Fields. Selina was quite right to be standoffish in public, for who knew where the danger might come from? Any of the people out on the Fields could have been in the pay of Lord Steyne—and they might be looking for evidence of an attachment between George and Selina.

Once all the children had enjoyed a turn on Trigger's back, they swarmed round George and thanked him profusely.

"How many of you have ever ridden a horse before?" George said. "Put your hand up if you have."

Not one child put their hand up.

Poor creatures! They would benefit greatly from the chance to learn.

"You have given the children such a wonderful opportunity today, Mr. Fitzgerald," Mrs. Godwin said, "and I thank you. Do you not think, Miss Templeton, that Mr. Fitzgerald has been very kind to give the children their first riding lesson?"

"Most obliging, I'm sure," Selina said, "however we must be going—to the far side of the field, where the sheep are grazing. Goodbye, Mr. Fitzgerald."

"Thank you so much," Edmund said to George, shaking him by the hand. "We will see you soon, I hope. You must come round to Number 1 to visit. And now I think of it, Mama is having a musical soirée tomorrow, and I insist that you be our guest; I will have the invitation sent directly."

Selina coughed. "I believe Mama said there was no space for any more guests. The evening is already full."

"This is the first I've heard of it," Edmund said. "Many apologies, Mr. Fitzgerald. I will make sure you are added to the guest list of the next musical soirée at Number 1."

How I would love to attend a musical gathering at the Templetons'. Selina sings like an angel! But she is right, the wall of ice needs to melt first; Lord Steyne must be defeated before I am free to woo my love.

Selina

SELINA WAS IN a total daze as her small party walked away from George and Trigger.

Hopefully the children will not notice how distracted I am, for they are but young; however, in faith I will find it hard to concentrate on looking at budding leaves and twigs and nature burgeoning all around us when I have just had the shock of my life—seeing George again so soon.

Mrs. Godwin encouraged the children to inspect an interesting clump of grasses some way off, leaving Selina alone with Edmund for a few moments.

"I say, Selina," Edmund said, "I wish I'd known Mama had said no more guests for the musical evening. I feel like a prize chump for asking George, only to have you contradict me."

"If you were more oft at home," Selina said, "you would know what was going on. You scarcely show your face at Number 1 anymore, Edmund. Instead, you are always out with your friends at your club or who knows where."

"Do not sound so disapproving, sister dear," Edmund said. "I may do what I like with my own life, may I not?"

Selina sniffed. "True, because you are male. Think what it is like for us females."

"I know lots of women who do exactly what they want," Edmund said.

"You may think they are doing what they want," Selina said, "but it may not be true. Women cannot be so open."

"Give me an example," Edmund said.

"Society rules that a man may propose marriage to a woman, but a woman may not propose to a man. We have to wait and hope."

"'Twould be ridiculous for a woman to propose to a man," Edmund said. "Everyone knows that! And no man would respect a woman who behaved in that unfeminine way. His only possible reply would be a firm 'no.' But women can use their wiles—to encourage. Last time I went to a ball, I noticed the women conveying their intentions by using their fans as signals—some special language, apparently. So do not tell me women are powerless."

"But this is what I mean," Selina said. "Why should women have to resort to play acting with fans to express their opinions? Why cannot we say things directly as we see fit and tell someone exactly what we think? Especially if the other person's behavior has been very poor."

"Selina, I have noticed the subject has changed from marriage proposals to bad behavior. Has anyone been unkind to you? If so, give me their name, and I will deal with it."

"That is my whole point," Selina said. "I want to deal with things myself."

I want to grasp the nettle.

The children ran back to Selina.

"Look at the grasses I picked!"

"Miss Templeton! I found a funny twig."

"And I discovered a little leaf sitting all alone on a piece of grass."

"Here is a tiny ant. Do you like it?"

Heavens! I am meant to be looking after these children, not debating with Edmund. I must concentrate.

"All these things you have found are quite wonderful," Selina said to the children who were pulling at her skirt and holding up their treasures for her perusal.

"Indeed they are," Edmund said.

"Yes," Mrs. Godwin said, "and many of these objects could be put into a scrapbook later."

"Not the ant," Selina said quickly to a small child who was looking rather sad—possibly at the thought of the insect being squished between the pages of a book.

"May I keep the ant as my special pet?" the child inquired.

Selina knelt down beside the youngster and gently explained that ants were much better off in their natural habitat rather than inside a house made for humans.

"We have plenty of ants in our home," the child said.

"Ah," Edmund said, "but I believe this is an outdoor ant who wishes to stay here with his brothers and sisters, having fun scampering about on the Crescent Fields."

The child seemed happy with this explanation and the party continued on their nature ramble.

How sweet Edmund had been. George had been very gentle and understanding with the children too; the man must have hidden depths. Who would have thought that the oft tongue-tied George would find it so easy to converse with little ones and enjoy giving them rides on Trigger? He treated them as gently as a father would.

Or he pretended to. For was not George a dissembler—a rake, capable of deceitful behavior? Today was doubtless a mere act—why, he had even pretended to take extra care with the boy who limped when lifting him onto Trigger, as though he had great concern for his welfare. How perfidious could a man be?

At the end of the outing on the Crescent Fields, the children thanked Selina and Edmund for helping them.

"We loved it!"

"Yes, especially riding on the horse. That man was really nice."

"I wish we could have riding lessons every day."

"Well done, children, for saying thank you so appreciatively." Mrs. Godwin beamed as she regarded her charges. "Now I must take you back to your homes, for your mamas will be anxious to see you. Goodbye, Miss Templeton—and Mr. Templeton. Thank you again."

Edmund and Selina strolled across the grass to Number 1.

"Mama will be anxious to see you, too," Edmund said to Selina. "You know how protective she is and how much she worries about you. She seemed extra wary today at breakfast and mentioned danger. What is going on?"

"'Tis nothing much," Selina said, "only that Lord Steyne has been seen around Bath again and he has a grudge against George. There is some silly rumor that George, I mean Mr. Fitzgerald, and I are attached, so Mama thought I might be in danger."

Edmund chuckled on hearing this. "'Tis totally obvious from

watching the two of you this morning that you absolutely loathe each other—which is odd, because there was a time I thought you were partial to him. Ah well! I am sure 'tis none of my business."

"Indeed, it is not!" Selina snapped. "Oh, I am sorry Edmund. Forgive me. I am a little tired this morning."

"Take a rest this afternoon," Edmund said. "You will feel better in no time."

He delivered Selina to the front door of Number 1.

"Are you not coming in?" she said. "It will be luncheon soon."

"No, I am going into the city to see who is around," Edmund said. "Please tell Mama not to expect me for dinner either. In fact, I might not be back this evening at all. Do not wait up for me."

With a bright smile, Edmund ran off down Brock Street.

LATER THAT AFTERNOON, Selina lay on the sofa in the withdrawing room. She had attempted to look at some of her music, but her voice felt scratchy and tired, so she decided to read her new novel. It would have been good to see Kitty. However, a message had come from Number 2 saying Kitty was still feeling a little out of sorts, and Doctor Jenkins had advised bedrest. There was nothing to worry about—'twas merely the sickness of early pregnancy—but she was to avoid all excitement, and that apparently included seeing her best friend.

Selina opened the first volume of *Emma*. Goodness! The heroine was certainly a strong character. She seemed very convinced she was right about all sorts of things. Pride could come before a fall, however, so perhaps later on in the story Emma would be proven mistaken.

Would it be wrong to have a quick peek in the other two volumes to see if this supposition was correct? Selina flipped through the pages of volumes two and three. Ah yes! Emma would be cut down to size for making things worse for others— and for herself. That would teach her not to poke her nose into matters that were none of her business.

Was this what I did when I went to the gaol? Perhaps I did not make matters worse—but I certainly didn't help any of the prisoners, which had been my primary intention.

Selina slammed the third volume shut. No, she was not going to look at the ending to see whom Emma married—Mr. Knightley or Mr. Frank Churchill. But it would turn out well for Miss Emma Woodhouse, that much was certain, for characters in a romance novel were guaranteed a happy ending. In real life, there was no such certainty.

However, I have nothing to worry about because I am perfectly happy to embrace a single life. I am resolved to find contentment in fulfilling the needs of others—as I helped the children this morning on the nature walk. How privileged I will be, married to my vocation of helping people; this will be enough to sustain me for the rest of my life.

Won't it?

Self-pitying tears threatened, but Selina gritted her teeth and continued reading, the gentle prose soothing her into a calmer state.

And ere long, her eyes closed, the volumes slipping from her lap.

Her dreams were vivid—and they were all of George.

She was chasing after him up a high mountain, yelling one minute how shameful his behavior was and the next pouring out her love and asking him to marry her. George did not seem to hear her entreaties, but continued his journey, on and on, over many treacherous mountains and then down into a valley. He swam right across a wide, green lake, and when he got out on the other side, he stood for a while in the wind, his wet shirt clinging to his chest. How magnificent!

Then Selina followed him into a deep chasm and through to a dank cave, watching in horror as he walked under a mighty stalactite. There was a person perched near the stalactite, hacking at it with an enormous axe. Lord Steyne—the fiend! The lethal point fell towards George . . .

Selina woke with a start.

"My dear," Lady Templeton said. "Have you had a good sleep? I didn't like to disturb you earlier, for I thought you could do with a rest."

Selina sat up on the sofa. "I was tired, Mama—but feel much restored."

"This is pleasing news," Lady Templeton said, "for I wondered if you might like to accompany me to the theater this evening. Your papa was to go with me; sadly, I fear he still has rather a sore head from last night."

"I would love to go to the theater," Selina said. "Thank you, Mama."

If nothing else, the spectacle will distract me from my preoccupation with George. I refuse to waste any more time thinking about a worthless man who will never be mine.

CHAPTER EIGHT
George

L ATER THAT DAY, George and his parents traveled by carriage to the Theatre Royal in Beaufort Square and made haste to take their seats.

"Thank goodness—we have made it in time," Mrs. Fitzgerald said as they reached their box. "I began to fear we would not get through the crush."

"I have to apologize again," Doctor Fitzgerald said to his wife, "for 'tis my fault we are so late. George and I came across such an interesting case this afternoon that we quite forgot the time."

"Yes, sorry, Mama," George said.

In truth, George would much rather have stayed with the patient, learning what he could and helping the poor fellow who was inflicted with some sort of degenerative disease. But George's mother adored the theater, and so George and his father had reluctantly left the patient and hastened home to get ready to go out for the evening.

"What do you think was wrong with our last patient?" George said to his father.

"Hard to say, exactly," Doctor Fitzgerald said, "although I have seen cases like this before, when I was a young doctor in London, and I have a few theories. A most interesting case . . ."

"Hopefully the course of treatment you recommended will

alleviate some of his suffering," George said. "Now, how can we prevent this sort of disease in others? Is there something the man could have done differently that meant he would not have caught the disease?"

"There's the question!" Doctor Fitzgerald said. "Possibly his occupation has not helped—for I have known others who work as he does who have been afflicted in a similar way. Then we must consider the mind, which can sometimes influence the body. The illness might stem from within."

"You mean he is ill because of his thoughts?"

"I think it is worth considering, yes. 'Tis possible the man has suffered some sort of disappointment and, years later, this has resulted in his incapacity. You are on the right track, George, with your most interesting question about how the man could have avoided the illness. We physicians are often so concerned with treating a disease that we do not always stop to consider how we could have prevented it."

"Yes, for educating the public properly about the workings of their own bodies and minds would surely help people to avoid disease."

"There is some talk in London circles that over indulgence in alcohol should be warned against," Doctor Fitzgerald said.

"What about tobacco?" George said. "Is that harmful?"

"It has not been proved to be," Doctor Fitzgerald said. "Personally, I do not recommend it to my patients."

"Are you two going to talk about your work all evening?" Mrs. Fitzgerald said.

Mrs. Fitzgerald was very proud of her husband's skill and popularity with his patients, and now she was even more proud that George was well on the way to becoming a doctor. However, George was aware she occasionally found it all a bit too much—and probably felt outnumbered by her husband and her only living child both being medical men.

"I beg your forgiveness, my dear," Doctor Fitzgerald said to his wife.

"Yes, Mama," George said. "We will endeavor to talk about much lighter subjects for the rest of the evening, I promise you. What is this play we have come to see?"

"My dear George!" Mrs. Fitzgerald said. "I cannot believe you do not know the name of the play. I have mentioned it *many* times in the last week. You have seemed rather distracted of late."

George mumbled another apology.

"We are here to see *Romeo and Juliet*," Mrs. Fitzgerald said.

Doctor Fitzgerald inserted a couple of his fingers into the neck of his shirt and pulled. "The valet always ties my cravat too tight these days. It must be the latest fashion to be half strangled."

"There is no point in trying to be fashionable, in my experience," George said.

The image of his tight pantaloons would haunt him for some time to come. That and the grotesquely high collar which had jabbed into the side of his face every time he turned his head; but he had come to like his new hairstyle very much—mainly because it required virtually no maintenance. An occasional run through with his fingers seemed to do the trick.

Ah! If only Selina were to run her fingers through my hair again, as she did yesterday on the Crescent Fields—how happy I would be!

Doctor Fitzgerald sighed. "So! We are to see a tragedy."

"A romantic tragedy," George murmured.

I am to be subjected to a tale of star-crossed lovers—not what I am in the mood for, no, not at all, for 'tis too close to home. I wonder what will become of me and Selina? Everything depends on the wall of ice melting—and that cannot happen until Carter has defeated Lord Steyne.

"You will enjoy it, my dears," Mrs. Fitzgerald said to her husband and son. "Both leads are very well thought of—I heard many good things about them in a friend's drawing room a few days ago. And apparently the production is outstanding—superlative costumes."

Doctor Fitzgerald leaned back in his seat. "Let us hope 'tis not too depressing. I did so enjoy the production of *A Midsummer Night's Dream* we went to last season; comedy is more to my taste."

As Romeo and Juliet started on their journey from first bliss-ful love to unforgettable loss, George looked around the theater at the audience. It took a while for his eyes to adjust to the low light, but he was determined to do everything he could to help defeat Lord Steyne. Why should Carter be left with all the responsibility? Granted, he worked for the government and seemed to have very special skills—but should not everyone be trying to help seek out Lord Steyne? For Selina's safety was at stake. George did not care that his own life might be threatened—his concern was only for his beloved Selina.

He scanned the audience with his opera glasses. Would Lord Steyne dare to show his face in the theater? Might he come in disguise?

"You're supposed to be watching the stage," Mrs. Fitzgerald whispered to her son.

George nodded, waited a while, and then resumed his search of the audience, hopefully with more discretion. What he discovered fair took his breath away, for seated in an opposite box were none other than Lady Templeton and Selina.

Why was Selina here? She should be safely cocooned at home. And she had not mentioned that she would be going to the theater. What was going on?

She scarce said two words to me when we met by chance on the Crescent Fields earlier today. How foolish I am to imagine she would tell me what her social engagements were for this evening.

George stared at Selina for quite a few minutes through his glasses, drinking in her beauty. She was wearing a low-cut evening gown with some jewels sparkling softly at the base of her throat, her hair threatening to escape confinement in the most charming and natural way. Her eyes were fixed on the stage—she seemed to be concentrating on every word that the young lovers were saying. Although there were many attractive ladies in the theater this evening, Selina shone as a diamond would amongst cut glass. No one could match her! Ye gods! What George would give to be beside her in her box right now. He would softly reach his hand towards hers under cover of darkness. Ah! The feel of her soft skin, her fingers in the palm of his hand . . .

This would not do! George must stop staring at Selina immediately. What if Lord Steyne or one of his spies was in the theater this evening? What would they think to see George behaving thus? Where was the wall of ice?

George resumed scanning the audience for any hint of Lord Steyne—and saw none. 'Twas a shame, for George would have liked to fight him.

In the interval, Doctor Fitzgerald said, "Shall we go and find a drink and further company?"

"Yes, my dear." Mrs. Fitzgerald looked into the auditorium and waved at a few friendly faces. "I can see many of our acquaintances—let us go and mingle."

George's parents stood up and looked at their son expectantly.

"Are you not coming, George dear?" Mrs. Fitzgerald said.

"I think I will stay in the box, for I am feeling a little fatigued."

George moved his chair to a shadowy corner at the back of the box and slumped down as low as his tall frame would allow. 'Twas best to keep out of sight. And best to feel the chill of the wall of ice.

"George, you have not been yourself for some while," Mrs. Fitzgerald said. "There is no need for you to isolate yourself in the interval."

"Yes, 'tis your duty to socialize," Doctor Fitzgerald said. "I do not see why you should be allowed to escape the chattering masses when I cannot."

Normally George would have found this remark of his father's mildly amusing and would doubtless have replied with some banter of his own. This evening, however, he felt indescribably weary and did not even have the energy for a half smile. It was very draining, having to act all the time—to pretend he did not adore Selina and want to be with her every waking minute.

"Do not tease our cherished boy," Mrs. Fitzgerald said to her husband. She put her hand on George's shoulder. "You must do as you wish, my dear—but do not forget we are always here if you wish to talk."

Damnation! For now George had worried his mama. She must think he had some secret sorrow that he needed to confide.

Although 'tis true, I do have a burden on my mind. Perhaps I should converse with someone. Maybe Henry?

No, 'twould be better not to burden Henry, for he had enough on his mind at present with his family increasing. George should keep his own counsel. And although Carter would also be sympathetic, 'twould be unfair to distract him from his vital government work.

George shook his head. He had to be his own man and cope with whatever hand fate dealt him. The situation was hard—although hopefully would not last forever. The danger would lift one day, and then George would be able to continue his campaign to woo the most delightful young woman in the world.

I feel like a caged bird, stuck in this box. Damnation! Another five minutes of this tedium and I will have to escape to stretch my legs in the corridor.

Selina

GEORGE'S BEHAVIOR IS outrageous! Not content with allowing his eyes to sweep over every young woman in the theater during the performance, he is now hiding at the back of his box like a criminal, slumped unattractively in his chair. Not that I am at all interested in how he behaves or looks—because I never wish to see him again in my life.

What cruel fate had resulted in George pitching up at the theater at exactly the same time as Selina? The man was a monster; he had even used his opera glasses to study the faces and maybe other parts of the ladies in the audience. There should be a law against it.

How could Selina have been so wrong about George? She had been totally fooled by his kind manner—which she now knew had been an act. Selina blushed as she remembered how unwisely she had pursued George after Henry and Kitty's dinner party, first to the stables and then along the Gravel Walk. Why, she had even asked him if he had thought she was a lady of the night. How amused he must have been at her naivety! How angry she felt about this.

I suspect Mr. George Fitzgerald is a man of the world, of the sort that Mama has often warned me about.

And yet they had kissed but yesterday under the tree, and it had seemed so sweet. Oh, how was it possible that Selina longed for a man who had proved himself to be worthless? What sort of person did that make her?

There was a gentle knock on the door of the box, and a footman appeared with a tray of drinks and sandwiches.

"I thought we would stay here for the interval," Lady Templeton said to Selina. "'Tis easier when there are no men in our party. Besides, my dear, I wanted to have a talk with you. Call it a mother's instinct—but I fear all is not right with my lovely daughter."

Lady Templeton patted Selina's hand.

I do not want to talk to Mama, but instead desperately need to be on my own for a few minutes to compose myself.

Selina cleared her throat. "'Tis a wonderful idea to stay in the box for the interval. However, I need to visit the ladies' retiring room and will be back shortly."

Before Lady Templeton could suggest that she should escort her daughter, Selina had slipped away and fled down the corridor. She ran past groups of people going to have a drink and socialize—on and on she raced, not quite knowing where her feet were taking her, until at last she found herself in a distant corridor and leaned against the wall to draw breath. The chatter from other theatergoers subsided as everyone moved towards the main meeting rooms and the bars.

If I could have but a few minutes alone, I think my heart would stop pounding.

After a while, Selina began to feel a little better and set off to rejoin her mama. Eyes down, she walked briskly back along the corridors, when all of a sudden she collided with . . . no! It could not be. George?

"Miss Templeton! Should you be alone in the corridor? Where is Lady Templeton?"

How dare he ask these questions! What business was it of his if Selina was alone or not? And why did he keep looking behind him all the time? Whom did he expect to see? Perhaps he had planned an assignation with some other young lady. That would be it—of course! Any minute now some misguided young woman would appear, expecting George to embrace her.

As he embraced—and kissed me—but yesterday.

Or maybe a married lady would appear, one who was searching for amusement. Married women sometimes met up with rakes—or so Selina had heard. She did not want to think what sort of betrayal this meant—or what the married lady and George might do together. Or maybe—horrors!—George had arranged an assignation with a lady of the night. Actresses, it was whispered, sometimes . . .

Selina felt thoroughly confused and completely out of her depth. She still could not fully believe that George could be so deceitful—one minute tenderly embracing her and the next denying he had any feelings whatsoever for her. Not for one minute did she doubt that what the servant girl, Martha, had told her was true. George had definitely denied there was any affection between them. Why did he say it? Why blurt out something like that in front of Selina's papa, her brother, and Carter? Something so private?

Selina would never understand men. If women were allowed to stay at the dining table when the bottle of port went round after dinner, none of this muddle would have happened.

"I must leave you," George said. "Goodbye, Miss Templeton. I know not when we shall meet again."

Why did George seem nervous? This did not fit with the picture of him as a confident young man about town able to trifle with the affections of any young lady he wanted. George's character truly was an enigma.

In a flash, Selina decided to have it out with him—she would ask George why he was behaving in this bizarre fashion. Why had he led her on by kissing her, only to deny any feeling for her in front of members of her own family on the same day? And then this morning, on the Crescent Fields, why display such indifference towards her?

Selina took a deep breath and closed her eyes. She was going to tell him what a blot on the face of the earth he was—but first, she needed to dig deep to find the courage . . .

When Selina opened her eyes, George had disappeared. How typical of the man to behave like a rat in the street running from danger! He must have guessed she was about to tackle him about his atrocious behavior and taken the coward's way out. Such a pity women could not challenge men to fight in a duel.

For I wish to meet George at dawn in a remote place and shoot him.

A vision of a lifeless George lying on the ground with a bullet hole between his eyes appeared, and Selina began to sob. She would tell George what she thought of him. She would, she would . . .

What do I think of him? I must face the truth, which is that I love him with my whole heart and soul. I hate him as well, for what he has put me through—leading me on, trifling with my affections—although if things were different, how happy I would be to become his wife, to be joined with him . . .

Selina ran round the corridors looking for George, even though she knew she would never have the courage to speak to him. For it was against nature for a woman to declare her passion, was it not?

And besides, I do not wish to declare my passion to George. I want to tell him how much I hate him and that I won't have anything to do with him ever again. I wish to condemn his behavior and make him squirm as I list all the ways he has misbehaved. He should be in a court of law—in the dock. I could be the chief prosecuting counsel.

Any judge in the land would condemn George for how he had behaved. He should be transported to Australia for the rest of his natural life—or at least clapped in irons for a reasonable length of time. He could be sent to Bath City Gaol, and then Selina could visit him with a food basket—he might then repent of his actions and declare that she was his one true love after all.

Selina eventually found herself back on the corridor where her mother would doubtless be waiting a little anxiously in their box. The sandwiches were a tempting thought—for hatred could be a hungry business. Selina put her shoulders back and marched the few remaining steps like a soldier going into battle. She had her feelings firmly under control now.

But before Selina reached the door to her box, she saw George again, looming in the corridor. What was he doing hanging round here? His box was right over on the other side of the theater. Before Selina could say anything, George turned abruptly, muttering as he came towards her,

"A thousand apologies, Miss Templeton. I mistook the route—and definitely did not mean to be on your side. Perish the thought! 'Twas a slight confusion, that is all, and now, I am going straight back to my box. Immediately!"

George brushed past Selina in his haste to get away, causing her to stumble in surprise. His arms went out to steady her, her own arms went onto his shoulders, then he reached round her waist to help her balance. Their faces were so close! Selina lifted her head and gazed into George's icy green eyes which suddenly did not seem cold, but instead meltingly attractive. Two pairs of lips moved closer together, and after an agonizing wait of a handful of seconds, the pair began to kiss with passionate abandon. Selina's breath came in short, ragged gasps as she felt George's muscular strength against her.

What bliss! George's sweet lips upon mine! And I can feel his heart beating fiercely. Nothing else matters . . .

But reality soon kicked in—there was a lot else that mattered, and mattered intensely. Selina struggled free from George's grasp and stood before him, eyes flashing.

"I hate you, George Fitzgerald. I hate you more than I've ever hated anyone in my whole life."

George

YE GODS! SELINA had obviously felt the same magnetic pull that George had felt when they'd stumbled into each other. Some feelings were so strong that one had to give in to them without thought. But now Selina had come to her senses. How impressive that she'd had the self control to stand back and tell George that she hated him—for the benefit of anyone who might be listening or watching.

George looked around the corridor. There was no one else there. However, Selina was right—one could not be too careful. He would take his lead from her.

"I care nothing for you," he said in a very loud voice, for he heard footsteps approaching. The interval must be over—people were returning to their seats.

"There is nothing between us," George shouted, before striding off in the direction of his box.

Selina let out a heart-rending sob as he walked away. This seemed a little at odds with the scene they were both endeavoring to act out. Could she be genuinely upset—about something else?

George shook his head and wished once more that he had sisters so that he could understand the fairer sex better. Perhaps Selina had felt overcome after their unexpected encounter and had somehow become a little hysterical? Although George's father had once told him that the notion that women were hysterical creatures was, in his opinion, very much mistaken.

"They are the stronger sex in many ways," George's father had told him. "They approach childbirth courageously."

George had seen babies being born as part of his work with his father, and he had already found the whole experience quite awe inspiring. He crushed the thought that appeared in his mind—of what it would be like if he married Selina, if they had a family together. Time enough for all that. Lord Steyne must be defeated first, and then George must work out a way to woo Selina properly.

Heart hammering, George slipped back into his seat. Damnation! His parents had already returned, and now there would be an inquisition to find out where he had been.

"I thought you were going to stay in the box," Mrs. Fitzgerald said. "And where exactly . . ."

"Leave the poor boy alone," Doctor Fitzgerald said. "If he changed his mind and wanted to go and socialize, 'tis no business of ours. He is an adult, after all."

Mrs. Fitzgerald opened her mouth as if to speak, then her husband reminded her that the production was about to start again.

"Ah yes, how delightful!" Mrs. Fitzgerald said as the curtain went up. "This play is always fresh, however many times I watch it."

A strange harrumphing issued from Doctor Fitzgerald. 'Twas obvious George's papa did not hold *Romeo and Juliet* in quite the same high esteem that his wife did.

As the tragic love story unfolded, George became exasperated with the impending sense of doom. Why must some stories end badly? Why did Shakespeare think that people would be entertained by such an aggravating twist of fate? Could not Romeo have only pretended to die—as Juliet had done? For then when Juliet awoke, Romeo could also awaken, and there could be a happy ending.

Or perhaps even if Romeo did manage to kill himself and

Juliet awoke to find his corpse, instead of killing herself, why could she not mourn him for a time and then try to make a new life for herself? Would it not be possible for her to build a different future? One heard of people making a happy second marriage after the death of their partner. So why all this unrelenting gloom?

George shook his head. His alternative ending to the play would be unlikely to be quite as popular as Shakespeare's, for George was no creative genius. The truth was that George was far too tender-hearted to enjoy watching people in torment.

He did not like to see animals suffering either. There had been a time a few months past when Trigger had been afflicted with an infection caused by a vicious thorn embedding itself into the side of the horse's leg. George had stayed by Trigger's side night and day until the danger had passed.

"You undoubtedly saved his life," Doctor Fitzgerald had told George. "Your thorough cleansing of the wound and exemplary nursing of the animal were first-rate. I am proud of you, my son."

Trigger was George's best friend in the world. He had known him since he had been a tiny foal. In fact, George had seen Trigger being born in his father's stables at Newton St. Loe. And since then, there were many times that George had whispered the details of something that had been troubling him into the horse's ear. Trigger was an excellent listener, for he never contradicted or offered advice, but instead gave George the space to work things out for himself—in the comforting presence of a friend.

Trigger accepts me for who I am; that is all I ask.

Was it possible that Trigger would be able to help George in the next phase of his campaign to win Selina's heart? The children yesterday seemed very taken with George's horse and would all benefit from riding lessons—particularly the young boy who had trouble walking. Could helping the children be phase four?

Or had phase four already occurred in the form of the unexpected passion George and Selina had experienced in the corridor? The scene was right at the front of George's mind—and yet somehow he was finding it difficult to face, instead musing about alternative endings to *Romeo and Juliet,* and riding lessons.

However, think about it he should! George had just kissed Selina passionately. And she had matched his hunger. How wild she was—abandoned. The attraction between the pair had been impossible to resist. What would it be like to be married to such a woman? George thanked God the lights in the theater were dim, for his cheeks flamed so much they could practically be considered a fire risk. He looked up into the shadows of the magnificent paintings on the ceiling above. 'Twould be a crying shame if such fine works of art were to be consumed in a fireball.

George lowered his eyelids and peered through his long lashes across the auditorium at his dearest love. Hopefully, this meant no one would see exactly where his vision was directed.

A slight movement caught his attention—someone was entering Selina's box! George leapt to his feet, eager to rush round in case a lowlife ruffian was planning to abduct Selina—ah, but no need. 'Twas Lord Templeton. How pleasant that he had managed to join his party, even at such a late hour.

George reached for his opera glasses. Lord Templeton was not alone, instead accompanied by Carter. And a conversation was going on. Selina was smiling and looking so dashed pretty that George had trouble restraining himself from climbing onto the edge of his box and yelling out his affection and admiration. Here, in the theater! In front of everyone. But that would never do. He must not draw attention to any communication between himself and his heart's desire, on account of the danger which might even now be lurking in the shadows.

Selina was staring across the auditorium and waving at George now, grinning broadly. She looked so happy! What in heaven's name was going on? Lady Templeton had her finger to her lips—she seemed to be telling the other occupants of the box to quiet down.

Faces in the stalls looked up towards the source of the commotion, and then all became magically calm again as the drama of

Romeo and Juliet moved inexorably to its devastating conclusion.

As George and his parents walked through the crowded corridors, they were surrounded by excited chatter.

"Brilliant performance!"

"Perfectly cast."

"And the costumes! So authentic!"

"I was affected deeply by the ending . . ."

"Yes! When he drinks the poison . . ."

"And she stabs herself . . ."

Huge lanterns lit up the outside of the theater, giving the panelled pilasters and carved garlands a fairytale appearance. George looked around surreptitiously for Selina—but no sign of her. He urgently needed to know why she had waved at him so exuberantly.

Doctor and Mrs. Fitzgerald stepped into their carriage which was waiting at the edge of Beaufort Square, and then as George was about to follow, Carter appeared.

"Mr. Fitzgerald. A quick word, if I may?"

"Of course," George said. "I noticed you arrive during the production. Is everything all right? There seemed to be quite a commotion breaking out in the Templetons' box."

"More than all right," Carter said. "To cut the story short, Lord Steyne is in custody. I managed to track him down today to his house in the Cottage Crescent. He was hiding out in a stable, just as you had suggested after dinner last night. I had a few friends with me, so we arrested him and took him to the Constable."

"Excellent news!" George said. "What will he be charged with?"

"For the moment, he is accused of threatening Signor Allegretto, but I feel sure there will be other crimes that will stick. Do not worry about that now. Concentrate on the wall of ice, which is redundant now Lord Steyne is languishing in the City Gaol."

"I don't know how to thank you."

"There is no need. Oh, and before I forget, Miss Templeton

has a particular invitation for you. She asks that you attend the Templetons' musical soirée tomorrow evening."

"So that was why she was looking happy," George said. "I did notice from my side of the auditorium. She must be as pleased as I am that the wall of ice has come down."

"That's what I thought too," Carter said, "although when I mentioned it, she said she didn't know anything about the wall. Of course, that particular scenario was hatched by us after dinner when the ladies had withdrawn. She hasn't seen Henry today, and Lord Templeton rose very late and obviously did not tell Lady Templeton about it. Miss Templeton was very pleased when I explained all about it just now, though. She said it explained a lot."

George frowned. "I do not fully understand how . . ."

Carter slapped George on the back. "Avoid overthinking! There is no more wall of ice, so you and Miss Templeton are free to make eyes at each other as much as you want. Accept your good fortune. 'Tis the perfect opportunity to get on with your courting."

"Good advice—which I will follow. Thank you again."

George watched Carter melt through the crowd and then got into the carriage.

"Are you feeling better?" Mrs. Fitzgerald said to her son. "I heard Miss Templeton's name mentioned and I wondered . . ."

"I've been invited to a musical soirée at the Templetons' tomorrow evening," George said. "I am greatly looking forward to it—you know how much I love Bach and Mozart."

Doctor and Mrs. Fitzgerald exchanged a look whose meaning George could only guess at. However, they seemed pleased.

Later, alone in his bed, George stared up at the ceiling, totally unable to sleep. Joy should have been suffusing his being—yet he was troubled by what Carter had said about the wall of ice— namely, that Selina had known nothing about it. George put his hands over his head and stretched out. What was it *exactly* that was bothering him?

If Selina did not know about the wall, did not know that we should keep our distance and act as if we did not like each other—why then was she so unfriendly this morning on the Crescent Fields?

Perhaps with her quick intelligence, Selina had taken her lead from George? For he had been remarkably abrupt and unfriendly. Yes, that must be it—she would have realized very quickly that George's behavior was mere playacting and that she should also dissemble. In short, she must have known that the pair must show no fondness for one another when in the company of others—until Lord Steyne was under lock and key.

However, the niggle in George's mind remained stubborn— and persistent.

Selina told me this evening that she hated me. We were totally alone at the time, so there was no need to act: there were no others.

What if she really does hate me?

CHAPTER NINE

Selina

WHEN SELINA WOKE the next morning, she felt an instant excitement at the thought of the musical soirée planned for that evening. George would be coming to Number 1! Perhaps, if everything worked out, she would manage to snatch a kiss with him. Their first kiss at her family home . . .

The busy sound of servants rushing hither and thither came floating up the stairs. There was so much to get ready for the entertainment—furniture to be rearranged, rooms to clean, fires to make, food to prepare . . .

How wonderful it had been last night at the theater to find out that George had only been playacting when he had been so cold towards her. Carter had given Selina a succinct explanation of the necessity for the "wall of ice" when he had come to the Templetons' box in the Theatre Royal last night. From then on, everything had begun to slot into place. At last!

How I wish I could have flown across from my box to George's to embrace him, in front of the cream of Bath society. How Mama would have scolded me—and what fun it would have been!

Lord Templeton had invited Carter in for a drink when their carriage reached the Royal Crescent after *Romeo and Juliet*, and Selina had taken the opportunity to have another whispered conversation with him when her parents were otherwise engaged, for she was determined to clear up the final reservation she had about George's intentions.

"I have been a little worried about something Martha told me," Selina said to Carter, "for she was outside the dining room when you men were talking after dinner and heard George deny there was any affection whatsoever between him and me."

"Oh, that!" Carter had said with a laugh. "George may have uttered those words for the benefit of listening servants, but I can tell you that no one in the room believed him. No, not your father, nor your brother Henry, and certainly not me. We all know love when we see it."

"That is such a relief," Selina had said, "for I had begun to think George must be a rake."

"George? The man is no rake. There has never been the slightest whiff of scandal attached to his name—and I would not shy away from telling you if there was, believe me. I assure you, the only other creature he has ever fully given his heart to is his horse. No, in my opinion, George is a most sincere young man. A good fighter, too."

"How glad I am to hear you approve of him," Selina had said.

Carter had gone on to explain that he considered George's character the ideal foil for Selina's more extrovert personality. This chimed with what she had already begun to work out for herself, namely that opposites could work well together, especially as far as romance was concerned.

Yes, Selina's conversation with Carter last night had been most satisfactory, clearing up as it did any lingering doubts she had harbored.

'Twas ironic that Selina had not been sure George was right for her until she thought he could never be hers. And strange that it took a crisis to make her realize all she wanted was to marry him and that her initial worries over whether they were suitable for each other were nothing of any consequence.

I thought him a boastful show-off and a tedious companion at Kitty and Henry's dinner party. He was either talking incessantly of his skill at cards or acting like a tongue-tied dullard . . .

Now Selina realized that George's keenness to impress her had caused him to veer between boastful babble and a distracted silence. How could she hold that against him? For was it not a delightful quality to have such strong emotions that one behaved a little erratically, not to say wildly?

And when I thought he was being cold towards me, he was acting out of great love, so anxious was he to shield me by creating the wall of ice. Protecting someone is not a fault. Medieval knights of old defended their ladies.

George was a very good actor, that was certain, for Selina had been totally taken in by his coldness and disdain. And George in his turn must have thought Selina was a good actress, for she had been rude to the point of bluntness.

I told him I hated him! He must've found that quite amusing, knowing that I was only doing it because of the wall of ice.

There was a complication that Selina supposed one day she would be able to articulate to George—that in reality, she had thought he did not care for her one jot. She had not known he was playacting. However, that could all be saved for another day—and would be a mightily complicated situation to explain. Selina's brain hurt even just thinking about it. A veritable Gordian knot.

Selina's task today was to convince George she loved him and that what was between them was not a mere physical attraction but something lasting—something with a future. She had the ultimate aim of encouraging him to make a declaration. And she knew how to do it. She had a plan—a musical one. And she knew it would work.

LATER THAT SAME morning, Selina was pleased to welcome Kitty to Number 1; she was longing to see her friend and keen to enlist her help concerning a plan to show George how much she loved him.

"How are you?" Selina asked when Kitty appeared in the

entrance hall.

"Much recovered."

"You are in an interesting condition! So exciting. Many congratulations! But are you sure you are in good health? You look a trifle pale."

"I am feeling considerably better. You must have wondered what was wrong with me outside Hunter's."

"We worked it out," Selina said. "That is, George and I did. Of course, Henry already knew."

"I'm sorry I did not tell you before," Kitty said.

"I understand," Selina said. "'Tis a private matter and still very early days."

The two young women stood at the foot of the staircase, and Selina smiled.

"Are you quite sure you are well enough to attempt the climb? Should I ask one of the footmen to carry you up?"

"If you do, I shall scream!"

Giggling like schoolgirls, the two friends hurried up to the withdrawing room.

"Now," Selina said, "if you are sure you feel well enough, I would appreciate your help. I need to decide what I am to perform at the musical soirée this evening, and I'm relying on you to help me choose."

"Gladly," Kitty said, "although I am surprised you have not sorted out a piece yet. Has Signor Allegretto not suggested anything?"

"He has," Selina said. "A fairly new song by Schubert—about a rose. 'Tis very charming, and I was happy to sing it, but now my circumstances require a slight change."

"This sounds interesting," Kitty said. "Tell me more."

Over the next ten minutes, Selina explained to Kitty everything that had been happening with George—including the wall of ice misunderstanding.

Not absolutely everything! Some things are too personal to mention—like the scene under the tree in the Crescent Fields and another in the corridor of the theater last night . . .

I have re-lived these moments of bliss a thousand times already; however, it is still too soon to share them.

"I sense there is something not yet revealed," Kitty said to Selina.

"Maybe! Oh, Kitty, I am so happy now that I know the reason for George's recent coldness."

"And what is this plan of yours?" Kitty said. "Tell me, why must you change your music?"

"Music can communicate feelings in a way that words cannot. I intend to show George how much I love him by singing to him—and for this, I need to find and rehearse a special song. I was thinking of an aria from *The Marriage of Figaro*. You know the one Susanna sings, about anticipating joy?"

"Oh, yes!" Kitty ran over to the pianoforte and strummed the opening bars. "Full of intrigue—and heartfelt love. Perfect!"

"I hoped you would think that was suitable," Selina said. "Here—I have the accompaniment ready. Would you play it through with me?"

"Gladly. And would you like me to play for you this evening?"

"'Twould be lovely," Selina replied, "however, Signor Allegretto is to attend this evening. Mama insisted, as he has been so loyal to our family—and he said he would like to play for me."

"Splendid," Kitty said. "I always enjoy hearing him play."

The two friends spent a delightful half hour rehearsing the song until they were satisfied with the result.

"How will this make George love you?" Kitty said. "Granted, it is a fine love song, but I do not quite see . . ."

"Ah!" Selina said. "When I sing, I intend to look directly at George. Then he will know how much I adore him."

Kitty creased her brow. "That could be considered a little improper. I do not think your mama would approve."

"I see your point," Kitty said, "for my mama does disapprove of many of my bolder ideas. Let me think about it again."

"I know," Kitty said, "why do you not fix your gaze upon a different man, one whom everyone would know you are not in love with, and sing it to him? Then George will realize how lovely it would be if he were to feel the full beam of your affection. My goodness! By the end of the evening, you could be an engaged woman."

By the end of this evening? I can scarce believe it. And one day, maybe I will be in the blessed state that Kitty finds herself in—carrying a child.

"But on whom should I fix my gaze?" Selina said. "For if I fix it on another young gentleman, George might get the wrong idea. Besides, I do not think my parents would approve of this either."

"Since when has your parents' disapproval stopped you doing anything you wanted?" Kitty said.

"Quite often!"

"I tell you what, why not stare at Signor Allegretto?" Kitty said.

"What a good idea. No one would ever think I was in love with him. He is far too old, and anyway, he is my teacher. He will be thrilled to see how beautifully he has taught me to show affection in my face as part of a performance. And hopefully George will see how much love I am capable of."

"I do hope this game of yours works," Kitty said with a giggle. "'Tis rapidly becoming more complicated than the silliest opera plot—and that is a hard act to live up to. And be assured, I will not tell anyone of your plan to capture George's heart—not even Henry."

"Thank you, Kitty. I know I can rely on your discretion." Selina clapped her hands in delight. "I have a very good feeling about this and cannot wait for the evening's entertainment."

Will it not be wonderful for George and me to have all our misunderstandings behind us at last? And then we can start to court properly and get to know each other in a civilized fashion, instead of snatching moments of bliss in between scenes of high drama.

George

GEORGE TOOK HIS father's carriage from Devonshire Buildings to the Royal Crescent that evening. He could of course have walked the few miles or ridden over on Trigger. However, attending Lady Templeton's music soirée was a significant moment in his courtship of Selina.

There was still the worry burrowing into his mind, though. Selina had said she hated him—and that had not been because there was anyone around to impress with her playacting, for George and Selina had been quite alone in the theater corridor at that time.

Is it possible that Selina was so stirred up by the emotions of the moment—and that exquisite kiss—that her brain simply confused two emotions and she meant to say something else? Had she really intended to say she loved me?

George looked out at the rapidly flowing River Avon as the carriage passed over the bridge into the city. He must be rational. It simply was not possible that Selina would confuse love and hate. The emotions could be close to one another, but Selina was a very clever young woman fully in control of her mind.

Wasn't she?

Granted, she took risks by frequently walking out onto the rooftop above Number 1; that balustrade was quite low. And she had put herself in grave danger when visiting Bath City Gaol by not thinking through the full consequences of her actions. However, being a little hotheaded and impulsive was very different from saying one thing and meaning the exact opposite. To do such a thing must surely indicate some sort of derangement. A temporary insanity? There was such a thing in medical literature—it was possible that Mrs. Leigh Perrot had suffered from this sort of condition when she had allegedly taken lace from Smith's in Bath Street years ago.

But Selina? George saw no evidence of any behavior that would give cause for medical concern. He could seek advice from his father, although that would mean revealing what had happened in the corridor at the Theatre Royal. Inconceivable!

George could consult some of the medical texts in his father's library on his return this evening—they might have something of interest there.

After a little more overanalysis, George realized the farcical direction of his thoughts.

Good Lord! What am I thinking? Would I rather Selina was suffering from some sort of delusion rather than face the fact that she hates me?

Would it not be easier just to follow Carter's advice from the night before? *Stop overthinking*, he had said to George. And embrace your good fortune. Yes, this was what George would do. Switch off his inquiring mind, embrace his good fortune—and hopefully Selina too—and continue with his attempt to win Selina's heart and mind. This was definitely the best course of action. And attending the musical soirée could conceivably be phase five in George's attempt to win Selina's heart.

George received a warm welcome from Lord and Lady Templeton at the front door of Number 1 and then sped up to the withdrawing room where Henry greeted him.

"George! How wonderful to see you. I'm afraid you'll have to be put up with some of my playing this evening—but there will be many more accomplished performances from others for you to enjoy, I promise."

"You are too modest," George said, "for you are a fine musician, Henry, as well you know."

"At least you will not have to put up with any musical offerings from me," Edmund said as he said joined them. "Mama always labelled me the least musical child in the Templeton household."

"I remember how she used to try to persuade you to practice more," Henry said to his brother.

"Yes," Edmund said. "There were many battles fought over my pianoforte scales and arpeggios. A hopeless cause! I simply did not have the aptitude, nor the interest. What about you, George? Were you forced to learn music?"

"I was not," George said. "My parents took me to many concerts, and I enjoyed playing the piano a little, but it was more the outdoor life for me as a boy—I loved to help out at my father's stables."

"Ah, yes," Henry said. "The stables. I remember you have spoken of this before."

"Is it not unusual for a doctor to run stables?" Edmund said.

"My father is interested in the health of all animals," George said, "including humans—and horses. He is never happier than when looking after the new foals."

"I believe your best friend is a horse," Edmund said with a smile.

Kitty and Selina were warming themselves at the fireplace at the other end of the room, for despite it being spring, the weather was still chilly. They were deep in conversation, every now and then pausing to smile and giggle before resuming an animated discourse.

If only I knew for certain she were to be mine, how happy I would be. I am on the edge of a precipice, with blissful love waiting for me in the clouds above. One false step, and I will plunge into the chasm, instead of flying to my love.

Selina looked at George across the crowded room, her eyes luminous and mouth curved into a beatific smile. She looked truly divine—both irresistible and unattainable all at the same time.

Then she whispered something into Kitty's ear.

"It looks as if my dear wife and sister are hatching a plot," Henry remarked.

"You never know quite where you are with those two," Edmund said. "They are as thick as thieves—and have been since childhood. Do you remember how they always tried to outwit us,

Henry, when Kitty came round to play with Selina?"

"Do I!" Henry said.

"They would have put Machiavelli himself to shame," Edmund said.

"Did you know Signor Allegretto is coming this evening?" Henry said to George.

"No! What a pleasant surprise," George said. "I look forward to seeing him again. He must be mightily relieved that Lord Steyne is locked up, after being terrorized by the villain."

"Absolutely," Henry said. "And Signor Allegretto is to accompany Selina when she performs this evening."

"I heard them running through the piece but half an hour ago," Edmund said. "Exquisite! I put my head round the door, and they were both so completely wrapped up in the music, gazing into each other's eyes, that they did not even hear me come in. You should have seen Signor Allegretto's face! He seemed enraptured with the beauty of the music."

As long as it was only the beauty of the music Signor Allegretto was enraptured with—for I could be jealous if I thought he had eyes for my Selina.

"What was Selina singing?" George asked.

"Don't ask me!" Edmund said. "'Twas in Italian, I know that much. It might have been Mozart, from an opera—but I am not entirely sure. I'm a bit of a Philistine, although I know enough to know that it was damned fine."

"I look forward to hearing the piece," George said.

"That's not all, though," Edmund said. "I got the distinct impression that Selina was involving Signor Allegretto in some sort of plot of hers."

"Lord!" Henry said. "Is there no end to our sister's machinations? Could you hear what they were saying, Edmund?"

"Barely. They were muttering something about love—that sort of nonsense. They looked a bit shifty, if I'm being honest."

Not good . . .

"Perhaps they were translating the words of the song?" Henry said.

"Possibly," Edmund said. "Anyway, they stopped talking as soon as they saw me standing there. Oh well. No doubt all will be revealed."

"'Tis time to take our places, I think," Henry said. "George, you sit in the front row next to Edmund. I'm going to sit with Kitty and Selina. We musicians have chairs reserved at the side so that we are ready to go on when it is our turn."

There were many splendid items performed that evening. Henry launched the concert, playing quite exquisitely on his violin, accompanied by Lady Templeton. Several gentlemen and ladies sang, there was a charming flute air, then Henry and Kitty performed a rousing pianoforte duet which had everyone tapping their toes.

How well matched they are musically and in every other way—and what joy they have waiting for them in their life together.

Kitty was looking far better than she had that day outside Hunter's—the roses were beginning to creep back into her cheeks.

Very soon it was time for the last item; Selina was performing a Mozart aria accompanied by her singing teacher. Signor Allegretto sat down at the pianoforte with a flourish and gave Selina an encouraging smile as she walked on.

"Ladies and gentlemen, I am going to sing an aria from the opera *The Marriage of Figaro*. It is sung by Susanna at the end of the final act, and is a beautiful declaration of love to her future husband. I had originally chosen a different song . . ."

Here Selina paused to smile at Signor Allegretto.

". . . but with my music teacher's blessing I have changed the program, for the sentiment contained in this Mozart aria is so close to my heart that I could not miss the opportunity to sing it to you."

Selina stood poised in front of her music stand, while Signor Allegretto played the introduction.

"Deh vieni, non tardar, o goija bella . . ." she sang.

The two performed as one. Signor Allegretto followed her every breath, easing the tempo slightly where necessary and creating a beautiful accompaniment to cushion and nurture her glorious voice.

Selina sang most of the song from memory, leaving her free to gaze into Signor Allegretto's eyes. She was so much inside the character of the song that one could be forgiven for thinking she was actually in love with her teacher.

What I would give for Selina to look at me like that every day for the rest of my life.

At the end of the performance there was a rousing burst of applause from the audience and many shouts of "Encore!"

"Thank you, thank you," Selina said. "And now, if you are sure you would like an encore, I will sing the song I had originally intended to sing this evening—by Schubert, about a little rose."

This time, Selina did not direct her gaze at Signor Allegretto, but instead allowed her bewitching eyes to rove over the audience. Was she lingering overlong on one or two of the men? Flirting? Jealousy flooded George's being. He wanted to jump to his feet and scream that Selina was his and his alone. Instead, he decided to stare fixedly at the floor, unwilling to bear full witness to her brazen behavior.

A chill came over him. He should not have been surprised.

"I hate you, George Fitzgerald," Selina had said in the theater corridor. *"I hate you more than I have hated anyone in my whole life."*

And the way she had looked at Signor Allegretto in the Mozart aria—why, they had more or less declared they were in love! Had not Edmund as good as hinted this before the concert, saying he had caught the pair whispering about love? And Selina had once said that Signor Allegretto had waxed lyrically about how lonely he felt sometimes in his lodgings and how he longed for a lady companion. Was Selina now Signor Allegretto's lady companion? Could it be that when George and Selina had encountered Signor Allegretto in Hunter's, the two lovers had been toying with George? Selina had been very keen to sit with

Signor Allegretto. Was the whole sorry story about Lord Steyne threatening Signor Allegretto a lie? Or at least an exaggeration?

George's head hurt as the implications of this betrayal—if there had been a betrayal—stacked up and shifted memories of other events inside his head.

Selina was not the woman George had thought. He still ached for her and loved her with his whole being—he always would. But it was obvious that he had been fooling himself. Selina did not care for him. Whether or not she had any real interest in Signor Allegretto, or any of the other young men there, was unclear. She could have been merely flirting and teasing. However, one thing was certain. George and Selina were finished—'twas not the match made in heaven George had previously supposed.

"Now, ladies and gentlemen," Lady Templeton said, "I am pleased to announce that refreshments are available downstairs in the dining room. If you would like to make your way . . ."

George fled down the stairs as if desperate to be the first for supper—but in reality, he was on a different mission. He would not stay where he was not wanted. 'Twas time to leave. As he wrenched open the front door, he heard a voice calling from above.

"Mr. Fitzgerald? George!"

Selina ran down the stairs after him.

George's heart had been dealt such a blow that his eyes became a little moist.

Dash it all! I will not stay to let a woman see me cry.

"Goodnight, Miss Templeton," he croaked. "Please give my thanks to your parents."

And with that, George fled down the steps to his waiting carriage.

Selina

SELINA PURSUED GEORGE across the cobbles, leaving the front door to Number 1 wide open.

"George! George!" she shouted. "Why are you leaving?"

What has gone wrong? I sensed a change in him while I was singing.

Selina ran to the very door of George's carriage and pulled at his sleeve as he was about to ascend the step.

"George! Please! Are you unwell? Why are you leaving me?"

He did not answer, but wiped his eyes quickly as if he were troubled by dust. Then he nodded—barely politely—and said,

"I am afraid I must go home now, Miss Templeton. Thank you for a charming evening. I believe you have had enough fun at my expense. Goodbye."

'Twas as if a shutter had come down over him. During Selina's performance of the aria from *The Marriage of Figaro*, George had looked captivated. Then all had changed dramatically during the encore, which he did not seem to enjoy at all. Perhaps he did not rate Schubert as highly as Mozart? And what could he mean, saying she had been having fun at his expense? Oh, what was going on?

"Selina!" Lady Templeton called from the front door. "Come back this instant! You will catch your death. What are you doing?"

"Coming, Mama." Selina spun round to face Lady Templeton. "I'm bidding farewell to Mr. Fitzgerald. A moment longer . . ."

When Selina turned back to the carriage, George had already taken the opportunity to hop inside and give the order to his driver to proceed. Selina waved to the departing carriage, but there was no answering gesture from George. In fact, he seemed to be looking in entirely the other direction.

"Mama sent me out to collect you," Edmund said to Selina, appearing at her side. "You should not be here alone. Apart from anything else, 'tis freezing."

"I had not noticed."

Selina followed Edmund back to the house and went into the dining room.

"Well done, Miss Templeton. You gave a very fine performance," one of the gentleman guests said.

"Yes," another said. "'Twas truly sublime. I actually thought you were in love with your music teacher at one point, such was the depth of your emotional interpretation."

"I thought you were enamoured with me, when you sang the encore," the first gentleman said. "You caught my eye in such an agreeable manner—and that of several other gentlemen too, I think?"

"Yes," the second gentleman agreed. "We are all hopelessly under your spell now."

On another occasion, Selina would have enjoyed these rather flirtatious compliments, however this evening she could not think of any witty put-downs at all.

"Excuse me," she said to the two young gentlemen. "I see that my friend Mrs. Templeton is waiting for me over there. I must have a word with her—and tell her how much I enjoyed her performance."

"Oh, yes," the first guest said. "'Twas a fine duet she played with her husband."

"Miss Templeton, perchance you will be playing a duet with a husband of your own one day soon?" the second guest said.

"Indeed," the first said. "We are all yours for the taking."

Selina gave the gentlemen a withering look before striding across the room to where Kitty stood waiting.

"Did it work?" Kitty said. "I noticed you were outside with Mr. Fitzgerald. What was he saying to you? Does he know how much you love him? Have things been resolved? And why did he leave so early? Was he unwell?"

"Which of these questions would you like me to answer first?" Selina said to Kitty. "I cannot cope with being so inundated."

Kitty stared at Selina, then put her hand on her arm. This had the effect of causing tears to spring up in Selina's eyes.

"Upstairs," Kitty whispered. "Now. Shall we go to your chamber?"

A few minutes later, Selina was sitting on her bed being comforted by Kitty, tears flowing freely in the privacy of her room.

After a while, she pulled away from Kitty and blew her nose on a handkerchief.

"Breathe," Kitty said. "In your own time—what has happened?"

"What has happened is that I have ruined everything. I thought I was being so clever, showing George my love through the language of music—whereas all I was doing was trying to snare him using a trick. 'Twas dishonest and foolish. And now he dislikes me intensely. He might even think that I'm in love with Signor Allegretto."

"Absurd!" Kitty said. "That could never be true."

"I have heard comments from other guests," Selina said. "'Tis the appearance I created. They said they thought I must be in love with my teacher. Then they said they thought I must be in love with them!"

"They must have been jesting," Kitty said. "Surely they would not dare to suggest anything so improper? Oh, I feel bad about this. This was my fault, as 'twas I who first suggested you should sing to Signor Allegretto."

"The blame lies entirely with me," Selina said. "Besides, I ran the idea past Signor Allegretto before the performance. He knew full well that I would pretend to make eyes at him, so that George would know I was capable of love. Signor Allegretto agreed that it would be good to make George a little jealous—for then he might realize he had feelings for me, not only physical feelings, but love. Deep love—the sort of love that might prompt a man to propose marriage."

How foolish and immature it all sounds—what a blunder I have made!

"Oh, how I regret my actions," Selina continued, "for instead of easing the path of love, I have made George think so little of me that he felt compelled to flee. He must think I am a scarlet woman, making eyes at my teacher, whereas in fact I only wanted to show him how my heart is full to the brim with love—for him. In the encore, I allowed my gaze to sweep across the audience, but when I tried to catch George's eye, he was staring at the floor . . . oh, what a mess!"

"There must be a path out of this," Kitty said. "Let us consider the facts. What indications have there been as to George's feelings?"

Selina blushed crimson. "I need to tell you about two incidents that I have not shared with anyone yet."

"This sounds interesting! Tell me all."

Selina gave her best friend in all the world a full account of how she and George had kissed under the tree on the Crescent Fields and then at the theater so recently, almost by accident.

Kitty's eyes grew round as saucers, then she grinned. "Well done, Selina! You are a dark horse. What wonderful romantic trysts!"

"Do not breathe a word of this to anyone, will you?" Selina said. "Promise?"

"Of course I won't," Kitty said.

"If my parents knew about this, they would be very angry with Mr. Fitzgerald—and also with me. I fear I would never be let out of the house again for the rest of my life."

"I will not even tell Henry, even though he is my dear husband."

"Good," Selina said. "Do not tell Henry, because I suspect he would think it was his duty to challenge George to a duel to defend my honor."

"Although your honor is worth defending, I would be rather heartbroken if Henry had to lose his life to defend it. No, we must think of an alternative."

The two friends sat side by side in silence for a while.

"I have thought of what to do," Selina said, "or perhaps I should say what *not* to do. I will no longer try to hatch any plans or schemes, for so far, recently at least, they have all gone wrong. Instead, I will try the direct approach. I love George and still cannot help feeling that the situation is one gigantic misunderstanding. I want the chance to talk to him face to face, woman to man."

"Would it not be better to wait and see what happens?" Kitty said.

"No! I have spent my whole life waiting for things to happen and then sneaking around, hatching plans, or dressing up as someone else and trying to get my own way through subterfuge. I will approach George on equal terms—for only then will I know whether there is any hope."

"You are braver than I am," Kitty said.

"I am sure I am not." Selina stood up. "However, I am hungry. Dearest Kitty, thank you for your help. Let us go down to supper. The others will be wondering where we are."

They walked arm in arm down the stairs to the dining room.

"There you are," Henry said to Kitty. "I missed you—I cannot be away from you for long."

"Excuse me for stealing your wife," Selina said. "We had important matters to discuss upstairs."

"Yes," Kitty said. "And I can confirm that the very important matter has been resolved—more or less."

"Well," Henry said, "there is an important plate of meat over there that needs your attention now, ladies, and some fine salads, too. Would you both allow me to serve you?"

"How kind," Selina said.

"Thank you," Kitty said.

As they walked over to the table, Henry whispered in Selina's ear,

"You have not fooled me, sister dearest. I know that something is troubling you. Just say the word if there's anything I can do."

"There is something," Selina said. "I wish to visit Beechen Cliff tomorrow. I have a fancy to walk around the summit and look across the city."

"'Tis not likely you'll be able to make that journey on your own," Henry said. "I can just imagine Mama's face if you proposed hiking up there by yourself."

"This is where your help comes in," Selina said to Henry. "I would like you to accompany me—and Kitty too, if she pleases."

"Did I hear my name?" Kitty said. "And talk of a trip to Beechen Cliff? I would not miss that for anything. I love walking on that noble hill—'tis one of my favorite places."

"One of mine, too," Edmund said, joining the group. "I am happy to be part of this outing."

"Good," Selina said. "We will go there tomorrow."

"A magnificent idea," Henry said. "I am sure Papa will be happy for us to take his carriage. Shall we set off around ten in the morning? Would that suit? I think Kitty and I can be ready by then."

"That sounds uncommonly early to me." Edmund sighed. "I will have to make a special effort."

"Ten o'clock it is, then," Selina said. "And afterwards, who knows, we might drop in on George, for he lives nearby, does he not?"

"In truth, he does," Henry said. "'Twould be very fine to see him. I need to ask his advice about a horse, as a matter of fact."

"I intend to ask him to marry me," Selina said, "as a matter of fact."

"Very amusing! Such a droll sense of humor," Edmund said to Selina. "I know you care not a jot for the man—I was there on the Crescent Fields when you met George on your nature ramble with the children, remember? You could not have been colder towards the poor fellow, nor he towards you. And George did not linger long at the soirée tonight, did he? He could not get away fast enough. 'Twas like watching the release of a greyhound at the start of a race."

Henry scratched his head. "I do not agree with Edmund about the lack of feeling between the pair of you, but of course he does not have the full picture . . . indeed, I had thought that given time and opportunity, George would . . . although given his character, patience is needed . . . However, Selina, I know for certain that you are joking when you say you will propose to George tomorrow."

"How do you know?" Selina asked.

"Why, 'tis simple." Henry smiled. "Ladies do not propose marriage, do they? Therefore, you must be jesting. You are always jesting!"

"'Tis time for another drink," Edmund said. "Would you care to join me, Henry?"

"I'd be delighted."

How little my brothers suspect. 'Tis quite comical, really.

Once the women were alone again, Kitty placed her hand on Selina's arm. "I think this is your best plan yet. I wish you luck."

"I am fully determined to take the reins," Selina said.

I will control my own destiny from now on—not wait for things to happen to me.

CHAPTER TEN

George

"YOU ARE HOME early from your musical soirée at the Templetons,'" Mrs. Fitzgerald said to her son. "Are you quite well, George?"

"Your face is a little flushed—perhaps you are feverish?" Doctor Fitzgerald put his hand on George's forehead. "Ah! Nothing much there to alarm me, physically at least. But something has upset you."

"There is nothing wrong," George said.

Doctor Fitzgerald pursed his lips. "You do not need to accompany me on my medical visits tomorrow—I can easily manage on my own. Instead, I prescribe a day off. Do whatever you want. Whether you read a book, go for a long walk, or visit the stables at Newton St. Loe, will be your decision. Your mind needs a break."

"Thank you, Papa," George said. "I appreciate your concern. I think I will go and have a word with Trigger now."

"You do that," Mrs. Fitzgerald said. "He has missed you—and missed going out to be entertained in a drawing room. Trigger does not get asked to many musical soirées."

If George had not been in such low spirits, he might have found this remark amusing, however, in his present state of mind he could only manage a lopsided grimace at his mother's wit before stumbling out of the room.

He went out to the lane behind the house, and from there, across to the small stable in the backyard. George put his arms around Trigger's neck and sobbed gently into his mane. There was no need for words. Hugging his best friend—his horse—was enough.

After a while, George felt a little restored. It had been such a shock, finding out that Selina was in love with Signor Allegretto. Or perhaps she was in love with one of the many young men whose eye she had caught as she sang her encore?

Was love even the correct word? Had Selina merely been flirting in the Templeton drawing room, spinning a web to trap admirers? Could she actually feel the emotion of love? She certainly knew what physical attraction was. George groaned as he remembered her sweet kisses, her soft, lithe body in his embrace . . .

The loving feelings had seemed so real—but George had been deluding himself. Because his feelings were of deep, true love, he had assumed Selina must feel the same. It was his fault—he had been mistaken. He had assumed the situation was as he had wished it to be.

Trigger neighed softly, and George ruffled his mane and stroked his nose.

"Selina has not been deceitful," George said in Trigger's ear. "She has been direct—for did she not say that she hated me? And this has turned out to be true. 'Tis I who am the fool, for I was deluded. Ah, how I wanted to believe she loved me—how I still long to believe it."

George's beloved Selina had not been guilty of any crime. Had she? She had never declared that she was in love with him— although she had shown by her kisses that she found him attractive. George felt puzzled, for in his world, one did not behave like that unless one's intentions were honorable. He leaned against Trigger.

I am so naïve. There are many in this world who can enjoy physical intimacy that is virtually meaningless. Some of my friends boast of their feminine conquests in a shallow way—and it stands to reason there must be women who behave like this too.

George kicked angrily at some straw.

I never thought Selina—my Selina—would be like this. 'Tis my own fault—for I invented a story in my mind whereby she was my true love, and I see now that she was toying with me.

What to do next: that was the question. George would take great pains to keep apart from Selina until his heart had mended.

But my heart will never heal—I will carry this sorrow to the end of my days.

If George kept out of her way, at least he would not have to see her flirting with other men. And then one day, she would marry. George would not stay in Bath to see that. He would go to Bristol, to London, abroad, another planet—anywhere, to get away.

But he could not do that—he could not leave his parents and Trigger. At least living out of the city, on the other side of the river, George was far enough from Bath that he need never come across Selina—if he was careful. He would accept no social invitations, go to no concerts; he would not attend the Pump Room, nor any balls at the Upper Rooms. In short, he would dedicate himself to his medical work—although he would have to be careful not to undertake any house visits that were anywhere near the Royal Crescent or probably the whole of the center of Bath.

George would definitely be able to help out more at his father's stables in Newton St. Loe—there was no reason on earth why Selina would ever venture there. And he would start tomorrow, by rising early and putting in a full day of work, helping with the horses. Some of the mares were in foal and due to give birth in the early summer. An extra pair of hands and some medical knowledge to help make sure their pregnancies were progressing well could be useful. And had George's papa not already encouraged him in this course of action?

"So, old boy," George said to Trigger, "we will be setting off early—before dawn."

George closed the door of the stable gently and went back across the lane and into the house.

"Are you feeling better?" Mrs. Fitzgerald said.

Had his mama really been waiting for him in the hall all this time?

"Yes, thank you, Mama," George said. "There is nothing for you to worry about."

"I do not like to see you unhappy, George dearest," his mother said and held out her arms to him.

George stood within his mother's embrace for some time as she rhythmically patted his back.

"You know you can tell me anything," Mrs. Fitzgerald said, "and you also know you do not have to tell me anything at all if you do not want to."

"I know, Mama," George said. "Thank you."

George told his mother of his plan to go to the stables in Newton St. Loe in the morning, and she seemed to think it was a good idea.

"Mind you take some food with you," she said. "'Tis hungry work."

"I will," George said. "I do love you, dearest Mama, and have not said this often enough. I know how much you and Papa care for me, how you have always cared for me—I am grateful to be your son."

"You are very precious, George," Mrs. Fitzgerald said. "As our only child, you mean everything to us. But even if I had ten children, I would still feel the same, for you are my George, my dear one. And I think I already know what you will not tell me— that you have been disappointed in love. Am I right?"

George nodded.

"You are not to worry," George's mother said. "Sometimes these things work out unexpectedly. And if it was not meant to be, there will be someone else for you."

"There will never be anyone else for me but Selina!" George cried out passionately. "If I cannot marry her, I will not marry anyone."

"Selina? Miss Selina Templeton, I presume?"

"The very one," George said.

"And are you completely sure she does not care for you?" Mrs. Fitzgerald said.

"I am now," George said hoarsely. "I thought she cared—but I was mistaken."

"'Tis easy to be mistaken in these matters," Mrs. Fitzgerald said. "You could be mistaken now."

"No," George said, "I am certain, for she told me she hated me. And now I must retire, for I am close to dropping. It has been a tiring evening."

As George trudged up to his chamber, he heard his mother saying something about love being close to hate.

GEORGE ROSE EARLY as planned the next morning and tiptoed down to the kitchen, intending to take a few slices of bread and some cheese wrapped in a napkin. To his surprise, he found Cook already up and about, apron on, putting the finishing touches to a sizeable hamper.

"Mrs. Fitzgerald was most particular that you should have plenty to sustain you for the day," Cook said. "You take this with you now—there's some nice cuts of beef and lamb in there, and all sorts of sandwiches and cakes, fruit too, and some ale."

"Thank you so much," George said. "There's far too much here for one person, but I appreciate all the trouble you've gone to immensely."

"Make sure you have a nice day—you deserve it," Cook said.

It was still dark outside, with no one about. George saddled Trigger, managed to affix the hefty hamper to the horse's back, and was soon cantering along the main road. 'Twas time to be positive. And time to think of others—of the horses he would be helping today and the men he would be working with.

When George arrived at the stables on the edge of the village of Newton St. Loe, he made sure Trigger was settled and then offered his services.

"You are always welcome, Mr. Fitzgerald," one man said. "And today, you have come at the perfect time, for we are a couple of men short through illness. There is much to do, and we will be glad of an extra pair of hands and also for your medical knowledge."

"And I will be glad to help," George said.

He took his jacket off, rolled up his sleeves and set to work.

After a while, a vast pot of tea was brought out to the men, and they pooled what food they had between them for a shared breakfast.

I love being here—the simple life, sharing food with other workers . . .

And I love doing something for the welfare of animals, just as my work with Papa helps men and women live healthier, longer lives.

Soon all the men were back at work, firm friends now with George and delighting in working as a team. Many compliments were made about the massive hamper bursting with delicious food, and George was asked to convey the men's compliments to the Fitzgerald's cook and their thanks to his parents on his return home.

Despite it being only March, it was such taxing physical work that George became glowing hot as he toiled. Glancing around, he decided to follow the example of his comrades and unbuttoned his shirt to cool down.

If only I could cool my passion for Selina this easily.

Selina

"THE WATER LEVEL is high for this time of year." Henry looked out of the carriage window at the very full river. "Bath could be flooded soon—'tis becoming too common an occurrence."

It was a quarter past ten in the morning, and the Templeton carriage was traveling south out of Bath over the River Avon—with Henry, Kitty, Edmund, and Selina inside, bound for Beechen Cliff.

And then we will go to Devonshire Buildings to see George . . . How I long to see my love and sort out this preposterous misunderstanding.

"You are quiet this morning, Edmund," Henry said.

Edmund opened one eye as he lay slumped on the seat. "I am still half asleep. Why you wanted to leave so early, I have not the slightest idea."

"'Tis the best part of the day, the morning," Henry said.

"Not for me," Edmund said. "I am somewhat of a night owl."

"Look at the view!" Kitty said, pointing out of the window. "I can see right across to the Royal Crescent."

The horses strained and snorted as they pulled the heavy carriage up Holloway.

"It seems unkind to make the carriage carry us right to the top of Beechen Cliff," Selina said. "Why do we not dismount and make the rest of the journey up the hill on foot? The carriage can wait for us on the flat at the top of Holloway."

"A sensible idea," Henry said, "although I think Kitty . . ."

"I am not ill, Henry," Kitty said. "Please do not treat me as if I am made of glass. 'Twill do me good to have a walk."

"If you are sure," Henry replied.

After a bit of grumbling, Edmund too dismounted from the carriage, and the four young people completed the rest of the journey on foot.

"'Tis beautiful up here," Selina said. "The air is so much fresher than down in the city, and we are away from all the smoke."

And I am nearer to my love, George . . .

"I think I should bring Mrs. Godwin and the children here one day," Selina said. "It would be a wonderful outing for them. Do you know, some of the children have never set foot outside the city?"

"Fancy that," Henry said. "I suppose 'tis true the poor have fewer opportunities to travel and are without the luxury of carriages and horses."

"That is another thing," Selina said. "I think the children should all have riding lessons."

"Yes," Edmund said. "They could have riding lessons with George—he was very patient with them when he gave them a ride on Trigger the other day."

Kitty stopped walking. "Despite what I said earlier, I think I would like to sit down for a few minutes. Henry and Edmund, you go on ahead, continue your walk, and I will sit here with Selina and rest awhile."

"You're sure you are all right?" Henry said to his wife. "You would say, if anything was wrong?"

"Of course," Kitty said. "I would like to sit down for a while; that's all."

"We will keep you within our sight," Henry promised.

"Shoo! Off you go and leave me and Selina to converse," Kitty said.

"Leave you to gossip, more likely," Edmund said.

"True!" Henry said with a smirk, and then the two brothers strode off at a brisk pace.

"Was it a mistake to come up here?" Selina said. "I am sorry the steep climb is a little too much for you."

"There is no need to be sorry," Kitty said. "This is a heaven-sent opportunity to have a private chat before you put your plan into action. Come—sit next to me on the bench."

Selina settled next to Kitty, then sighed. "Do you still think 'tis a good idea? You do not think it is too shocking for a woman to take charge?"

"I think George will suit you very well," Kitty said. "I also think he needs a bit of encouragement. He's obviously gotten quite confused about something—we know not what exactly—therefore it will be good for you to have the chance to talk to him alone and explain how you feel."

"That is precisely what I think—and after all, I have nothing to lose. Oh, if you could have seen how George looked at me yesterday—or rather did *not* look at me. He did everything he could to avoid eye contact and could not wait to escape in his carriage. For all I know, he's planning to leave Bath. I must tell him how I feel today, no matter what the consequences.

"And before you say anything else, Kitty, I am fully prepared to accept whatever happens. I know he may reject me and carry on behaving in this cold and unfeeling manner. However, if I do not try, I will never know. I do not wish to have any regrets."

"You are brave," Kitty said. "In your shoes, I'm not sure I would have the courage."

Selina laughed and pointed at her stockinged feet. "I'm not in my shoes! I kicked them off as soon as we sat down."

"Of course you did!" Kitty said. "You always do."

"What are you two laughing about?" Henry said as he returned with Edmund.

"Selina, you have been partners in crime with Kitty since first she came round to our house as a child," Edmund said.

"I remember," Henry said. "And Edmund and I used to have long conversations about why we thought girls spent the whole time giggling."

"Did you ever decide why that was?" Selina asked.

"We did not," Henry said. "But sometimes we used to try and listen to what you were saying, to find out what was so funny."

"We had no luck eavesdropping, though," Edmund said. "You always seemed to sense when we were near."

Selina sprang to her feet. "Well, if everyone has had enough of these stupendous views, I think we should move on to the next stage of my plan, er, I mean our journey. We must go to see George in Devonshire Buildings."

"I don't mind paying a call at the Fitzgerald house," Henry said. "I always like chatting to George—although he might be out at work with his father."

Edmund sniggered. "Ha! As long as Selina does not propose! The idea . . ."

"They still do not know what is going on, though 'tis staring them in the face," Kitty whispered to Selina, who laughed.

"There you go again!" Edmund said. "Whispering and giggling. Come on, Henry. Race you back to the carriage. The ladies can follow on more sedately—with their secrets!"

'Twas not far to Devonshire Buildings; during the short carriage ride, Selina found herself increasingly tense as the possibility of seeing George loomed. She bit into her lip as fiercely as she dared to stop it trembling and clenched her fists into tight balls.

Soon she was walking up the path of the Fitzgeralds' home. Behind that very front door lived the man she wanted to marry. Selina had not worked out yet how she would contrive to be alone with George; she knew Kitty would be tactful and melt away if need be, but as her brothers seemed to think the whole thing was a joke, they would be unaware how much she longed for the necessary privacy to propose.

Brothers can be so annoying! Sometimes I wish I could pull a lever and they would disappear through a trap door.

The Templetons were greeted by Mrs. Fitzgerald.

"How delightful to see you all," she said. "I am afraid to tell you that George is not at home today. He's at my husband's stables in Newton St. Loe—he does this from time to time, to be away from everything and work with the animals."

I had not planned for this! Oh, what am I to do next?

"Nevertheless, you are very welcome," Mrs. Fitzgerald said. "Please, come up to the drawing room, and I will arrange for coffee to be sent up."

"I thank you," Henry said, "however, we will not trespass on your hospitality. I'm sure you have many things to do today."

Selina held her breath. Was this how her great plan was going to end?

Mrs. Fitzgerald smiled. "I insist you come upstairs to the drawing room. 'Tis quite a journey from the Royal Crescent, and

I would not feel comfortable sending you back without refreshment. Please! Follow me. Mrs. Templeton and Miss Templeton—if you would like to come first?"

"I thought I heard voices," Doctor Fitzgerald said, coming out of his study.

"Have you time to join us for coffee, my dear?" Mrs. Fitzgerald said. "The Templetons have come to visit. They were hoping to find George here, but no matter. I am delighted to say they are staying for coffee."

"Wonderful news," Doctor Fitzgerald said. "Let us all go upstairs forthwith."

"Perchance first," Mrs. Fitzgerald said to her husband, "the two Mr. Templetons might care to take a quick look at the fossils in your study?"

"Splendid!" Doctor Fitzgerald said. "I am always very happy to show my collection to visitors. Fossils are a passion of mine; such an interesting glimpse into the past . . ."

Upstairs, Mrs. Fitzgerald invited Selina and Kitty to sit down, and within a few minutes a tray of coffee arrived.

"What was it you wanted to see my George about?" Mrs. Fitzgerald asked, looking directly at Selina.

"Mrs. Fitzgerald," Kitty said. "Might I be excused . . . the ladies retiring room . . .?"

"Of course, my dear," Mrs. Fitzgerald said. "The maid will show you."

Is Kitty being tactful? Leaving me free to converse with the woman I hope will be my future mother-in-law?

Once alone with Mrs. Fitzgerald, Selina decided to be bold. As she had said before to Kitty, what had she to lose?

"I want to see George because I love him," Selina said. "I wish to marry him."

Mrs. Fitzgerald clapped her hands together "Marvelous! I had hoped that was the case."

"Sadly, 'tis not a trouble-free path," Selina said, "for there is some silly misunderstanding between us. I cannot explain the circumstances, for 'twould take too long, but I think George might believe that I love someone else—or even that I am incapable of love. Neither of which are true."

"Then you must go and see him at the stables," Mrs. Fitzgerald said. "'Tis not far to Newton St. Loe, and you have a carriage. What are you waiting for?"

"You approve, then?"

"Of course I do," Mrs. Fitzgerald said. "I know my George—and I know he loves you. Sadly, he thinks he stands no chance of winning your heart—so you need to go to him and enlighten him. 'Tis obvious, at least to me, that he adores you."

Just then, Kitty, Henry, Edmund and Doctor Fitzgerald all entered the room.

"What an amazing collection of fossils you have amassed, Doctor Fitzgerald," Henry said. "I am impressed by your dedication—there is such variety."

"Thank you," Doctor Fitzgerald said. "Ah! Coffee."

"And Bath buns," Edmund said. "How fortuitous—for I missed breakfast."

"Thank you, Mrs. Fitzgerald," Selina said, accepting a coffee.

"Sugar?" Mrs. Fitzgerald offered.

"No, thank you, I am trying to give it up. We all are, after Mr. Fitzgerald alerted us to the efforts of the Anti-Saccharites in his speech."

"We certainly know all about that," Doctor Fitzgerald said. "George hardly left the house for days on end while he was researching for his speech at the Quaker Meeting House—although I believe in the end he did not deliver the original version."

"What he said was apt and to the point," Selina said. "And since then I have had the good fortune to read his full speech and think 'tis magnificent."

"Absolutely," Doctor Fitzgerald said. "We are very familiar with his words, as he practiced his oration here before delivering in Bath."

"George was determined to do his best," Mrs. Fitzgerald said. "It seemed he had a mission. I think he was keen to impress."

Mrs. Fitzgerald is trying to tell me something . . .

"The Templetons are going to Newton St. Loe," Mrs. Fitzgerald said to her husband.

"Are we?" Henry said.

"'Tis news to me," Edmund said.

"Of course we are," Selina said, "for that is where George is today. And did we not plan to see him?"

Edmund choked over his coffee. He was obviously finding something very amusing. Henry merely looked thoughtful. Was he beginning to realize Selina was serious?

"You would be doing me a favor if you did go to see him," Mrs. Fitzgerald said, "for although I sent him with a little food, I feel there was not quite enough for a tall, strong man of his healthy appetite to last the whole day."

"Are you sure, my dear?" Doctor Fitzgerald said. "For I thought Cook said she had risen early to prepare quite a feast for George. A large hamper was how she described it. He will have enough to share with the men."

"Perchance I am mistaken. However, 'tis no matter." Mrs. Fitzgerald beamed at Selina. "The important thing is that I know how much George would welcome a visit from his friends."

She is encouraging me! George's mother has given me her blessing.

George

"TRIGGER, MY OLD friend," George said, "here, I have fresh water for you and a bag of oats and hay."

George was taking a short break from his work to make sure that Trigger was comfortable. There had been the sound of a carriage arriving a few minutes ago, which meant there were visitors around, perhaps inquiring about the possibility of buying some horses.

"Ah, Trigger! If only Selina was arriving—how sweet that would be. You see, I love her, with all my heart. Something has gone wrong between us—I know not what—all I know is that I would give anything in the world to have her in my arms right now."

Trigger made no answer, save gently nuzzling George and licking his neck and chest.

"I must go back to work in a few minutes," George said to Trigger. "Perhaps I had better do my shirt up again if there are visitors to the stables, for it does not look good if I am to go around half dressed."

Suddenly there was a slight scuffling noise from the next stall.

"Who is there?" George said. "Show yourself."

"'Tis only me," Selina said, stepping forward.

Ye gods! Selina? Here in the stables? How is this possible?

Selina stood before George, her bonnet in hand, a bright smile upon her face and eyes sparkling like the sun upon the sea. She looked glorious! Was she a vision? Was George so lovesick that he was hallucinating?

George reached out and touched her shoulder.

"I am here," Selina said. "I am really here."

"How? Why?"

"The *how* is easy to answer. I came by carriage with my two brothers and Kitty. We called to see you at Devonshire Buildings, and your mother told us you were spending the day here."

Selina took a step towards George.

"The *why* is also very easy to answer: I am determined to speak my mind. I love you, George Fitzgerald."

"You, you love me?"

I must be dreaming! And yet, did Signor Allegretto not tell us both in Hunter's that we were in love with each other?

"How much did you hear—of what I said to Trigger?" George said.

"Enough to know that you love me too, although please do

not think you will escape from telling me so to my face. 'Tis not enough to tell you a horse that you love someone—you must tell the lady herself."

George put his arms around Selina. "I love you, to distraction."

The pair embraced passionately. Selina put her arms inside George's shirt onto his bare back and pulled him towards her. Hot and fervent were the kisses between them. George wanted this moment to last forever—for if it came to a conclusion, surely the spell would be broken?

They had been here before, sharing kisses and wordless embraces—this had always been followed by disappointment and heartbreak. So far, at least . . .

"I know what you are thinking," Selina murmured. "No, George, do not pull away from me. Let us lean together, that is it. There is so much between us to explain, for example, the wall of ice. I did not know about this and so I saw no reason for your coldness towards me—and I thought you might be a rake waiting for a lady in the theater corridor. 'Tis no wonder I told you I hated you! I was carried away by jealousy—and did not mean those cruel words."

George buried his face in Selina's shoulder.

"George! You are laughing! Why?"

"Because you thought I was a rake. Nothing is further from the truth. I have eyes for only one woman—you." Then he frowned. "What about your Signor Allegretto?"

"I cannot believe you think I would be in love with Signor Allegretto! He's a dear friend, and the best music teacher in the world, but really, me and Signor Allegretto? Impossible!"

"At the soirée, it seemed . . ."

"I was trying to put all my emotions into the music; I could not look at you, not in front of everyone at the musical gathering, so I gazed at Signor Allegretto . . . and then in the encore . . . oh, I know it all sounds like nonsense, but believe me, George, I love you through and through."

"You love me?" George said softly. "Say it again, my darling."

"I love you."

Very soon, all the doubt and confusion, the muddles and misunderstandings, were swept away as Selina and George listened to each other. All the twists and turns of their tangled romance became clear. George even outlined the five phases of the campaign he had planned to win Selina's heart, which unaccountably made her helpless with mirth for quite a while.

"And I promise that when we are married," George said, "I will not try to control you—make you wear your shoes in the house or decide when you go out or who you see."

"And I promise I will not mind that you are a little shy sometimes, and that you like to wear muddy breeches at the dinner table."

"There is one thing we have forgotten," George said.

"Ah, yes. The proposal. I came here intending to ask you to marry me, in fact I told your mama as much—more of that another time, for I know I am to have the most delightful mother-in-law in the world."

"Well, shall we propose together," George said, "since we are determined to break away from convention?"

"A most suitable idea," Selina said. "Will you . . ."

". . . marry me?" George finished.

Two pairs of lips met to seal the deal.

"I must ask your father's permission, of course," George said.

"Naturally. That would be the correct etiquette. But know this: if he does not give his permission, I will run away with you."

"Run away? What on earth is going on?" Henry said, striding into the stable with his wife and brother.

"Hell's teeth, George!" Edmund said. "Do your shirt up, man! 'Tisn't proper."

"And perhaps you should unhand my sister," Henry said.

"Yes, indeed. And care to explain why you two seem so close?" Edmund demanded. "I thought you hated each other."

"I knew you did not hate each other," Henry said, "but my

goodness, something mighty strange is going on if Selina is talking about eloping. Why would that be necessary?"

"I see all is resolved," Kitty said, "and I offer my warmest congratulations to you both."

Selina's brothers took a little while to fathom the situation, but ere long, first Henry and then Edmund were beaming and offering sincere felicitations to the happy couple.

It was decided that everyone would go back to Bath, to Number 1, where George could formally ask Lord Templeton for Selina's hand. Selina tried to argue that she should travel with George on Trigger, but Henry and Edmund managed to persuade her that it might give her parents less of a shock if she arrived home in a carriage rather than on horseback with George. Particularly if George continued to wear his shirt open.

Very soon the happy party were returning to the city, with George riding beside the carriage gazing at Selina—who in turn locked her eyes to his.

Once they reached the other side of the river, Henry called out to George.

"I say! With all the excitement it went clean out of my head; I am tasked with collecting some new gloves for my mama from one of the shops on Pulteney Bridge. You will not mind, George, if we take a small detour?"

"Not at all," George said.

I am grateful for the slight delay, for it gives me a little while longer to formulate in my mind what I must say to Lord Templeton when I ask for his daughter's hand in marriage. 'Tis not every day I have to make such an important speech.

"You must not be worried about talking to Papa," Selina called to George.

Selina is a mind reader! How well she knows me.

"Papa is very fond of you," Selina continued, "and he will be pleased to get rid of me at last, I am sure."

"That's true," Edmund said, "for Selina, you have been on the shelf for far too long."

I will have to get used to this banter, for I am to be part of the Templeton family. I cannot believe my good fortune!

The carriage stopped outside Chillington's on Pulteney Bridge, and George dismounted from Trigger, then Selina and Henry dashed inside to collect the gloves. Selina reappeared a few seconds later and gave George a particularly loving embrace in front of many astonished passers-by.

"I will be away from you for only a few minutes," she said to George. "Can you bear it?"

"I will try," George said. "Hurry, my love! Quick! Into the shop before you are recognized. We should not be so intimate in the street."

Selina rushed back into Chillington's to join Henry.

George looked to his left, towards Great Pulteney Street. There seem to be quite a commotion going on.

"What is happening?" George said to a man running onto the bridge.

"'Tis Lord Steyne," the man said. "He escaped from prison but ten minutes ago."

"Yes," another man said. "He took the chance to slip out of the back gate when in the yard—word is he bribed his gaoler, else how would he have been able to get away?"

"He's been seen in Laura Place," the first man said.

"There he is," the second shouted. "See? On the other side of the carriage way. He is standing as bold as brass in the middle of the shops—outside Chillington's."

Lord Steyne stood directly opposite George, glaring at him.

"Damn you, Fitzgerald," he bellowed. "You thought you've got rid of me, didn't you? I will have my revenge. You destroyed my reputation in this city—and you will pay."

"There is nothing you can do to me," George said.

"Maybe not," Lord Steyne said, "but perhaps I can do something to the personage you love—Miss Selina Templeton, that spoilt, wilful chit of a girl."

Almost before George realized what was happening, Lord

Steyne shot into Chillington's.

With a howl of rage, George ran into the shop after him. Too late! Lord Steyne had already grabbed Selina and twisted her arm behind her back.

"Do not come near," Lord Steyne hissed at George. "If you do . . ."

I cannot bear it! That fiend has my darling Selina!

Selina managed to slip from Lord Steyne's grasp and flung herself at the open sash window. Surely she was not going to try and climb out? That ledge looked far too narrow. She was adept at standing on the roof of Number 1 behind the balustrade— however this was entirely different. The central arched window of Chillington's was directly above the swollen River Avon—and if Selina fell in, she might be swept over the treacherous weir.

George leapt to the window and pulled Selina to safety, passing her to Henry for shelter; then, teeth bared, he wrestled furiously with Lord Steyne, forcing him to the ground with admirable strength and a strategic blow to the back of the knee.

"Prepare to meet your doom," Lord Steyne snarled as he squirmed on the floor, producing a pistol from about his person and directing it at George's heart. "You trouble making, interfering, good-for-nothing b—"

The end of Lord Steyne's insult went unheard as with a tremendous roar, George kicked the pistol out of Lord Steyne's hand and across the room, causing the weapon to discharge a bullet into a pile of gloves.

"Apologies," George said to the shopkeeper. "I will, of course, make full recompense if you would be kind enough to send me a bill for the damage."

Someone had called the Constable, who now burst into the shop and pointed at Lord Steyne.

"Arrest that man!" the Constable barked and several men rushed forward to do their duty.

Lord Steyne was having none of it and jumped onto the window ledge in a surprisingly nimble way for a man of his age.

"I refuse to go back to Bath City Gaol—'tis nothing but a vile hellhole!"

"Be sensible, Lord Steyne," the Constable said. "You cannot escape. And 'tis not that bad a gaol. You should see some of the others."

"The food is terrible," Lord Steyne said. "I will not spend another night in that place."

There was a sudden loud whinny from Trigger—and suddenly, Lord Steyne lost his balance and fell backwards out of the open window. There was a splash as his body hit the river, followed by a stunned silence in the shop—then everyone ran to the windows to look down at the rushing floodwaters.

"He'll be carried downstream," Henry said, "and will live to fight another day."

"No, more likely he has been dragged under the water," the Constable said. "Justice has caught up with that monster at last. Look! There is no sign of him surfacing. Lord Steyne is no more."

SELINA REFUSED TO complete the journey to Number 1 in the carriage, but insisted on riding with George on Trigger. And all the way back to the Royal Crescent, George held her tightly and whispered in her ear how much he loved her.

Lord and Lady Templeton were waiting at the door of Number 1 as the carriage arrived, followed by the engaged couple on horseback.

Henry jumped out of the carriage first.

"Apologies, Mama," he said. "I forgot your gloves from Chillington's—but when you hear the reason why, you will not mind at all, and will rejoice heartily. And Papa—I believe that Mr. George Fitzgerald has something terribly important he would like to ask you in your study."

EPILOGUE

GEORGE AND SELINA were married in June of that same year, 1816. After a splendid reception at Number 1, they made the short journey to the exceedingly generous wedding gift Lord and Lady Templeton had bestowed upon them—Number 3 Royal Crescent, their new home.

"Will it not be wonderful to be so close to Henry and Kitty," Selina said, "especially when their new baby is born in the autumn?"

"Absolutely," George said, "and I am thrilled that your father is able to accommodate Trigger in his stable at the back of the Crescent. My dear horse is going to enjoy giving riding lessons to Mrs. Godwin's class of children, I know it. And talking of Trigger . . ."

"Yes," Selina said, "we must get ready to set off on our adventure. 'Tis time to change out of these fine garments, for we will not need them where we are going. I have packed a blanket and some food—let us hope it is not too chilly tonight. We have had virtually no summer this year so far—extraordinary, is it not?"

"Not as extraordinary as the fact that we are now wed and will soon be joined together," George murmured, taking Selina in his arms. "I will light a fire to protect us against the night chill, although I do not think we will be cold."

George and Selina had decided that they did not want to

spend their wedding night in their marital bed, however splendidly furnished their new bedchamber at Number 3 Royal Crescent was. They had a much better idea—a notion that chimed most pleasingly with their mutual wish to break free.

Once all the servants had turned in for the night, George and Selina crept out of the back of Number 3 and ran round to the stable.

"Hello, Trigger," George said softly.

"Are you surprised to see us?" Selina said as she stroked the horse's nose.

Very soon, George and Selina were galloping away northwards through country lanes and across fields to a secluded grove of trees.

"The ideal spot," Selina said. "You have chosen well, George."

"Indeed I have," George said and kissed his bride.

Trigger was soon tied to a tree and happy with a bag of oats.

"Here, take my hand, my love," George said as the married couple walked to a private patch of grass.

Selina spread the blanket on the ground while George lit a simple fire. The pair sat in silence for a while, staring into the depths, then Selina held out her arms to George.

He embraced her tenderly, whispering, "I love you—and at last we can be together."

"I cannot wait! I will love you forever and a day, George. You complete me."

"And, dearest Selina, you allow me to be myself."

Very soon, the time for words was over. And there, under the stars, they became one.

The End

About the Author

Jenny grew up in Bath, in the west of England, and spent much of her childhood exploring this beautiful city and wondering about the kind of people who lived there centuries ago. She was an avid reader from an early age, inheriting the love of a good story from her Irish grandmother.

After studying music at college, teaching in secondary schools for a number of years, and starting a family, Jenny finally found the time to pursue her dream of writing.

She now lives in London with her husband, writes short stories for UK women's magazines, and has had a number of romantic comedy novels published.

Website – jennyworstall.wordpress.com
Facebook – facebook.com/jennyworstall
Twitter – x.com/JennyWorstall
Amazon – amazon.co.uk/stores/Jenny-Worstall/author/B007IVNY1G
Instagram – instagram.com/jennyworstall